Harriet Rutland was the pen-name of Olive Shimwell. She was born Olive Seers in 1901, the daughter of a prosperous Birmingham builder and decorator.

Little is known of the author's early life but in 1926 she married microbiologist John Shimwell, with whom she moved to a small village near Cork in Ireland. This setting, transplanted to Devon, inspired her first mystery novel *Knock, Murderer, Knock!* which was published in 1938. The second of Harriet Rutland's mysteries, *Bleeding Hooks*, came out in 1940, and the third and last, *Blue Murder*, was published in November 1942. All three novels are remarkable for their black comedy, innovative plots, and pin-sharp portraits of human behaviour, especially concerning relationships between men and women.

Olive and John were divorced in the early forties, and Olive remained single for the rest of her life, without apparently publishing anything further. She died in Newton Abbot in 1962.

Also by Harriet Rutland

Knock, Murderer, Knock!
Blue Murder

HARRIET RUTLAND

BLEEDING HOOKS

With an introduction
by Curtis Evans

DEAN STREET PRESS

'I sent a message to the fish:
I told them "This is what I wish."

The little fishes of the sea,
They sent an answer back to me.

The little fishes' answer was
"We cannot do it, Sir, because—"'

'I'm afraid I don't quite understand,' said Alice.
'It gets easier further on,' Humpty Dumpty replied.

Through The Looking Glass

INTRODUCTION

Bleeding Hooks, the second detective novel by Harriet Rutland (the pen-name of Olive Shimwell (1901-1962)), was originally published in February 1940, just sixteen months after *Knock, Murderer, Knock!*, her acclaimed debut, which first appeared in November 1938. In the intervening year, 1939, Olive Shimwell gave birth to a son, Alan, just a few weeks after the outbreak of the Second World War. Rumors of war and the reality of a pregnancy seem not to have unduly hampered Shimwell in the writing of her second detective novel, however, for it is as impressive a piece of mystery mongering as her first. *Bleeding Hooks* was highly praised at the time in both the United Kingdom and the United States (its US title was the prosaically literal-minded *The Poison Fly Murder*); yet the novel since has bafflingly remained out-of-print for seventy-five years, making its 2015 republication by Dean Street Press all the more welcome.

Bleeding Hooks is set in Aberllyn, a Welsh fishing village, at an inn named The Fisherman's Rest (owned, perhaps predictably, by a couple named Evans). Gathered this season at The Fisherman's Rest are the novel's "murderee," Mrs. Ruby Mumsby, a vulgar, outsized woman who obviously fancies the human male rather more than the finny breed; Mrs. Partridge, her daughter Pansy and her daughter's boyfriend, Florence Vyvyan Gunn (the aggressively modern young couple despise their given names and instead go by, respectively, Pussy and Piggy); Mr. and Mrs. Pindar; General Sir Courtney Haddox and his possessive spinster sister Ethel; Mr. Weston, his nervy son Claude and Claude's pet performing monkey; garrulous Major Jeans, an adept in the design of fishing flies; and Mr. Winkley, a Scotland Yard man, expert at piecing together miscellaneous facts, who is enjoying a fishing holiday after having solved that unpleasant affair at Presteignton Hydro, related by Harriet Rutland in *Knock, Murderer, Knock!* Also on the scene are the officious Police Constable Thomas Lloyd, the snappish Dr. Rippington Roberts, and Mrs. Mumsby's much put-upon Welsh ghillie—i.e., fisherman's guide—John Jones, who has grown heartily tired of fending off his employer's lascivious advances ("Every ghillie in Aberllyn knew that she was man mad.")

Death disturbs The Fisherman's Rest when the objectionable Mrs. Mumsby is discovered lifeless by the lake, a salmon fly embedded in her hand. Dr. Roberts pronounces that the woman must have died accidentally from the shock of this vicious wound, but the ever-curious Mr. Winkley has his doubts, as do Pussy and Piggy, who are bored with the routine at The Fisherman's Rest and accordingly are eager to play, in the classic manner of Agatha Christie's Tommy and Tuppence before them, amateur detectives, though Pussy demurs when Mr. Winkley refers to her and Piggy as Bright Young Things. "To her, Bright Young Things were antiquated," wryly notes the author, who herself was of the Roaring Twenties generation. "Most of those whom she knew had already become 'hags,' and by this time had acquired several babies or divorces, or both." Addressing both Mr. Winkley and Piggy Gunn, Pussy, echoing the bravado of Christie's Tuppence in *The Secret Adversary* (1922) and *Partners in Crime* (1929), pronounces that she is determined to detect, whatever Mr. Winkley may say about it: "This is the first bit of excitement I've had in three weeks, and I'm going to enjoy it properly. Of course I'd rather sleuth with you two, but if you don't want to go on with it, I shall ask in the hotel for volunteers. I should think they'd jump at it. But whatever happens, I shall sleuth."

While Pussy and Piggy attempt surreptitiously to interrogate suspects at The Fisherman's Rest, Mr. Winkley determines to his satisfaction that Mrs. Mumsby expired not from the shock of inadvertently grasping a wickedly barbed salmon fly, but from prussic acid poisoning, the fly having been coated in the deadly stuff. Mrs. Mumsby was heartily disliked by almost everyone staying at the inn, but who could have so despised her as to want to kill her? Or is there some other motive in the offing? Mr. Winkley finds himself not only having to deal with the enthusiastic amateur sleuthing of Pussy and Piggy but a mystery problem that proves even more barbed that he initially thought.

Bleeding Hooks was as well-received as its predecessor, garnering critical praise, like *Knock, Murderer, Knock!*, for its humor and sophistication. In the magazine *Saturday Review*, Harriet Rutland's American publisher placed an illustrated ad extolling the virtues of novel, under the punning headline, "Hook on to a good mystery!" "Good sport—especially for angler-philes," pronounced the celebrated humorist (and mystery critic) Will Cuppy in the *New York Herald Tribune*, continuing the fishing puns. In fact *Bleeding Hooks* is one of the finest classic British mysteries of which I am aware that incorporates a fly fishing background--this subgenre includes Josephine Tey's *The Singing Sands*, Ngaio Marsh's *Scales of Justice*, Cyril Hare's *Death Is No Sportsman*, Ronald Knox's *Double Cross Purposes*, Nigel Orde-Powlett's *The Cast to Death* and John Haslette Vahey's *Death by the Gaff*—yet it also offers readers a superb example of the English "manners" mystery, with incisive and amusing social observation of well-conveyed characters in an interesting setting. No wonder *Bleeding Hooks* charmed British and American readers alike, the latter presumably willing to overlook this slur on one of their greatest (and greatest selling) native fictional sleuths:

"You know that American criminal lawyer, Perry Mason...?"
"That gas-bag!" exclaimed Mr. Winkley.

Will Mr. Winkley emulate Mr. Mason and land a clever criminal in Bleeding Hooks? Read on and see.

Curtis Evans

CHAPTER I

General Sir Courtney Haddox, wearing a discoloured trench coat over innumerable out-at-elbow woollen cardigans, and a deflated fishing bag slung over this, entered the front door of The Fisherman's Rest, walking a little stiffly in his heavy rubber waders. He stood for a moment, his tight skinned, purplish-tinged face thrust forward like an ill-tempered vulture's, as he peered at the other end-of-season visitors who were already grouped round the catches of fish arranged on the floor in the centre of the hall.

He heard his sister's voice raised above the murmured conversation of them all. It had the croaking harshness of a corncrake's, and, like a corncrake's, seemed capable of going on for ever.

"...because 'Tight Lines!' always seems to be such a silly expression," she was saying, "and I do think that 'Happy Landings' would be much more suitable, because the line might be tight for a minute but you still might lose the fish, but if it were landed safely in the boat, you'd be sure to bring it in with you, but perhaps the Air Force thought of it first..."

The General winced.

For the hundredth time he regretted the impulse which had induced him to bring Ethel with him on his annual holiday to the little fishing hotel in the Welsh village of Aberllyn. From the first, her behaviour had proved almost unbearably embarrassing. Every morning she insisted on walking with him to the boat at the head of the lake, and waved him off with a red silk parasol. She inquired, in the ghillie's hearing, whether he was wearing enough underclothing, and had once made him retire behind a wall to put on the ribbed bodybelt he had forgotten. And every evening she was waiting for his return to greet him with false gaiety, or to overwhelm him with undeserved praise.

As soon as she saw him now, she broke off her conversation, a proceeding which entailed no difficulty since it was always so pointless, and bustled towards him.

Her grey hair was cut in a thin fringe across a low forehead, and she wore a girlishly colourful Viennese frock singularly ill-suited to her horsy features and forty-eight years.

"Any luck, dear?" she gushed, then, without appearing to notice the impatient shake of his head: "Mr. Gunn and I have been having a most interesting talk about huntin' and fishin' and shootin' – at least, we hadn't got to the shootin' yet, had we?"

General Haddox glanced at the loose-limbed, tousle-haired young man whose expression seemed clearly to indicate that where she was concerned he infinitely regretted the omission, and asked the inevitable question of the day.

"Do any good today?"

"I'm afraid not, sir," replied Gunn. "Just a few brownies that the ghillie made me put back because they were under the pound. That ghillie has very large ideas, I can tell you. But Mr. Pindar hooked a salmon, and I shot a few hundred yards of film when he was playing it, so the day wasn't entirely wasted."

"Did he, by Jove?" The General was suitably impressed. "I've been looking for salmon all day and never even saw one. Where did you get him?" he asked, turning to the bronzed, good-looking man who was standing with his arm linked through his wife's.

"Well, I didn't get him at all as it happens." he replied. "I hooked him by accident off the black rocks at the end of the lake on a ten-foot-six trout rod – Hardy's 'Perfection', if you know the type – and a 3x cast."

"That would give you a bit of fun," nodded the General.

"It did. He made a swirl as big as a clothes-basket, and led me a hell of a dance for an hour and twenty minutes, then he broke me. I'm not feeling too pleased with myself, I can tell you. But we had no gaff, so I had to try and play him to a standstill."

"Hard luck!" said the General. "If your cast had been heavier you might have brought him in. I remember once –"

They were interrupted by a squeal from Miss Haddox.

"Oh, Courtney! Are these your fish? Why, they're four beauties, and all speckled. They're quite the nicest fish I've seen this evening. The others have such ugly jaws and look so black, but these are a lovely colour, all golden brown. And you said you hadn't caught any. You naughty boy! My brother's so modest," she said, as she beamed at the little circle of people.

The purplish tinge on the General's face became almost royal in tone as she thus drew attention to the four brown trout which he, as a man who fished exclusively for salmon, should, by all the unwritten laws of fishing, have left in the lake.

"Had to kill 'em. Swallowed the hook," he murmured brokenly. "Don't put them down here; give them to the cat," he said sharply to the ghillie, who touched his cap with one sympathetic hand while he removed the offending brown trout with the other.

The uncomfortable silence which followed was broken as the hall door swung open to admit Claude Weston, the youngest of all the visitors at present in the hotel. He threw his fishing bag on to the floor, regardless of a protesting rattle from his reel, flung his young, graceful body into a chair, and puffed out a weary sigh.

"God, I'm tired!" he exclaimed, running a slender hand over his copper-coloured hair.

"What's wrong?" asked Gunn. "No fish?"

Claude's gesture indicated despairing assent.

"My father is bringing in a few miserable corpses," he said. "He is also," he added as an afterthought, "bringing in Mrs. Mumsby. She seems to have had all the luck."

"Did Major Jeans do any good on the upper lake?" asked General Haddox, addressing no one in particular.

"I don't think he's in yet," replied Mr. Pindar, "but I should call it a miracle if he brought much out of that little mountain lake today. The light was too bright."

"I like it a bit bright myself," returned the General, "but then I only fish for salmon. The trouble today was that there wasn't enough wind."

A tall, thin man, wearing the dark pin-stripe suit which betokened a recent arrival to the hotel, joined them.

His skin was pink, his hair and moustache fair, the latter stained brown at the straight-clipped edge with nicotine, and matched by the skin between the first and second fingers of his left hand. His eyes, of a mild blue, regarded the fish with an interested and experienced look as he bent down to examine them more closely. In return, the eyes of the visitors expressed the curiosity which the fish were past feeling.

"What did you do today?"

It was Mr. Pindar who asked the superfluous question.

The stranger straightened himself, drew a contemplative stream of smoke from his cigarette, and replied with the self-assurance of a regular visitor.

"Oh, I've only just arrived. I hope to get a few tomorrow though, if you people have left any in the lake. What's the fishing been like lately?"

"Rotten," replied Mr. Pindar.

"Damned bad as usual," said General Haddox.

"Hopeless," said Gunn.

A ghillie who had just come into the hall was adding a string of small sea-trout to the fish already on the floor, and finally laid a large, fat brown trout beneath.

Claude Weston got up, regarded it affectionately.

"An ill-favoured thing, but mine own," he quoted.

"Why, that's a lovely fish!" exclaimed Miss Haddox. "Did you catch it all by yourself, Claude?"

"Oh no," he replied. "It committed suicide on the end of the hook. I swam out to rescue it, but it was too late. But don't spare a thought for it, lady, it's only a brown trout – of no value, commercial or otherwise, in these parts!"

A man of average height, with dark, sparse hair, his face rather grey and drawn as if he had had a tiring day, joined them, and put an affectionate arm round Claude's shoulders.

"More nonsense, Claude?" he asked.

Claude turned.

"Oh, there you are, Dad. What an age you've been. Have you been trying to drown old Mother Mumsby in the lake?"

"No, she's safe so far," replied his father in the same bantering tones. "She went straight upstairs."

"She always does," said Miss Haddox spitefully. "It's because she's so annoyed at not catching any fish, though I must say that she ought to be used to the idea by now, for she hasn't caught more than once since we've been here. It just proves what I've always said, that the only reason she goes fishing at all is because it's the only chance she gets of being alone with a man!"

"Whose fish are those?" asked General Haddox hastily as a sturdily built, dark-haired ghillie pulled five fair-sized sea-trout out of his creel, and knelt down to arrange them.

"Mrs. Mumsby's, sir," he replied, looking up.

"Yes, we know," said Miss Haddox. "But how many of them did she really catch?"

"Four," replied the ghillie. "It was a good day for her indeed."

"Four?" Miss Haddox was incredulous. "But you don't mean to say that she's missed the opportunity of telling us all about them? Why, she –"

"Here's the Major," said her brother rather unnecessarily, as Major Jeans trumpeted himself into the hall.

"Hallo, hallo! What ho within, what ho without! But not without fish, I hope. What's anyone done today? Such a nice, bright, happy day with trout all over the lake and all under the lake and everywhere except out of the lake! Did you have a pleasant picnic, boys and girls? By Jove! I bet those fish are pulling their little whiskers and slapping their fins in glee at being left in peace for another day. What did I get? Gather round me while I tell you. Ten little brownies. Herrings! Sprats! 'Calloo callay, he chortled in his joy.' I'm a bloomin' murderer!"

He slapped his hands together and rubbed the palms against each other as if he were a brewer sampling hops, and his lean, wind-chapped face beamed at them all.

"Major Jeans."

The stranger moved forward.

"Eh? Who? Why, God bless my fishy soul, if it isn't Winkley!" He clapped him on the shoulder, and shook the proffered hand. "Come down to tickle the trout, have you, eh? You won't find them so ticklish this year. Well, well, you're as welcome as the mayfly in May. Come and have —"

He bustled Mr. Winkley down the corridor leading to the bar.

And now that the last fisherman was safely within the hotel, and the last fish scrutinized, the little group of people dispersed as quickly as clouds on a windy day, and went to their several baths.

CHAPTER II

Mrs. Ruby Mumsby knotted a red spotted tie under the shirt collar of her blouse, as badly as only a woman could knot it, and, holding her breath, tucked the blouse down the top of the riding breeches which clung steadfastly to her too-protuberant stomach.

Her name was not Ruby, but she had chosen it in preference to her baptismal name of Gladys during her early theatrical days, because she thought it suited her better. Whether other people agreed with her depended entirely on their opinion of rubies. If they considered the stones blatant and gaudy in appearance, the suitability was at once obvious, for Mrs. Mumsby was blatant in manner and had a gaudy taste in dress. Her present appearance in such sportsmanlike attire was due to a desire to appear suitably dressed in the eyes of the

men in the hotel who had come down for the fishing. The fact
that she merely succeeded in looking obscene was the fault of
her figure, and her mistaken idea, somewhat prevalent among
women, that the feminine form, though discreetly restrained
beneath evening gowns, should remain *au naturel* under
sports clothes. As she dressed, her heavy, swelling breasts
swayed slightly at every movement, and touched the hands
which were busy about her wide waist.

Not a whit perturbed by the reflection which the rather
specked mirror showed her, Mrs. Mumsby struggled into a
suede golf jacket, assured by the tag at the back that it was
O.O.S., added a knitted scarf of a particularly violent shade of
mauve, and, since fish have a notoriously keen eye for bright
colours, discarded a vivid green beret for one of more subdued
hue, and pulled it at a roguish angle over her peroxided curls.
She smoothed the lipstick on left wing of her mouth with a
gentle finger, and surveyed the effect in her magnifying mirror
with some pleasure.

And indeed, if she could have been a cameo all her life, she
would have been a handsome and attractive woman, and might
have inspired the exotic *amours* about which she so often
dreamed, for it was not for nothing that she visited the most
expensive beauty salons several times a year and submitted to
blissful hours of face-slapping and beauty masques. But while
her face responded to treatment, despite its natural tendency
to plumpness, her body only expanded the more, and although
what little aesthetic sense she possessed urged her to slimness
by way of the Hay diet and the Women's League of Health and
Beauty, her love of food kept her fat.

She gave a sigh which developed into a chuckle as she
surveyed herself in the long mirror of the wardrobe.

The trouble is that I don't take myself seriously, she
thought. *Soft in more ways than one, that's me. If I could only
hate my figure enough, I'd give up luxuries, and half-starve
myself on raw beetroot and wheat biscuits. But why bother?*

My figure hasn't scared any man off yet, and if you're made big, you'll be big whatever you eat, that's what I say.

Her annoyance was not unmixed with a sense of satisfaction.

She, at least, was a woman; a little too obviously perhaps, but you couldn't have everything. She didn't know what women were coming to these days. Just look at that saucy young piece, called Pussy, in the hotel at the present time – no chest, no hips, no bottom, nothing to satisfy a man. She often wondered whether the girls of today possessed the requisite female organs in their thin, elongated bodies, but presumably they did, since they occasionally produced children under the same circumstances as their fore-mothers had done.

For some reason the thought of children depressed her. She wondered whether she would ever become a mother again. It was a sad thing to lose a child, though some people might think her a hypocrite for saying so... But there, everything was going to be all right. She held all the trumps, and if she played her cards well, she was bound to get what she wanted. A little threat here, a few tears there, a firm hand and a charming smile, and the game would be hers. Then she would begin a new life with a new companion. It wouldn't be easy to accomplish. She would have to be clever. But then she was – far cleverer than some people gave her credit for.

She gave a final pat to her beret, then, gathering together her fishing tackle and mackintosh, she went out of the room.

As she moved carefully down the wide, curved stairs, there was a sudden commotion in the hall, where Major Jeans was standing with the party of four Welshmen who had arrived early that morning from Cardiff for the end-of-season fishing.

"Hide, boys," he hissed. "Here comes the Merry Widow!"

They grabbed their fishing bags and spare coats, and made a dive for their rods which were standing, ready for use, outside the front door.

"Well, tight lines!" they called over their shoulders.
"Bleeding hooks!" grinned the Major.

CHAPTER III

By the time that Mrs. Mumsby had descended the last stair, the only person left in the hall was the girl whom she had so recently condemned in her thoughts.

Although she was in her early twenties, her figure had an immature appearance, her breasts, no larger than those of a heavyweight boxer's, lacking the feminine curves so dear to Mrs. Mumsby's heart. Her green eyes had the slumbrous look of a well-bred cat. Her beaked nose, small, dimpled chin, and mouth whose true shape could only be guessed at beneath a too-liberal application of greasy lipstick, did not make for prettiness, but certainly she was attractive, an air of painstaking grooming compensating for what her features lacked. Her hair was well-brushed and waved, and gathered into a neat roll in her neck, and at first sight this struck an incongruous note, until one realized that it served to counterbalance the prominence of her nose.

She sat in a fireside chair in front of an electric stove which simulated a coal fire, its hidden fan casting little flickers of light through the useless embers. One hand was thrust into the pocket of her man-tailored coat, and her legs, clad in chocolate-brown slacks, were stretched out in front of her.

She did not look up as Mrs. Mumsby approached, and, after a second's hesitation, the widow passed behind her chair into the little office which led out of the hall.

A few minutes afterwards, the girl was vaguely conscious of the murmur of voices coming from the office, but they did not disturb her deep perusal of the large *Manual of Sexual Psychology*, which rested on her lap. Gradually, however, the voices increased in volume until she could not fail to take notice of what was being said, for few sounds are so penetrating as the raised voices of two angry women.

"I think you must have made a mistake, Mrs. Mumsby."

"Mistake? Me? You know perfectly well, Mrs. Evans, that I never make mistakes. I tell you I left that bottle on my table when I went out fishing yesterday, and when I came back, half of it had gone."

"I hope you're not suggesting that I —"

"You know very well what I'm suggesting." The girl could almost see Mrs. Mumsby standing against the counter in that rather barmaidish attitude of hers, her large breasts vibrating with anger. "I'm telling you that if a lady leaves a bottle of whisky in her bedroom, it's your business to see that it's not tampered with. If this is the result of my making friends with you and asking you into my room for a chat and a drink —"

"Mrs. Mumsby! If you're not satisfied with this hotel, you know the remedy. I'm sure we shouldn't like to keep you here against your will and it's no pleasure to us to take your money if you're dissatisfied."

"If it occurs again I shall certainly leave, but let me remind you, Mrs. Evans, that if I do, you and that precious husband of yours won't get a penny of my money!"

As Mrs. Mumsby stormed out of the office, the girl looked up. Her nonchalant attitude and her all-embracing glance seemed to be full of studied insolence, whereas in reality they merely expressed a supreme contentment with the world in general and with her own state in particular.

As if in reply to a challenge, Mrs. Mumsby sauntered towards the fire.

"I've just been giving Mrs. Evans a piece of my mind," she said. 'These hotel people are all the same. They get slack if you don't keep them up to scratch. I live here all the year round, you know, except for two months in the South of France in the winter, and when there's no one else in the hotel, they can't do enough for me, but as soon as other people come, I have to go to the wall. I can't stand that sort of thing."

"I must say I don't blame you," replied the girl indifferently.

"Aren't you fishing, today?"

"No, I never fish."

"Isn't your friend, Mr. Gunn, going out either?"

"Oh yes. He's going out with Mr. Pindar."

"Mr. Pindar. That's the naval gentleman, isn't it?"

The girl took a last puff at the Russian cigarette she was smoking and threw it carefully behind the fire.

"Is he? I'm sure I don't know."

Mrs. Mumsby looked arch.

"Well, I don't know either, if it comes to that. It's just my idea, you know. It couldn't be right, of course, or he'd be more than plain Mr., but he looks so much like a sailor, don't you think? You can always tell."

The girl yawned.

"Can you?" she asked in her bored voice. "Perhaps you know more about sailors than I do."

Mrs. Mumsby eyed her sharply to see whether this remark was double-edged, but her thirst for scandal overcame her doubts, and she went on:

"It's his profile and his eyes. Naval officers always have such handsome profiles, and their eyes have that far-away look, through gazing over the seas. So romantic, I think."

The girl had met naval officers at sherry parties, and secretly thought that splicing the mainbrace had more to do with that far-away look than the sea.

"All men in love have that romantic look in their eyes," she replied in the full experience of her eight years of adolescence. "He's obviously terribly in love with his wife. Mrs. Evans says that they're on their honeymoon, and she seems to have a way of smelling out a honeymoon couple."

"Mrs. Evans!" exclaimed Mrs. Mumsby. "What does she know about it? What does she know about any of us, if it comes to that? Exactly what we tell her and nothing more. Well, she may think that they're honeymooning, but it's my belief that the pair of them are not married at all!"

But the girl's patience was exhausted. She liked the Pindars.

"You're nothing but a mischief-making old cat!" she exclaimed.

Mrs. Mumsby's anger was not modified by the truth of this statement. Her eyes blazed at the girl, and for a second she could not speak.

"If I were your mother," she said at length, "I should take you across my knee and spank you."

"Grandmother, you mean," said the girl sweetly. "Here's the ghillie with your lunch. You'd better be quick and go out, or you'll miss all the men."

Mrs. Mumsby choked back with difficulty the first words which rose to her lips, and when she spoke her voice was hoarse with anger.

"That's a typical remark," she said. "You modern girls can think of nothing except men, and you imagine that all other women are like you. All you think and talk and read about is sex, sex, sex. Look at the book you're reading now! I've heard you and that boy-friend of yours telling each other filthy stories – of course we all know what both of you are here for. You don't know what platonic friendship is. I can go out for a day on the lake, have my lunch with any man I see, come in with my fish, and have a drink at the bar with any of them, without expecting to be treated like a woman. But you, with all your aping men's clothes and habits, you couldn't sit in a boat with a man without trying to vamp him. And that's your idea, I suppose, of sport."

"*Vive le sport*," cried the girl.

Mrs. Mumsby gave up the unequal contest, and stamped out of the hotel, followed by the grinning ghillie.

The girl looked down at her hands and found to her surprise that they were trembling.

"What have you been doing to the Merry Widow?" inquired a soft voice, and at the sound of it, the girl gathered her body together and jumped to her feet.

"Oh, hallo, Mrs. Pindar," she said. "Come and sit down."

The newcomer was one of those rare women whom everyone thought beautiful. Her hair was the colour of heather honey, her eyes amber, and her complexion sun-kissed. She was tall and large-boned, and her every movement was graceful. She seemed to glow when she moved, and her entrance into any company was habitually greeted with the silence of admiration. Her voice was soft, her manner charming, and she was, above all, entirely free from self-consciousness or self-admiration. She might have been any age between twenty-five and forty, and there was about her the unmistakable aura of a woman who loves and is loved. She was dressed in perfectly cut, hand-spun tweeds, an Italian scarf, and Henry Heath hat; her shoes were hand-made. A platinum wedding-ring, very new and bright, gleamed on her left hand; she wore no other jewellery.

"I won't sit down, thanks," she said. "I promised to meet Miss Haddox at the corner of the lake road, but I think I'll let Mrs. Mumsby get ahead first. Your mother is supposed to be coming too. Do you know where she is?"

The girl shook her head.

"I haven't seen her since eight o'clock," she said, "when she came and ticked me off for ordering breakfast in bed. She says I'm too young for that sort of thing. Such rot! I never can see why you should have to wait until you're sixty before people give you your breakfast in bed."

"It costs extra in a hotel," remarked Mrs. Pindar practically.

"So it does. Of course I never thought of that, and we do rather have to count the sixpences. But why couldn't Mother say so instead of saying I'm too young? That's just like her. She never will say things straight out."

Mrs. Pindar smiled.

"Perhaps you won't like it when she does," she said.

"Perhaps not. Mrs. Mumsby didn't like the truth."

"What did you say to her?"

The girl laughed, and offered her cigarette-case.

"Oh, I was baiting her a bit," admitted the girl. "She accused me of immoral behaviour with the boy-friend, and I let her have it good and proper. Talk about the pot calling the kettle black! Why, she'd ran after anything in trousers, old or young. All the men in the hotel are scared to be left alone with her, and then she has the cheek to turn round and accuse me!"

"It's because she envies you," replied Mrs. Pindar. "When I see the two of you side by side, I can sympathize with her, poor woman. It must be pretty awful to have a figure like that. I always think she would look rather handsome if she dressed in darker clothes, and dieted a bit."

"Her face is all right," said the girl, "although that make-up of hers is too blue. It's her foul mind I don't like. A minute ago she was telling me some rigmarole about your husband being a naval officer, and said she didn't believe you were married."

"Oh!"

The girl stooped to pick up the cigarette which Mrs. Pindar had just dropped, and did not trouble to consider whether the exclamation was one of surprise or indignation.

"I shouldn't take her too seriously," she said, turning with the cigarette in her hand. But, to her amazement, she found that Mrs. Pindar was already on her way to the front door.

The girl stood gazing after her for a moment. Then she shrugged her shoulders, threw away the half-smoked butt, and settled herself philosophically in her former position in front of the fire.

CHAPTER IV

She was aroused by two heavy hands which grasped her shoulders and levered the chair on which she was sitting almost to the floor, so that her thin legs assumed a perpendicular position which might have proved embarrassing if she had been wearing skirts.

"Let me go, you low hound!" she screamed, kicking as hectically as any elderly spinster defending her honour. "Piggy, let me go!"

One of her hands clutched wildly at the vast bulk of the man behind her, found his armpit, and began to tickle.

"Stop it, you little devil!" he yelled. "Blast you, Pussy, stop it! I shall let you fall!"

"Put me back, then."

An armistice having been declared by mutual unspoken consent, the girl's chair was raised until it stood once again squarely on all four legs. The girl jumped up and hurled herself at her companion, and they indulged in a rough-and- tumble, from which they both emerged, tousled and panting, and grinned at each other in the perfect understanding of their joint forty-five years.

The boy crossed his fingers.

"Now, *pax*, Pussy," he said. "There's someone coming. If you start on me again, I'll murder you."

The girl looked at him admiringly.

"Kiss Pussy, then," she coaxed, holding up her half-open mouth, luscious with lipstick.

Piggy Gunn complied without hesitation, then stepped back, and with the automatic habit of long use, pulled a handkerchief from his breast pocket, and wiped his reddened mouth.

He had a long, large body, on which his legs and arms seemed to be strung as loosely as those on an anatomic skeleton, so that when he waved an arm about, as he frequently did when talking, you almost expected it to detach itself and fly over your head. His hair was light brown, and his features so regular that his face was a difficult one to remember among the similar indeterminate features of the hosts of young men in their twenties today. His eyes were hazel, flecked with brown, and the flesh around them was so crinkled that he appeared to have eyelids both below and above them. Like the girl, he wore brown slacks, sports shirt, pullover and checked jacket; but in addition he had scattered around the hall the innumerable and rather shapeless cardigans and mackintoshes so essential for late autumn wear on the lake. Near his feet a fishing bag spilled fly and cast-boxes.

The girl looked at him critically, pulled at his green tie patterned with beer tankards, fished a lipstick out of her handbag, and began to repair the damage to her lips. She barely finished before she caught a glimpse of a familiar face in the mirror of her jewelled flapjack.

"Oh, hello, Mummy," she drawled, while Gunn stood to sudden attention with the deference of a young man towards a prospective mother-in-law.

Mrs. Partridge was short and slight, with greying hair carefully waved back from a centre parting, and eyes as brown and soft as a doe's. She was dressed for walking in a short tweed skirt, tailored coat, woollen oversocks, and brogue shoes of chrome leather. She carried a strong ash walking-stick, and looked healthy, neat, and businesslike. In colouring, in character, and in looks, she was the very antithesis of her daughter.

"Pussy dear," she said, "you're coming for a walk with me. We'll take sandwiches, and get a cup of tea somewhere. Breakfast in bed and reading over the fire first thing in the morning will do you no good. You're too young to be lazy. Besides, you'll lose your figure."

Pussy pulled a face, and ran to close her book before her mother could read the title. She had tucked it under her arm, and was about to go upstairs to put on her walking shoes, when Mr. Weston walked down, carrying the usual accoutrements of trout fishing.

Pussy greeted him with her most genuine smile. She admired Mr. Weston, much as she had admired Douglas Fairbanks, because of his athletic build and charming manners. If his breeches and sports coat gave the impression of having been cut by a theatrical tailor, at least he had the figure which could wear them, and he was altogether such a kind, unassuming man that a slight exaggeration in clothes and manner did not disturb anyone who met him.

There was a certain awkwardness about his movements which was due to the fact that he used his left hand too frequently, and at first sight, one did not perceive that the right one was so crippled as to be little more than a sleeping partner to its fellow.

"We're blithering mugs to go out day after day like this," he remarked after he had greeted them all. "Any fool can see that we're going to have another flat calm, with the sun blazing down on the lake as if it were midsummer instead of October. My son and I have been here for over a fortnight, and we've caught four sea-trout between us, on an average, every other day. That's pretty bad for the best sea-trout lake in Wales. This place doesn't seem to understand the weather forecasts! When it isn't blowing a gale, it's a flat calm. Yet we all go out every morning, full of hope that it's going to be better than yesterday, and it's always worse instead. Blithering mugs, that's what we are!"

"I think it's pretty much the same everywhere," said Gunn. "It's the uncertainty of it all that entices us out day after day, and the perpetual hope that we shall eventually strike a perfect fishing day, and bring in a trout big enough to be stuffed and kept in a glass case, like the one upstairs on the landing which Mr. Winkley caught. That's fishing, that was!"

"The Fisherman's Prayer," remarked Pussy. "It's all right, Mother, it's quite proper," she laughed, as Mrs. Partridge looked apprehensive.

"Lord, send a fish that even I when telling of it may tell no lie!" supplemented Gunn.

"I think all this talk of exaggerating their catches is rather a libel on fishing people," said Mrs. Partridge. "I've always found them very honest and rather modest, too. When anyone tells you about having hooked two fish at the same time, for instance, and one getting away, well, that does happen, doesn't it?"

"Oh, certainly," replied Mr. Weston, "especially the part about one of 'em getting away. After all, no one knows why salmon and sea-trout take a fly or a bait in fresh water. Old Walton seemed to have got as near the truth as anyone when he said they take them for sheer wantonness."

"But surely it's because they're hungry," protested Pussy.

Mr. Weston shook his head.

"No," he said, "they never feed in the fresh water; they only come back to spawn. They stoke up when they're in the sea, and live on their humps like camels until they get back again – if they do. Their flesh is pink through eating shrimps."

"But why do they ever leave the sea?" asked Pussy. "It seems so silly to run away from food."

Gunn guffawed.

"Of course, you would find that difficult to understand," he mocked, "but the answer is that they can't help themselves. If a sea-trout or salmon was hatched out in one of the little lakes beyond the big one here, and then went out to sea to grow up, some instinct would bring it back again to that same little lake when it wanted to spawn."

Pussy didn't believe him.

"Do you mean to tell me," she asked, "that because I was hatched out" – Mrs. Partridge looked hurt – "in the Isle of Wight, I shall have to return..." She broke off abruptly as a dark, flying shape hurtled through the air towards her.

"Omigod!" she screamed, and clutched at Gunn with one hand while with the other she attempted to dislodge the thing from her shoulder.

"Ha, ha!" came a deep, sepulchral voice from behind them. "I likes to make yer flesh creep."

"Claude, you devil!" yelled Pussy. "Take your fiendish monkey off me! Take it off, I say! You know I can't bear monkeys. Dirty, flea-bitten things. Ugh!"

Claude Weston bowed gracefully from his slender hips. "Madam, it shall be as you command. To hear is to obey." He clicked his tongue at the little marmoset which sat rolling its

eyes and gibbering on the girl's shoulder. It immediately
sprang over to him, and he caught it in his arms, whence it
swung itself up to crouch on his head, and proceeded to
investigate his thick hair. Claude struck the conventional
attitude of an acrobat who has safely landed on the ground
after a successful hazard on a trapeze, and cried "*Allez – oop!*"

As he stood poised almost on his toes, he looked too slight
and pretty for a boy of eighteen. His hair, the colour of newly
burnished copper, was parted in the centre and curled back on
either side like the horns of a faun. Faun-like, too, was his slim,
graceful figure, his satirical smile, and the pale freckles
sprinkled over his creamy skin. His hands were white, long-
fingered, and supple.

He drew the monkey to his shoulder.

"She is unkind to you, my Petkins," he said, addressing the
monkey. "It is strange in one who has a heart of gold." He
made a sudden play with his hands towards Pussy, and
repeated, "A heart of gold," while, miraculously, there
appeared in his fingers a heart of gilded metal. He then
produced pieces of gold from her ear, her hair, her book, and
finally knelt down and tumbled a clinking stream of them from
what the Americans call the "cuffs" of her trousers.

"Up to your tricks again, Claude," she laughed, as he tipped
the whole collection into her pocket, which she found empty
immediately afterwards. "Are you never still?"

"He can't allow himself to be," smiled Mr. Weston, his
whole face expressing pleasure and pride in his son's
performance. "As soon as this holiday is over he has an
engagement to appear on a provincial stage. It is the beginning
of his career. I think he has a great future."

Claude struck another attitude.

"*Ecco!*" he cried. "Behold Claude, the Great
Claustrophobia!"

They all laughed at his foolishness.

"I wish you'd give an entertainment tonight," suggested Mrs. Partridge. "It's very dull after dinner here, and everyone would love it. Can't you persuade him, Mr. Weston?"

"He won't need persuading," replied Mr. Weston. "He brought all his outfit with him so that he could keep in practice. It will be an excellent opportunity to try out some of his new tricks. How about it, Claude?"

"To hear is to obey," Claude said again. "Do you hear that, Petkins? Tonight we work."

"I hope your tricks don't include any monkey business," said Pussy. "I know that you're fond of the little beast, but for God's sake, don't let it come near me again."

Claude addressed the monkey again.

"The lady doesn't like you," he said. "But never mind, my precious, all ladies are not alike. Come down and I will whisper a secret in your ear before we go a-fishing."

He sat down on a chair and held the monkey on his knee. They appeared to converse together.

"You're surely not going to take that little brute out fishing with you," remarked Gunn, putting his arm around the girl's shoulders.

"Don't stop him," said Pussy, rubbing her head against his chest like a sensuous kitten. "It will catch cold, and die on his hands, thank goodness."

"No, no!" cried Claude, making great pantomime with his hands. "Behold, the good magician thwarts the wicked witch. Lo! Here is a woolly coat knitted for thee, my Petkins, by the kind, fat hands of Mother Mumsby!"

With all the concentration of a child dressing a favourite doll, he proceeded to thrust the arms of the chattering monkey through the top of a blue-and-scarlet knitted coat.

Again they laughed at Claude's absurdities, but Mr. Weston did not laugh with them. The smile had passed from his lips, and the twinkle from his eyes. With a muttered exclamation, he turned on his heel and strode out of the hotel. They gazed after him without comment, but Pussy, for the second time that morning, wondered what there could be in the name of Mrs. Mumsby to cause people to act in so strange a manner.

As if he sensed her thoughts, Claude looked up and smiled. "Don't take any notice of Dad," he said. "He's like Grumpy. He thinks 'all females is p'ison'."

CHAPTER V

At first sight there was little to attract you to The Fisherman's Rest, standing, as it did, directly on the main road, with its front rooms protected only by spiked iron railings from the curious glances of passers-by. Tourists, were they motorists, hikers, or cyclists, frequented the larger Lakeside Hotel, which stood, as its name implied, where the big lake lay like a gigantic octopus and stretched its streamy tentacles through the mountain passes to smaller lakes more wild and bleak than itself. But people who visited Aberllyn for fishing always stayed at The Fisherman's Rest.

The reason was not far to seek.

Your true fisherman is a creature who likes to be understood, and it is not easy to understand him. He will turn out of a warm bed at seven o'clock on a bitterly cold morning, and will fish continuously until seven o'clock at night in conditions of acute discomfort as long as it is light enough to see his cast. He will sit in a boat, his cramped limbs little eased by the latest design in rubber boat-cushions, and will exist all day on a few sandwiches and a flask of tea. He will suffer being buffeted by gales and soaked to the skin by rain, or will sweat in the heat and have his skin blistered by the sun's rays reflected from the still water. He will do all this, and return day after day with an empty creel, grumbling at the fish, the weather, the water, the light, and yet will feel exhilaratingly happy.

But as soon as he enters his hotel, he demands immediate and endless comforts. Hot water, warm fires, dry clothes, a comfortable bed, good drink, a pleasing variety of food, and a goodly company of fishing folk, to whose ready ears he may recount the prize catches of past days, and with whom he may commiserate upon the atrocious scarcity of fish in the present.

When such a fisherman, unrecommended, looked for accommodation in Aberllyn, he invariably chose the Lakeside Hotel. To his unknowing eyes, it was a bigger, brighter, and better hotel. And why, he would argue, should he choose to walk or drive half a mile to the lake every morning when he could stay at a hotel where his boat would await him only a hundred yards away?

But by the end of a week, he would be inventing excuses for leaving the hotel of his choice and would beg for a room, however small and poorly furnished, at The Fisherman's Rest.

The bedrooms at the Lakeside Hotel were bright and large, but while visitors to The Fisherman's Rest were sleeping snugly beneath warm, cotton-covered eiderdowns, clasping hot-water bottles, and were awakened by a hot cup of tea provided free by the management, those at the Lakeside Hotel shivered beneath inadequate blankets under a silk bedspread, and drank luke-warm tea for which they were charged sixpence extra. While wainscots in the hall at The Fisherman's Rest were peppered with power plugs for electric fires which visitors could move about at their will, and the lounge was heated by two generous coal fires, one at either end, the "Lakeside" lounge held a feeble fire which barely warmed the five people who could first make a circle around it, and the hall was not heated at all.

The Fisherman's Rest had two bars: one within the hotel itself, complete with high stools, foot rails, and elbow room, and another with rough sawdust-strewn floor and an outer door for the village people. At the Lakeside Hotel, whisky and cocktails were referred to as "alcoholic liquor", and were kept in a locked cupboard in the dining-room, whence they were abstracted in a furtive way by the waiter, who had first obtained the key from the office.

The manageress of the Lakeside Hotel was a touchy woman who took offence at the smallest suggestion of criticism, but Mrs. Evans of The Fisherman's Rest was a most admirable hostess, with capable hands and an attentive ear.

In figure she was not unlike Mrs. Mumsby, save that her thighs were longer and her carriage thereby rendered graceful, so that where Mrs. Mumsby waddled, she sailed along as if she wore a dignified crinoline. While Mrs. Mumsby visited a hairdresser each fortnight in order to keep a tell-tale streak from the parting of her hair, Mrs. Evans' hair was unashamedly grey. While Mrs. Mumsby's complexion was applied, layer by layer, out of innumerable bottles, Mrs. Evans' cheeks were rouged only by bending over the kitchen range, and her nose was dull or shiny according to the slack or busy part of the season. Nor was Mrs. Evans a widow, although she might well have been one for all that the visitors saw of her husband. Occasionally they might glimpse a wizened, grey-moustached man flitting about the kitchen quarters in shirt-sleeves, but for the most part he had become a person whom Mrs. Evans kept about the hotel for the same purpose as a nervous spinster keeps a man's hat hanging in the hall. Whether he took a place in the background because of her stronger character, or whether she had been forced to develop her abilities on account of his weakness, was a thing which no one had yet succeeded in discovering. But everyone agreed that she ran the hotel with inspired ability, and that her greatest inspiration had been the hall.

Now the hall at the Lakeside Hotel was merely a hall and nothing else – a draughty entrance through which you must of necessity pass in order to reach any other part of the hotel. But the hall at The Fisherman's Rest was so important that most of the fishing visitors believed that the hotel had been built round it.

In the hall, you became acquainted with your ghillie on the evening before your first day on the lake; in the hall, you waited for the luncheon-basket which would sustain you until late evening; in the hall, you took a last look at your flies and casts to ensure the success of the day; in the hall, you left coats and fishing tackle until the precise moment of your departure; in the hall, you deposited your catch on your return, while an ever-growing group of fellow-fishermen stood around, admiring, weighing, measuring, and criticizing each fish as it was laid tenderly, every tail straight, by the ghillie who had netted it; in the hall, at nine p.m. precisely, Taffy, the patient porter, gathered each catch on to its labelled tin tray, and wiped down the scaly tiles; and in the hall, little clans of otherwise ill-assorted people talked over their after-dinner coffee, while the faint odour of the departed fish arose to remind them of the day's sport.

When visitors returned from dinner that evening, however, the hall had assumed yet another aspect. The fish had been cleared away, and the blue-and-gold loom chairs had been arranged in rows facing an alcove cut off by black velvet curtains. In front of these stood three small square tables covered in black baize, their edges braided with gold.

Claude, who had dined early, could be seen flitting in and out of the curtains, arranging the paraphernalia for his display of magic. He was dressed in an outfit which matched the colouring of the tables; black, tight-fitting trousers with harlequin pockets, and a wide-sleeved tunic of gold, edged with black. He looked like some gay, handsome troubadour who had stepped straight out of the illustrated pages of a child's fairy book.

He paused for a moment beside one of the tables, and flexed his wrists, making graceful little passes in the air with his long, white fingers. After the long, sunny days on the lake, he had had to supplement their whiteness by the application of theatrical lotion so that their effect against the dark curtains should not be spoiled.

As they all entered the hall, he moved to a chair in the front row, and patted the blue silk cushion.

"Come along, Mrs. Mumsby," he said, with his most charming smile. "You are the guest of honour. Without you, I cannot perform. I've saved this front stall specially for you."

"Claude, you dear boy...!"

Mrs. Mumsby, wearing a pale-blue satin dress which looked as if it might collapse at any moment and pour her fat, white body in a heap on to the floor, moved down the aisle between the chairs towards him, bridling with smiles. She tapped his cheek with a playful finger, and squatted down on the chair he had indicated.

Claude settled the cushion behind her broad back.

"Comfortable?" he asked, and raised her fingers to his lips.

"Magician?" growled Major Jeans. "Damned gigolo, I should say. Oh, I beg your pardon," he added as Claude's father brushed heavily against him and walked towards his son.

Mrs. Mumsby looked up and smiled as he joined them, but Mr. Weston was in too much of a hurry to respond.

"All ready, Claude?" he asked. "How about starting now?"

"Okay." Claude clicked his heels together and gave his graceful little bow which his present costume showed off to greater advantage than usual, and disappeared behind the curtains.

The rest of the audience arranged themselves in the chairs, and, try as he would, Mr. Weston could not jolly them into the front seats, so that Mrs. Mumsby, seated in the chair on the extreme left, remained in isolated possession of the front row until Mr. Weston himself took the corresponding chair on the right aisle – an arrangement in which no one perceived any significance.

First, however, Mr. Weston took possession of the stage and introduced Claude in a little speech which needed the glare of footlights and the atmosphere of the theatre to make it appear natural. He ended on a simple note.

"We all think that he has a great future in conjuring, but you are an intelligent audience, and I will leave you to judge for yourself. May I present my son, Claude the conjuror."

Claude, grinning broadly, skipped from the curtained alcove with the grace of a Nijinsky, and was heartily clapped by Mrs. Mumsby from the front row, and cheered by Pussy, Gunn, and Mr. Pindar from the back. The others, seated midway between these biased enthusiasts, preserved the lukewarm attitude of people who fear to commit themselves to indiscretions. But they soon perceived that the enthusiasm was well-deserved. They had all seen better tricks, for his display was old-fashioned in parts, but they had seen nothing to surpass the showmanship of Claude.

He was undoubtedly a poseur, and yet there was something so naturally frank about his whole bearing that, even in his theatrical garb, he did not fail to be likable. He was a born actor, and his continuous flow of nonsense added greatly to the show. Where other magicians spoke patter which sounded stilted through over-rehearsal, Claude's comments were uttered with a *naiveté* which might have been spontaneous. His remarks were as light as thistledown which blew audaciously from his mouth, and floated gently over their heads. And all the time his lovely hands were moving in company with his words, picking endless cards from the air, tearing them to pieces, and making them whole again; taking eggs from Sir Courtney Haddox's neck, and flags from Mrs. Pindar's ear; turning water biblically into wine, wine into milk, milk into ink; and making endless clinking chains of round, Chinese rings which had no visible joints.

Perhaps his greatest achievement was the conversion of Major Jeans from polite scepticism to enthusiasm, which was first made known to the audience by the Major's acceptance of a forced card with a jump in the air and a delighted:

"By Jove, the boy's a marvel!"

From that moment the entertainment was a success, and Claude embarked on a series of tricks which necessitated the co-operation of members of the audience.

Mr. Winkley and Mr. Pindar were beckoned, willingly enough, to the front, and asked to take in each hand the ends of two pieces of coloured cord which Claude had knotted together. Over the knot he tied a scarf of rainbow colouring, uttered some mumbo-jumbo so absurd that he did not attempt to give it any meaning, and told them to pull the cords as tightly as possible. Then he flicked off the scarf, disclosing the two pieces of cord in their original smooth lengths, with the two men somewhat foolishly holding the ends.

"Oh, Mummy!" cried the Major, to the disgust of Miss Haddox who occupied the next chair. "I know how he does it!"

Claude had not yet missed an opportunity. He did not miss this.

"For my next trick," he said, "I shall require the services of a very clever little boy."

Major Jeans at once gave his knitted pullover a tug, fingered his tie self-consciously, swallowed twice, got up, and walked over to Claude.

All small boys are an asset to a good conjuror; those who profess to know how his tricks are achieved are a particularly welcome gift. But no conjuror can ever have been gifted by the co-operation of so clever a small boy as Major Jeans now became. His curious, unbelieving eyes peered everywhere; he questioned every movement, and demanded that things should be repeated.

"Huh!" he growled when Claude produced a handkerchief from an egg. "I knew it was an imitation one wiv' an 'ole in it!"

Claude's air of disgust at being so cleverly found out was splendid, but even more splendid was the Major's consternation when the same spurned egg was cracked, and a genuine yolk and white fell into a glass.

It was all amazingly good fun, and an hour passed too quickly for them all, so that it was a pity that Claude should have chosen to end his performance on a different note. It was, after all, the only mistake he made throughout the whole performance, and it was, moreover, a mistake of youth, and of romantic youth at that.

He began by asking for the assistance of any lady in the audience, but it was so obvious that he meant Mrs. Mumsby that no one else made any attempt to move. Throughout the entertainment there had seemed a special sympathy between them, as though he had silently appealed for her appreciation at the successful conclusion of each trick, which she in her turn had given by heading the applause.

Now, as she stood beside him, smiling encouragement, and glancing from time to time at the audience, Claude began a highly romantic story of a poor youth who loved a rich Princess, which he illustrated with his tricks, giving to Mrs. Mumsby the various articles mentioned in the story, which he produced from the air. And even as Major Jeans had become the perfect foil, so did Mrs. Mumsby become transformed into the epitome of a conjuror's lady assistant. As each article was produced, she held it up first to the left, and then to the right, showed her teeth in a toothpaste smile, and backed away to place it with surprised hands on one of the little tables. When, finally, Claude produced a shoulder-spray of red roses, the emblem of his love for the Princess, and again kissed her hand, her tears of joy seemed real.

They all applauded loudly, for the show had been cleverly presented, but they did not go away half-amazed, half-laughing, as an audience should do. It was a trick of showmanship that Claude had not yet learned, and they made allowances for him, yet Mr. Winkley, for one, felt, unreasonably, that the evening had been spoiled.

They filed slowly away, and Mrs. Mumsby, with a last smile at the young conjuror, joined them fussily. She nodded to Mr. Weston, and touched the nosegay at her shoulder.

"He's such a *dear* boy," she said.

CHAPTER VI

The Big Lake glinted in the sunshine of the October morning. Light clouds skimmed gently over the blue sky and sent little shadows scudding across the surface of the water. The sun touched the crisp fields at the margin of the lake, and combed its way upwards with a caressing movement towards the barer crowns of the mountains. A light breeze touched the tops of the low bushes, and set their leaves a-quiver; it rolled the water into soft, regular waves across the lake to lap against the gravelled shore.

The guests from the Fisherman's Rest walked the half-mile along the rutted lane to the lake, with anticipation in every step. Each one paused for less time than usual at the boggy edge where the boats were beached, while they put up their rods and strung their green lines through the rings of smooth agate, affixing a 2x or 3x cast, as their fancy dictated, with its first three tentative flies.

"When the wind is in the west, then the fishing is the best," sang out Mr. Pindar, but for the most part they were too anxious to get out, to waste time in the exchange of morning pleasantries. In any case, the five boats now in use were too far apart, for those ghillies who were disengaged had already hauled their boats high up in the green fields beyond the bog, where they would be safe from the winter storms which might be expected along the west coast of Wales at any time after the first of November. The Lakeside Hotel was already closed, and this end of the lake, which had been so full of bustling activities earlier in the season, was now bleak and forlorn.

Amid much waving of hands and yelling of "Tight lines!" the boats moved slowly off, and after some sixty or seventy pulls on the oars, continued their journey down the lake by slow, steady drifts.

By noon they were all moving towards the lower end of the lake, in the bay which was most easily fishable when the wind was in the west, where the boats could lap softly over the waves from the shore towards the islands, where in July the sea birds have their nests, and ply their restless flight for food to the seashore and back, or towards the black edges of rock where the salmon and big trout lie.

The water was slight and choppy, what few white horses there were being ridden with a light snaffle. The light was bright but not too bright; the wind was steady but not too strong. The fish rose freely to the fly. It was, in fact, that rarity of rarities – a perfect fishing day.

Mrs. Pindar lay in the stern of the boat on the last drift of the bay while Mr. Pindar and the ghillie fished. Mr. Gunn had taken the girl, Pussy, up to Hafod-y-llyn this morning, and Mrs. Pindar had taken his place in the boat.

As she lay there in complete idleness, her thoughts played around the man in the bows, whose mind was fixed on sea-trout, and his attention on the top dropper of his cast, which he drew expertly through the surface water. She tried to regard him critically, and could find no fault in him.

Rather short in stature, his body was well-proportioned and sloped to the hips from broad shoulders. His hair, which was glinting brown and tousled in bed, was now black and shining with brilliantine, and brushed into deep, natural waves from the forehead. Black lashes, golden at their tips, turned back from expressive, tender, brown eyes, which denied the firm obstinacy of his chin. From temple to chin, the brown smoothness of his skin was puckered by a long, deep scar, which added some ten years to his age. His face had a look which was lean without being hungry.

Her thoughts were interrupted by the sudden jerk of the ghillie's wrist, which set the boat rocking. He pulled in the slack of the line fiercely, and reeled it up, as the top of the rod quivered, and dived, and bent. A silver-bodied trout shot up in a spiral-twisting leap from the water, and dived down again in a vain attempt to rid his jawbone of the barbed hook he had so gullibly swallowed. The ghillie dipped the rod in salute, then tightened up again and held it firmly, butt well down, in his roughened hand.

"Would the lady like to play it now?" he asked almost appealingly, and in response to Mr. Pindar's encouraging nod, she took the rod, which was now heavy with its writhing and restless burden.

For three breathless minutes she followed the ghillie's instructions as best she could.

"Don't be too hard on him, ma'am, he's a good fish, look, let him run. Now reel up on him, no, not too fast, lower your rod when he leaps out of the water; now straighten up. Hold him! Hold him! Give him the butt, keep the butt of the rod right down and hold your elbow in. That's right. Now reel up a bit on him. No, no, not too much: he's not played out yet. Go easy. Now reel up slowly. Keep him going, ma'am. Easy now, keep him going. Keep his head up, so that he won't see the net. Easy now. This way." He leaned over the gunwale of the boat so far that it seemed that he must lose his balance, slid his net gently under the fish, and lifted the squirming silver streak into the boat, laughing, "I have him now, ma'am. Slack out your line. He was a well-hooked fish, yes."

He took the slippery trout in his hands, and hit its black head expertly on the seat in front of him.

"A good trout." smiled Mr. Pindar. "What does it weigh do you think? Two pounds?"

"About one and three-quarters, sir," replied the ghillie. "It's a cock fish. Do you see the long, hooked under-jaw, ma'am? That's what he uses to dig away the gravel where the hen can lay her eggs."

"Well make a fisherman of you yet, darling," said Pindar. "What about a spot of food now?"

"Is it lunch-time already?" exclaimed Mrs. Pindar, glancing at her watch.

"My stomach never lies. I don't need a watch," laughed Pindar, and the ghillie spat on his hands and dipped his grey oars in the water.

He did not ask them where they wanted to land for lunch, for there was only one suitable part of the shore in this particular bay. Along the greater part of it, the banks descended by rocky steepnesses to the water, while in other places they overhung the lake, and dripped water from the hills over their mossy ledges. Only at the extreme end of the bay did the land edge the lake in little gritty beaches, where a boat could easily be punted ashore, and hand-pulled to safety. It was towards these miniature beaches that all the boats would eventually make their way from the last drift of the bay, as their occupants felt the need for food.

The Pindars were the first to land, and after them came Mrs. Mumsby, holding up excited fingers to show an exaggerated number of fish.

Major Jeans, half-way down the bay, had just lost a fish, and after the first storm of his anger had passed, it had left an air of gloom in the boat, for he openly believed that it was due to bad lakemanship on the part of the ghillie, while the ghillie secretly thought that the Major was losing his touch.

But the gloom was soon dissipated when, after the ghillie's warning, "Strike now, Major, and you'll be in him, man!" Jeans jerked back his hand, and heard the reel scream as a trout pulled out the full length of his line and half the backing. When his efforts to bring the fish back to the boat proved unavailing, the ghillie seized his oars and began to row feverishly after it.

"Must be foul-hooked, Major," he shouted. "You were a bit late in the strike, man!"

"You get on with your rowing, and don't talk so much," rasped the Major. "This is a bigger fish than any you've ever had in your boat, and it isn't in your boat yet."

Already, in his imagination, he was storing all the details of a titanic struggle to tell to his cronies in the United Services Club on foggy London evenings. But even as the trout made its third long rush for freedom, he felt a sickening slackening of line, and knew that he had one tale the less to tell.

"Hard luck, sir," said the ghillie after the Major had spoken his mind on fishing in general, and on those fish in particular which take the fly only that they may dash the hopes of hardworking fishermen.

But Major Jeans glanced at the nearing shore of the bay where two boats already lay unoccupied and bellied over, and indicated with a jerk of his thumb that he was ready for lunch.

"It was foul-hooked I think, indeed," reiterated the ghillie, as the Major helped him to beach the boat.

"Foul-hooked, my grandmother's false teeth!" retorted the Major. "It broke my asterisked cast!"

Claude sat in the bows of the fifth boat, and sang all the songs he could remember from Walt Disney's films. Like many other people he gave the credit for their composition to the cartoonist, for whom he had the greatest admiration, "because, like me, he is an artist". When he caught a trout, which he did on an average of one in two or three drifts, he stopped singing, and whistled softly, while the little monkey sat at the bottom of the boat, wearing his scarlet woollen coat, and patted the bodies of the dead fish.

As they reached the end of the last drift of the bay, he put his rod down, stretched himself stiffly, and began to massage first his hands, and then his knees in their greenish riding breeches.

"Stiff, stiff, I'm stiff, I'm a big stiff," he sang, to a "Snow-White" tune. "It's about time you caught a fish, Dad," he went on, leaning forward to count the trout in the boat. "Do you know that I've caught three to your one? And on a perfect day like this." He looked at his father over the ghillie's broad shoulder. "You look a bit tired," he said. "I hope you haven't been overdoing it again. Let's go and have lunch."

General Sir Courtney Haddox played his fifth trout with increasing exasperation.

It really was most annoying to catch trout, day after day, when you were after salmon. You'd think that any self-respecting trout would ignore anything so large and gaudy as a salmon fly, but no! it seemed to attract all the tiny fish in the lake. It was especially annoying because old Jeans thought him a fool for going for salmon in October. The proper time to get them, the Major said, was in May and June. But he knew different. He remembered one season when he had brought in a salmon every day for a fortnight, and he'd be damned if he'd fish for trout just because everyone else did. He couldn't see any sport whatever in trout-fishing; a salmon was the king of all fish, and one sixteen-pounder was worth all the trout you could catch in a season. Anyone could get trout, even beginners like young Weston, even Mrs. Mumsby, but you had to be a good fisherman to hook and play a salmon. It was your wits against his all the time: he might be sulking under the ledges for an hour, gradually fraying your cast, if you hadn't the requisite skill to inveigle him out into the open water. Let Jeans and Winkley bring in their large baskets of trout – he was the best salmon fisherman in the hotel and didn't think it boasting to say so. If he'd hooked the salmon that Gunn and Pindar had been bragging about yesterday, he'd have landed it even if he had only had a ten-foot rod; he'd have landed it if he'd hooked on a bent pin dangling at the end of a piece of stick! Let him just bring in one salmon before the end of the season: that would wipe the eyes of all the others, and justify at last Ethel's outlandish praise of his fishing.

His ghillie eyed him a trifle sourly.

He didn't really like fishing with the General, but his love of money had induced him to push himself into his favour, for Sir Courtney tipped lavishly when he left. Also, his other clients were usually impressed when they knew that he ghillied for General Sir Courtney Haddox, and their tips became increasingly large. But he often wondered whether it was really worth it, for it was a tiring job. For one thing, the General *would* fish for salmon at the end of the season, when they were black and out of condition, and never took the fly freely. For another, he would not allow his ghillie to fish in the boat at the same time as himself because he said it ruined the water for him. And so he had to sit on his behind all day, leaning idly on one oar, while he gazed endlessly at Sir Courtney's dipping line.

Sir Courtney thought he was a good fisherman, mused the ghillie, and what he didn't say in praise of his own fishing, his sister did. But he hadn't the adaptability of the best fishing gentlemen. Today, for instance, when the water was ideal for sea-trout, and the breeze altogether too light for salmon, Sir Courtney had insisted on fishing the ledges, almost as if he had an appointment there. In consequence, he was catching nothing but tiddlers of a size which any self-respecting child would have returned to the water.

He sighed, but, like most of his compatriots, he had learned to curb his impulses in the cause of mammon. So, instead of clipping Sir Courtney under the chin and putting up the trout rod which he always hopefully brought out in the boat with him, he eased himself on the seat, and glanced inquiringly at his employer, hands on oars, as a hint that it was time for lunch.

But the General was not ready for lunch. He did not, in fact, care whether he had any lunch or not. He had seen a slight swirl in the water about half-way down the drift, which might have been made by a salmon, and he intended to drift as nearly as possible over that particular spot all day until he saw it again.

But as he opened his mouth to tell his ghillie to pull again to the head of the bay, he caught sight of a red parasol waving violently on the shore.

"Lunch," he said briefly.

Ethel did not like to be kept waiting.

Mr. Winkley, who had just landed his eighth fish, lit his fifteenth cigarette, and looked across at his ghillie who was disentangling the tail-fly from the net.

"Any use going over that last drift again, David? I rose a few good fish, you know."

David glanced unnecessarily over his shoulder at nothing in particular.

"I wouldn't say it is, sir. You've only picked up one trout on the last two drifts. I should say the one o'clock rise is over, sir."

"Right. We'll give it a rest then. If we get as many fish again after lunch, we shall have a pretty basket to show in the hall."

"We shall indeed." said David; "but it was a pity you lost that big fellow. He'd be three pounds if he was an ounce, sir."

"Oh, I'll get one as big as that this afternoon, if that's all that is worrying you."

"'Twas a pity all the same, sir," persisted David. "They'd have made a grand pair, the two of them."

"Get away with you, you old ruffian," laughed Mr. Winkley. "You're never satisfied."

David spat on his horny hands and pulled on his oars with steady, unhurried strokes.

Mr. Winkley placed his rod in a horizontal position along the side seat of the boat, pulled out a yard or two of line, and placed a small lump of grey rock on it to act as a check. He did this as a matter of habit, without much expectation of hooking a fish on the trailing flies, then he slipped down on to the bottom boards of the boat, and lay there in dreamy placidity, surrounded by numerous navy-blue and gold cigarette tins of various shapes and sizes, in which he invariably kept flies, casts, and an occasional Silver Spoon or Golden Devon.

He fingered the flies of long-forgotten seasons which clung by their rusty hooks to the lapels of his tweed fishing jacket, and surveyed the lake through half-closed eyes, for the light reflected from the water was strong in spite of the sheltering brim of the old trilby hat which he rescued year after year from the lumber room.

He drank in the peace of the scene with the deep thirst of a town-parched soul. During the past week, London newspapers had been full of "Indian Summer" headlines, with the

attendant observations on city typists discarding their
stockings, and the usual predictions of "the hottest October for
forty years". The tube he travelled on had seemed stuffier and
noisier and more crowded than any other. His little office at
Scotland Yard, which always appeared to have been as much of
an afterthought on the part of the authorities as Mr. Winkley
himself, had seemed more stifling than any other part of that
illustrious building. His work had seemed more difficult, the
Assistant Commissioner more exacting... In a word, Mr.
Winkley had needed a holiday.

He lay and wallowed in the bliss of the sudden change; in
the exhilaration of the fresh, warm, sea-laden air, in the
pleasant contentment of having caught eight fish on his own
rod, in the peace of the quiet Welsh countryside. Already he
had half-forgotten the dust and noise and rush of London, had
half-forgotten his work, and crime statistics, and whether the
Irish gangsters would really carry out their threat for
Christmas Day, now that their cherished code (which he had
deciphered by luck and a knowledge of the islands in Killarney
Lakes assimilated during a disappointing week's fishing there)
lay locked in his desk. For three blissful weeks now he could let
his brain lie fallow, and think of nothing but Coch y Bonddu,
Orange Grouse, Red Palmer, Black Zulu – names which made
music for his fisherman's soul.

For him, now, Scotland Yard was non-existent. Fishing was
the thing!

CHAPTER VII

Mrs. Mumsby pulled the last piece of lobster out of its claw and
crammed it into her mouth. She flung the shell towards the
edge of the lake, where it immediately sank amongst the other
discarded coral-pink shells which fringed the margin of the
water, then she bit heavily into a hard-boiled egg, and looked
around her.

She knew that there must be at least four or five other people near the little beach where she was sitting leaning against a convenient grey rock, for few of them continued to fish after half past one without taking lunch, yet the only living creature within sight was a small black bullock which grazed incuriously on the short crisp grass a few yards to her right. She could not even see her ghillie, although she knew that he was somewhere within hailing distance, waiting for the last cup of coffee from her flask. She had noticed him a moment ago talking to one of the other ghillies – about fish, of course; these men never talked about anything else.

A murmur of voices came from the other side of the rough wall to her left, which was built of the grey stones which lay scattered everywhere in the fields and on the mountainsides.

No, there was no need for her to sit alone. She had only to walk a few yards to find company where she would always be sure of a welcome as long as she could talk about fish. But today she did not want company. Like a certain well-known actress, she wanted to be alone.

She had thought that things were beginning to go well with her at last, and that all her schemes were succeeding. But since last night she had not been so sure. She needed a little time to herself. She would have to think things out very carefully...

She stretched herself, and yawned so widely that the hinges of her jaw emitted a slight click.

I've eaten too much lunch, as usual, she thought cheerfully. *But it's a lovely day; I can have a nap for an hour if I like, thank goodness.*

She emptied the dregs of coffee from her thermos flask, added milk, and four lumps of sugar, and cooed for the ghillie.

With scarcely a sound he came towards her from behind a tall, neighbouring rock, and took the cup from her hands.

"You can see where my mouth's been, by the lipstick," she said, looking up at him coyly through the artificial eyelashes which cost her five shillings a pair, and came off in the rain. "Here, take some more to eat, John, and don't disturb me for half an hour at least. I'm going to have forty winks. I've had too much lunch."

She slapped her enormous stomach, giggled, and proceeded at once to make herself as comfortable is possible in a half-sitting, half-lying position against the grey rock.

The ghillie nodded in reply, picked up an unopened package of sandwiches, and made his way slowly out of sight in the direction from which he had appeared. He walked away until he was sure that he was well out of earshot, for he knew from experience that Mrs. Mumsby was far more likely to disturb him than he was likely to disturb her. He lowered himself on to the grass without spilling the coffee from the cup, and stirred it with one horny finger while he reflected, with true Celtic despondency, on the ills to which his life was subject.

The ghillie's name was John Jones, and you might have met half a dozen other men so named in Aberllyn. Like them, too, he was short and black-haired, and his face in repose was shadowed by a dark, brooding look which some people thought untrustworthy. But his eyes were a distinguishing feature, for one was china-blue and the other brown, like the eyes of a half-bred Merle Collie. Perhaps this was why he habitually looked at the ground when he was walking.

Like all the other ghillies, he hated working for Mrs. Mumsby. He knew of nothing more tiring than being in her company for six or seven hours each day, evading her attempts at seduction. Oh, it was no exaggeration. Every ghillie in Aberllyn knew that she was man mad.

She did not seem to understand that a man had his profession to think of. A ghillie was not a common boat-puller like those fellows who touted up and down on the promenades of fashionable seaside resorts, pestering people with their everlasting, "Nice day for a row, miss."

Any man could row a boat, but a ghillie had to be highly trained and experienced. He had to know the parts of the lake where the sea-trout lay, and their movements from the first run of those with the sea-lice on their backs, to their final journey to the spawning beds. He had to know where the best drifts began and ended, and how to row to them without disturbing the fish for others. He had to know when the wind was likely to freshen, so that he did not get caught in the middle of the lake by a sudden gale, for the lake was deep, and storms sudden, so that an inexperienced man might well drown there. He had to be a weather prophet, and know whether to persuade a faint-hearted client to go out on the lake or stay in the hotel. He had to know how to land a fish by net or gaff, and be equally proficient in the vastly different techniques of lake fishing and river fishing. He had to know always a little more than his client, and had to be a good psychologist into the bargain, so that he could restrain the over-enthusiastic, or cajole the hypersensitive man.

He had to do all this because his one object was to bring in as many fish as possible every day until he became known as a first-class ghillie, and so gravitated automatically to serve the best fishermen among the many visitors to the hotel. And John Jones reckoned that he earned his ten shillings a day and the two drinks supplied to him free every evening in the public bar of The Fisherman's Rest.

There were tips, too, reflected John, and Mrs. Mumsby was known to give larger tips than anyone else. Nevertheless he disliked working for her. It advertised too much that he was regarded as the least proficient of any ghillie now employed. In the season, she would have been unable to secure the services of any man except that old toper, Evan Griffiths, who was so deaf that he replied to every remark with a jerk of his head and a beery "Yes – yes".

It would not have been so bad if Mrs. Mumsby had been in the least interested in fishing, but she usually only tried for an hour, and then handed him her rod, and lay in the bottom of the boat, staring at the various parts of his anatomy, asking about his love affairs, and telling coarse stories which it would have been difficult to cap even in the Sailor's Club in the village. At first he had felt ashamed, but after a few days he had grown so used to it that he never listened, but merely punctuated the pauses, like Evan Griffiths, with an inane "Yes – yes".

He mustn't grumble. It all meant extra money in the Savings Bank, so that he was a little nearer to marrying Pegi. If Mrs. Mumsby wanted a few lessons in sex-appeal, Pegi, with her saucy black eyes and provocative mouth, and that heart raising twist of her short skirts, could give them to her.

He glanced up at the sun.

Mrs. Mumsby wouldn't be awake yet. There was time enough for him to do what he had promised.

He rose to his feet, cleaned out the cup with a piece of newspaper, put it in his outer pocket, and walked off.
Half an hour later he returned, and made his way reluctantly back to Mrs. Mumsby, gazing down at the ground until her preposterous body came into view.

Then he looked up.

Mrs. Mumsby lay where he had left her, her body contorted, her face purpled, and her eyes and mouth wide open. Beside her sat Claude's little monkey, patting her warm, dead body as callously as it had patted the cold, dead bodies of the fish, while, like the sound of a soul in agony, the cry of a curlew arose from the marshy ground beside the lake.

CHAPTER VIII

Police Constable Thomas Lloyd pedalled his bicycle slowly along by the lake towards Aberllyn village.

He was a dark little man of insignificant appearance even in uniform, yet when on duty, he assumed some small measure of dignity by virtue of his own egotism. He had all the pomposity and officiousness of Ernest the Policeman, without his geniality of manner, and he looked a man with a grievance, as indeed he was.

The nephew of the local postmaster, Thomas Lloyd had always had a desire to enter the police force. To that end he had pored over books, learned traffic regulations, first aid, the Morse code, and the answers to such General Knowledge questions as could not by any stretch of imagination be of use to a policeman. At length, after the usual training course, he had been detailed as constable to his native village by what he firmly believed to be string-pulling, and what was undoubtedly an oversight on the part of the police authorities. But any idea he might have had of achieving fame and respect through his local associations had quickly been dissipated. The people of Aberllyn remembered him as a sticky-fisted youngster who had gone barefooted to the little village school. He was still "that young Thomas Lloyd" to them, an object of fun rather than of dignity.

When he had warned the local midwife to keep her hens from straying across the road, she had laughed, and said, "Why, Thomas bach, you can't summons me. Didn't I bring you into this world before that lazy, good-for-nothing doctor came, and a sicklier child I never knew. Why, if it weren't for me you wouldn't be here today. Just you get along with your job and leave my hens alone!"

When he'd warned young Evan Jones that he'd lock him up next time he found him drunk and disorderly, Evan had only hiccupped in his face and said, "You're a nice one to talk indeed, Thomas Lloyd. Wasn't it you that first made me drink apple cider behind the hayrick on my father's farm?"

But perhaps his bitterest experience had been when, after lying in wait to catch the boys who were systematically robbing Farmer Owen's orchard, he had heard their shouts of "Run! Run!" change to "No, it's only Thomas Lloyd."

From that moment he had become ruthless, and was now the best hated man in Aberllyn. He never lost an opportunity of prosecuting man, woman, or child for an indictable offence, and filled twice as many note-books as any other member of His Majesty's Police Force in the British Isles, Irish Civic

Guards not excepted. At holiday times he stood on duty at the cross-roads close to The Fisherman's Rest, with an eagle eye for an "L", and a sharp instinct for the driver who had forgotten to renew his licence. In this way alone could he be sure of keeping his name in front of the authorities, so that he would ultimately earn promotion through attention to duty and be transferred from a district which had become loathsome to him to one where his origin would be unknown.

As he cycled along the dusty road, he searched his mind for some means of ensuring a fresh crop of prosecutions for the forthcoming District Court. A gap in the hedge showed him a vista of the lake glittering in the sun. He could not understand why there were no boats out there, until he looked at his watch and saw that it was two-fifteen, and guessed that it was the end of the fishermen's lunch-hour. He might call at The Fisherman's Rest, he thought, to see whether any visitors had forgotten to take out a salmon or trout licence. Mrs. Evans could explain, of course, that the licence had been taken out, but that the amount was to be added to the bill, which wasn't the law, as he'd often had to tell her. However, she and the doctor were the only two people in Aberllyn of whom he was afraid, and although he knew he would never dare to prosecute either of them, still the licence idea might be worth a drink, when he was off duty.

He spat into the dust of the road.

I'm wasted in a little village like this, he thought. *A man with my devotion to duty should be at the Yard by now. But the Bible truly says that a prophet is unhonoured in his own country. The trouble is that I've no chance to show the chief constable what a fine policeman I am. It's too peaceful in Aberllyn. All I can hope for is a few drunk-and-disorderlies, out-of-date licences, exceeding the 30-mile limit, bicycles without lamps, and an odd fight or two. It will take a few thousand convictions like that to earn promotion. What we want in Aberllyn is a nice juicy murder!*

He heard a shout behind him, and, looking over his shoulder, saw a man running towards him from a point in the road which he had just passed. He turned and cycled back, and recognized the man who was ghillying for the Westons.

"What's wrong? Somebody dead?" he asked hopefully.

The ghillie looked shocked.

He had expected to startle the constable with his news, but it looked as if he knew all about it already. But how could he know? And why was he cycling along the lake road at this time of day, when he should have been on traffic duty at the cross-roads? Well, it was none of his business, and it was best to keep in Lloyd's good books.

"Yes," he replied. "A lady from The Fisherman's Rest, name of Mumsby. She'd been fishing, and died after lunch."

"H'm. Surfeit of palfreys," was the constable's amazing reply. He had once read *1066 and All That*, and had taken it seriously. "You'd better fetch the doctor. He's fishing the river away back along the road. I passed his car not long ago: you'll see it standing by the road. And when you've found him you'd better warn Mrs. Evans and tell her to send a car to the landing-stage. Here, take my bicycle. You can leave it at the cottage when you've done. And mind what you're doing with it, man; it's Government property!"

Two minutes later he was looking down at Mrs. Mumsby's dead body, and there Mr. Winkley found him when he belatedly joined the little circle formed by Mr. Weston, Claude, Major Jeans, Mr. and Mrs. Pindar, and their respective ghillies.

The constable was already writing details in his note-book in a form of shortened longhand, legible only to himself. Like the old-fashioned stage policeman, he sucked his pencil from time to time, but had introduced a touch of originality by using one of the copying-ink variety, which left purple striations on his tongue and round his mouth.

"'I came back and found her lying dead'," he repeated, as he wrote the ghillie's final words. He looked up. "Can anyone corroborate that?" he asked.

"Yes... at least... I came next," said Claude. He passed a weary hand over his pale, clammy forehead. "Do you mind if I sit down?" he asked. "I've been sick, and I still feel a bit shaky. Seeing her like that..." He shuddered. "It upset me."

Mr. Weston moved nearer to him, and led him to a convenient rock where he could turn his eyes away from Mrs. Mumsby, and still face the constable.

"It was the lobster," said Mr. Weston. "You know I didn't feel so well myself after eating it today. It's a bit late in the season for lobster, and nothing upsets me so quickly."

"'Tis the voice of the lobster, I heard him declare

You have baked me too brown, I must sugar my hair,"

said Claude with a ghost of his usual manner. Then his voice changed. "Oh God! How can I be so callous? Mother Mumsby! Poor Mother Mumsby!"

Lloyd looked perplexed.

"Your mother, was she, sir? I didn't understand..."

"Oh no," said Claude. "I only called her that for fun. She didn't mind, you know. In fact she rather liked it. You see, she was always so kind to me."

"I see," said Lloyd, moistening his pencil. "Well, there's nothing to be done until the doctor comes."

But it seemed as if Claude could not stop talking.

"We must have been close to her all the time," he said. "We were sitting on the other side of that wall. I wanted to stretch my legs, so I took my rod and went to fish off the rocks. It's high up there, and I could see right down on to this part of the lake. I saw Mrs. Mumsby lying there, so I rushed down and – and she was like this!"

He buried his face in his hands and began to cry.

Mr. Weston put out a hand and stroked the copper-coloured hair.

"Poor boy!" he said. "You should never have seen her like that." He turned to Lloyd. "My son was very fond of her," he explained.

They were interrupted by a voice from the wall.

"Is anything wrong? Can we help?"

Sir Courtney Haddox walked through the gap in the wall, his lean head thrust forward. He turned to give a hand to his sister, then went on:

"We heard voices, and it seemed strange –"

"It's the Merry Widow," said Major Jeans. "She's had a stroke – or – or something."

He appeared to give some deliberate significance to the words, and Mr. Winkley intercepted a look which seemed to impart some warning to the newcomers.

Miss Haddox pushed forward and looked down at Mrs. Mumsby. She gave a loud cry, and running back to her brother, clutched him round the neck and began to laugh and scream alternately. Finally she threw herself on to the ground and arched her body in the stiff convulsions of hysteria.

Sir Courtney made sympathetic clucking noises and surveyed her with helpless concern. But to Mr. Winkley's critical eyes the attack looked too deliberate to be authentic.

Mrs. Pindar grasped her husband's arm.

"Take me away. I can't stand any more of this," she whispered, and he put his arm around her and led her gently towards the edge of the lake, where they sat with their backs to the others.

"Where's the doctor?" growled Major Jeans. "We can't stay here all day."

The constable's reply to what he assumed to be a reflection on his efficiency was luckily interrupted by the sound of a vehicle approaching along the road with a noise like an out-of-date threshing machine. It stopped with a squeaking of brakes which put a surprisingly speedy end to Miss Haddox's hysterics. She sat up, and took the cup of water which one of the ghillies was still holding patiently.

In a few minutes there appeared a brisk little man with long, silvered hair and bushy eyebrows, carrying a salmon rod in one hand, and a black leather bag in the other. His eyes were red, and his temper raw, from lack of sleep.

"Huh! Mrs. Mumsby, eh?" he exclaimed. "She might have known that I'd been up all night delivering twins. That woman never had any consideration for me." He came forward and looked down at the twisted body. "Huh!" he said again.

"Dead as a doornail! I told her that heart of hers would play this trick on her one day. Well, what's this?" he snapped, looking round at them all. "A Court of Inquiry, eh? Arrested anyone yet, Thomas? No? What's wrong with you then? Right arm paralysed?"

Dr. Rippington Roberts (his somewhat imposing name was due to the foresight of his mother who had decided before his birth that he should become a doctor, and had invented an imaginary family name to supplement the more ordinary Roberts) handed his salmon rod reverently to a ghillie, plumped his bag on the grass beside Mrs. Mumsby, and followed it rheumatically.

He made a formal examination of the body, then sat back on his haunches, and gazed at it in puzzled silence, while the others looked on as if fascinated.

"Anyone with her when she died? John? No, you wouldn't be."

Suddenly he pounced on Mrs. Mumsby's left hand, and turned it palm uppermost, revealing a wound in which was embedded a small object, barely recognizable as an artificial fly.

"That's it!" he exclaimed triumphantly. "I knew there'd be something to account for it. She was turning over her flies, and got one stuck in her hand. The shock of it killed her."

Thomas Lloyd waggled the point of his pencil up and down on his protruding tongue.

"But that would hardly be enough of a shock to kill her, Doctor, surely," he said.

"Huh! You know more about it than I do, do you?" snapped the doctor.

"No, no, Doctor, but I hope I know my duty," said Lloyd.

"I hope you do, man," retorted the doctor, "though if you do, I don't see how you happened to be here at all at this time of day. But that's just like you, Thomas. You always get there before me. You even got yourself born before I arrived." (This was a sore point between them.) "As for the shock not killing her, it was just the kind of thing I'd told her to avoid. Her heart was in a rotten state and any sudden pain like that would be too much for it. We all know that you've got a bee in your bonnet about people not dying natural deaths, but how else do you suppose they'd be likely to die in a peaceful place like Aberllyn? There's only one death that's likely to occur from unnatural causes. That will be by poisoning, and the person will be yourself. Just look at your tongue, man – God knows it's long enough! I've warned you that you'll poison yourself if you go on licking that pencil any longer. But you'll never learn. You made yourself sick as a child by licking all the gum off your uncle's stamps and I suppose you're too old to change."

A subdued murmur of amusement ran round the little circle of people whose day's sport had been so tragically spoiled. It relieved the tension among them, and they began to talk quietly together. The Major exchanged a few words with his ghillie, Miss Haddox became quite normal and took her brother over to join the Pindars, and even Claude managed to smile wanly at his father.

But Mr. Winkley stood still, looking thoughtfully down at the fly which protruded from the dead woman's hand.

CHAPTER IX

After the doctor had composed Mrs. Mumsby's twisted limbs, and had released the salmon fly from her hand, two of the ghillies improvised a stretcher and settled her body in the boat. The constable seated himself in the bows, and John Jones pulled towards the head of the lake, looking as unperturbed as ever.

"Charon," murmured Major Jeans.

"I beg your pardon," said Mr. Weston.

The Major started, as if he had not realized that he had spoken aloud.

"Fellow who used to row the souls of the dead across the what's-its-name, and take the coins off their closed eyes for fare. 'Per twopence per person per trip,' as Sam Small would say. That's it. Charon. I never could think of a good name for that fellow before –"

But Mr. Weston had moved away.

The other boats followed Mrs. Mumsby's in unstudied order, for despite the favourable conditions, everyone seemed to take it for granted that fishing was over for the day. Nor did it occur to them as strange that in this age of individuality they should all be moved to act in accordance with some ancient herd instinct. When the boats were beached, they set out silently, took off casts, reeled in lines, removed reels, took down their rods, and placed them in the khaki-coloured canvas cases, which were tied with as many bows as a bride's rest-gown.

Thomas Lloyd crossed over towards them.

"You'd better go back to the hotel." he remarked. "The car will be here soon, and John Jones and I will wait. It was a pity to spoil your day's fishing, but it couldn't be helped, indeed."

All, except Claude, formed a little group, and walked slowly, talking, towards the hotel. He followed a little way behind, whispering brokenly to his agitated monkey. Behind them came the ghillies, laden with luncheon-baskets, mackintoshes, spare rods, nets, gaffs and fish. They clacked together in Welsh.

Pussy Partridge and Gunn were standing outside the hotel, and greeted them boisterously.

"What ho! You look like a funeral. What brings you all back again so early?"

"Mrs. Mumsby is dead," said Major Jeans solemnly.

They roared with laughter.

"So you've really got rid of her at last," said Gunn. "I always said that woman would die an unnatural death."

"Which of you killed her?" asked Pussy.

They gazed at her in horrified silence.

"Well, you needn't all look so guilty," went on Pussy. "*You can't all have done it, you know, unless you set on her like a pack of hounds and tore her limb from limb, and I hardly think you're bloodthirsty enough for that, although I've heard each one of you say at different times that you could just murder that woman."

Major Jeans flashed a look of hatred at her, and stormed into the house. Mr. Weston passed without a word. Mrs. Pindar made a spasmodic little movement with her hands; Mr. Pindar propelled her gently towards the front door and glared at Pussy over his shoulder.

"Rotten bad form!" he exclaimed.

General Sir Courtney Haddox dropped his fishing rod and swore execrably. His sister ignored Gunn, and said icily to Pussy, "I suppose you think you're clever, but you're merely being offensive."

Pussy stared after them, and her arched eyebrows lifted until they nearly met the blonde widow's peak of hair on her forehead.

"Well!" she exclaimed. "What's the matter with them all?"

Gunn shook his head.

"It beats me," he said. "Let's ask Claude."

Claude walked slowly over the small grey river pebbles which covered the front drive of the hotel, dragging his coat along the ground, and looking the picture of misery.

"Hallo, Claude. What's happened? Lost sixpence and found a farthing?"

Claude halted abruptly.

"Mrs. Mumsby's dead," he said in a dull voice. "Heart failure, the doctor says, but she must have died in agony. She looked awful." He gulped. "I saw her... I..."

Gunn and Pussy looked at each other in consternation.

"And I thought they were joking," remarked Pussy. "We've certainly put our foot into it this time."

Gunn nodded.

"Both feet, hard," he replied. "Thank God for a sensible explanation anyway, Claude. From the look of them we thought someone had murdered her."

Claude stared at them in horror.

"Don't say that!" he cried. "Oh, don't say that!"

He dropped his coat, and rushed blindly into the hotel, slamming the door behind him.

Piggy Gunn blew out his cheeks like his Disney namesake and deflated them slowly.

"Well!" he exclaimed. "It's beyond me. Here we are, you and I, stuck in a lousy fishing hotel at the wrong end of the year amongst a lot of dismal Jimmies, and do we bring sunshine into their lives or do we not?"

"We do not," replied Pussy promptly. "If you ask me, it looks jolly fishy for them to act in that way, and a few gentle inquiries wouldn't be out of place. We might find more in this than meets the eye."

"Trust you to do that," returned Gunn, ruffling his tousled hair. "But don't forget that if you start asking questions, it might give other people the same idea, and before we know where we are, someone will want to know what we've been doing today."

"M'm," replied Pussy, with a knowing nod. "I get you. I hadn't thought of that."

"And what have you been doing?" asked a gentle voice behind them.

They jumped round as if startled by a shot, and saw the long, lean figure of Mr. Winkley sitting on a white-painted hotel seat, examining the flies in his old trilby hat.

Pussy ignored the question.

"You've been out on the Big Lake today. What have you got to do with this commotion about Mrs. Mumsby?" she demanded.

"Oh," replied Mr. Winkley. "Didn't you know? I killed her!"

The two young faces crinkled with mutual smiles.

"Sez you," retorted Gunn.

"Sez I," returned Mr. Winkley, grammatically.

CHAPTER X

"I must say I don't like the look of it," said Pussy seriously as she stumped out the stub of her Russian cigarette.

It was six o'clock the same evening, and she and Gunn were sitting alone among the empty tea-tables in the lounge.

"There's something wrong somewhere," she went on. "I can feel it in my bones."

Gunn slid his loose-limbed body still further back against the velvet cushions of an embossed hide chair, and sighed.

"Oh, for heaven's sake, Pussy," he said in an exasperated voice, "do stop harping on that string. You haven't stopped all day. Just because a handful of people look upset and uncomfortable when you accuse them of murder, you imagine there must be some truth in it."

"It isn't that so much," replied the girl, frowning lines into her smooth forehead. "It's Claude. He's making as much fuss over Mrs. Mumsby's death as I imagine you'd make over mine, and I can't believe he was ever in love with her. He's eighteen and she must have been forty-five if she was a day. Besides, she was almost repulsive with that great slug-like body of hers. There's something sinister about the whole affair, somehow, and I believe Claude knows it."

Gunn sighed again.

"If you ask me anything," he said, "I think old Claude is going crackers. Look what an exhibition he made of himself at tea-time, when old Fish-eyes said all that about Mrs. Mumsby being an exceedingly vulgar woman, *nouveau riche*, and no breeding. Why, he looked as if he could have gouged her eyes out when she blithered about the Lord removing her from this earth because she was no longer useful nor ornamental."

He paused, and they both seemed to hear again Claude's voice raised in his passionate outburst, "She wasn't removed. She died from shock. Shock, I tell you. Shock!"

"Well, of course, it was in pretty bad taste for her to say a thing like that when Mrs. Mumsby had only been dead a few hours. You know the old tag, '*De mortuis, nil nisi bonum*', or 'Don't call the dead names: they make good bones'. But, hang it all, nobody takes the Haddox seriously, and he ought to have had more sense. It just shows you that you never know where you are with these artistic blokes and their lily-white hands."

He glanced surreptitiously at his own hands, sunburnt and tingling, with their well-manicured nails slightly dirty for the sake of masculinity.

"That's it," said Pussy eagerly. "Shock. He's been talking all day about people dying from shock."

"But why shouldn't he?" said Gunn logically. "After all, he did like her even if she was a slug, and the doctor says that she died from the shock caused by getting that fly-hook stuck in her hand –"

"Well, I don't believe a shock like that would kill a mouse, even if it had a weak heart," retorted Pussy.

"Upon my soul," said Gunn, "you're the most obstinate, pig-headed woman I ever met in my life. You listen to a whole list of facts with a superior air, and then toss your head, and go off believing something quite different that you've invented yourself."

She laughed at him, and he wriggled uncomfortably.

"Oh, all right," he growled. "You think it's queer, but all the same it's none of your business. So what?"

"So I'm going to make it my business," said Pussy with her most engaging smile. "I do think there's something queer about Mrs. Mumsby's death, and I'm going to find out what it is. What's more, you're going to help me."

"Oh no, you can count me out, my sweet."

"If I do," said Pussy vindictively, "I shall knock you out first! Look here, Piggy, you're supposed to be staying here with us. Mother and I have come to this lousy place because you wanted to do some fishing –"

"But it was your mother's idea," protested Gunn.

"I know, but only because she wanted to give you something interesting to do to keep you out of mischief, and because she used to come here in the good old days, and she thought it was such a nice hotel, the poor lamb!"

"And so it is."

Pussy stamped a petulant foot.

"Of course it is, you boob, that's the trouble! It's too damned nice for words. No midnight parties. No cheery people. Nothing to do except catch a few miserable fish. If I stay here much longer I shall start growing fins and open my mouth like a trout –"

"If you'd only shut it as often..." murmured Gunn.

"Shut up, Piggy! I'm serious. I've gone for walks until I've worn holes in my shoes. I've looked at the sea till I feel in need of Mothersill's. I know the titles of all the sixpenny books in the post office, and if I look at the lake any more I shall go and drown myself in it. It's all very fine for you. You can fish and enjoy it, and you can amuse yourself pressing 'Go' and 'Stop' buttons on your cine-camera, but I shall go bats or cuckoo if I can't find some way of brightening up the daily round."

"So what?" said Gunn again.

"So I'm going to play murder."

"That soppy game!" said Gunn in disgusted tones. "Why, that went out with Bright Young Things. Be your age, Pussy. You don't seriously expect old Haddox and Co. to help you, do you?"

"Of course not," replied the girl. "I don't mean that old game, anyway. It's a new one I've just invented."

"Oh, all right," said Gunn. "I'll play. What do we do first?"

Pussy got up and stretched her boyish figure.

"We go down to the lake and find the spot where X marks the body," she said. "Come on!"

CHAPTER XI

Gunn gave full vent to his feelings as they bumped their way along the rough lane leading to the lake in the old two-seater car, which was the best he could afford on his allowance as a third-year medical student. He had christened it the "Iron Lung" for obvious reasons.

The evening was cold, and a heavy October mist rose from the lake and obscured the feeble lights from the headlamps. At times, the car scraped against a wall, and at times, a hedge clung to the cloth hood with thorny fingers. The lake was six miles long, and the bay where the boats had been fishing in the morning, some five miles away, although at their present rate of progress it seemed more like thirty.

At last Pussy stuck her fingers in her ears.

"For God's sake shut up, Piggy," she screamed. "If I hear any more of that language, I shall start, myself, and you know how difficult it is to keep my conversation clean in front of Mother. That's why it's such a strain to go for a holiday with her. Up to now my language has been as pure as the driven snow, but if I once let myself go, I shan't be able to stop when we get back to the hotel."

"Serves you right for dragging me out here," grumbled Gunn, but he stopped swearing.

"I had a look for the others in the hotel before we came out," said Pussy, "and as far as I could see, they were all there except the Pindars. You now, it was funny that she didn't come down to tea. He said it was because she was upset about Mrs. Mumsby, but I don't see why she should have felt more upset than anyone else. She didn't think much of her."

"I suppose what really happened was that Mr. Pindar killed Mrs. Mumsby, and his wife ran down to the lake while we were having tea, to remove the evidence," sneered Gunn. "I really do think..." He broke off abruptly and jammed on the brakes, which uttered wild squeals of protest, and the car came to a bucking standstill.

"When you've quite finished!" exclaimed Pussy. "That's my head, that was! Oh! There's a car here already. Didn't I tell you that there was something up? Why should anyone come down here in the dark unless they're up to some funny business."

"Speak for yourself," retorted Gunn. "But it is queer, I give you that. Of course, someone may have driven down to the bay this morning while their ghillie rowed the boat down to meet them. I've known people do that."

"But the car wouldn't still be here," objected the girl, "and besides, everyone was in to tea except Mrs. Pindar, and I don't think she can drive. Perhaps the car broke down."

"No one would leave it here all night," replied Gunn. "They would have sent the car from the hotel to tow it back. And if it had broken down recently, we should have met the driver walking towards the village. No one owns a car in these mountains, that's a certainty. Well, we can soon find out." He parked his own car close to the hedge, then switched off the engine, and climbed out. He put his hand on the radiator of the other car.

"It's warm," he said in a whisper. "Someone has just got here, but why didn't they leave the sidelights on?"

"Perhaps it's a petting party," suggested Pussy.

Gunn nodded.

"Perhaps," he said. "I'll go and have a look. You stay here." Pussy's reply was lurid, and lasted for several seconds.

"And whose idea was this, yours or mine?" she demanded finally.

"All right, you little guttersnipe," said Gunn, taking an electric torch, shaped like a pencil, out of his waistcoat pocket. "I smell red herrings, but come on, and don't make a noise."

He led the way slowly off the road on to the uneven, grassy land leading towards the lake, and threaded his way with sure-footed instinct round the large boulders which loomed up in front of them. Suddenly he snapped out the little torch, and in the misty silence which enfolded them, Pussy wriggled her toes, and felt possessed by an atavistic urge to run up a tree, and cling to the highest branch with a nonexistent tail. She looked in the direction in which Gunn, like a well-trained pointer, was set, motionless, and saw a blurred circle of light wavering about near the edge of the water.

"Somebody's lost something," she whispered inanely.

"It's probably Major Jeans looking for his grandmother's false teeth," hissed Gunn, moving forward. "Now is the time for all young men to go to the aid of the party!" He raised his voice and shouted, "Want any help?" and the light was immediately extinguished.

But Gunn was not a rugger three-quarter for nothing, and his adrenal glands were working at full speed. He stabbed the darkness with his pencil light, and with a superb tackle, he hurled his heavy body outwards and downwards to the spot where he had seen two legs. To Pussy's confused mind came the sound of a struggle which seemed to last for half an hour, but which was, in reality, almost non-existent.

"Don't touch my hands, you fool!" came a voice out of the darkness.

"Mr. Winkley!" gasped Gunn.

CHAPTER XII

Mr. Winkley looking exasperated, Gunn rueful, and Pussy Partridge smug and self-satisfied, eyed one another over glasses which held sherry, Worthington, and gin-and-lime respectively.

"I might have known that you two would come butting in," remarked the former. "You Bright Young Things can't keep

your noses out of affairs which don't concern you. It's the
result of all those wild Treasure Hunts, I suppose."

And that remark sealed Mr. Winkley's fate, for Pussy
violently disliked the appellation. To her, Bright Young Things
were antiquated. Most of those whom she knew had already
become "hags", and by this time had acquired several babies or
divorces, or both. Mr. Winkley, she decided, must be made to
pay for this lack of tact. Whereupon she conjured up her
sweetest smile, and asked artlessly:

"What were you doing down by the lake in the dark, Mr.
Winkley?"

Mr. Winkley sipped his sherry, and grimaced.

"Flavoured with blackcurrant," he grumbled. "Why is it that
hotels never can provide a decent sherry? A good, reliable
Amontillado doesn't cost much, and even if it's a little
unimaginative, it's at least drinkable. But the stuff they stock in
most hotel bars is pure muck."

"I know," agreed Pussy. "That's why I drink this" – holding
up the pale-green liquid – "although I know what you men call
it. But aren't you rather evading my question? After all, we've
already told you what we were doing down there, and Piggy has
apologized very prettily for bumping your head against that
rock. I think it's really up to you to explain yourself."

"Well, Miss Partridge – it is Partridge, isn't it?..." began Mr.
Winkley.

"Yes, but everyone calls me Pussy, even Mother, unless
she's annoyed with me," replied the girl, with an airy sweep of
her hand. "I suppose you think our names are silly – too
farmyard altogether, in fact – but they're not nearly so silly as
the ones our parents gave us. Our surnames are bad enough –
Major Jeans calls us, 'Game and Gun'. They couldn't do
anything about those, of course, but they might have had a bit
of sense over the others. Piggy's parents named him Florence
Vyvyan – the Vyvyan has 'y's, too! – and mine christened me
Pansy! Claude Weston isn't much better either. He's Claude
Lionel Everard, if you please. But I honestly think that mine

takes first prize. It wouldn't have been so bad if they'd chosen Viola, but Pansy...! I ask you! Do I look like a Pansy?"

Mr. Winkley gave an emphatic "No!" to the double implication of the question, and then continued, "Well, Miss Partridge, I must say that I quite fail to see that the way in which I choose to spend my evenings is any business of yours, and if Mr. Gunn goes about attacking everyone he happens to meet at night, he will soon find himself in the local gaol."

"Look here!" began Gunn, but the girl interrupted him.

"Very well," she said. "I don't mind if you choose to be secretive about it. It only shows that you have got something to hide, and I'm sure all the other people in the hotel will be most interested to hear where we found you this evening. You can't expect us to keep quiet about it."

Mr. Winkley leaned forward.

"Oh no!" he exclaimed. "You mustn't go around telling people. It's very important that you shouldn't mention it to anyone."

Pussy laughed.

"And who's going to stop me?" she demanded. "If you tell us all about it, I promise I won't breathe a word to a living soul, and you can absolutely trust both of us. But if you won't let us into the secret, we'll talk, won't we, Piggy? And how!"

Gunn looked uncomfortable.

"I'm afraid it's true, sir," he said. "Pussy's like that, and she's so pig-headed that you couldn't do anything about it, short of throttling her, and I've often been tempted to do that. If you keep anything from her, she'll go to any lengths to find out what it's all about, and she'll ask everyone she sees, and discuss it all with them. But once she's on your side, she'll be as mum as an oyster. Honestly, I give you my word." Mr. Winkley faced this predicament with great annoyance. He looked from the one face to the other as if to seek some assurance that he would not be relying on people of straw, and apparently he found it, for without more ado he said:

"It is most necessary, for reasons which I'm sure you're intelligent enough to see, that no one except ourselves should know that I was down by the lake this evening. Miss Partridge 'had a hunch' that everything was not straightforward about Mrs. Mumsby's death. Well, I had a similar hunch for different reasons. In my job, I've learned not to despise hunches. I'm a kind of – of research-worker" (the hesitation was scarcely perceptible), "and I find that hunches frequently succeed where logic fails. Will you have another drink?"

"No, thanks," said Pussy hastily. "Do go on."

"Hold your horses!" exclaimed Gunn. "That must be the first time in her young life that she ever refused a drink. Is this a record?"

"Shut up, Piggy! What was your hunch, Mr. Winkley?"

"I suppose it began by being just an inexplicable feeling, like yours." Pussy shot a triumphant little glance at Gunn. "When I saw Mrs. Mumsby's body, I felt that there was something wrong about it, something incongruous. Then it suddenly struck me that it was the fly which was sticking up in her hand."

"There!" exclaimed Pussy. "Didn't I say that it could never have killed her?"

Mr. Winkley shook his head.

"On the contrary," he said, "I believe that it did. It was the size of the fly which had impressed itself on my mind. I suddenly realized that it was a salmon fly."

"Oh!" said Pussy blankly.

"Don't take any notice of her," said Gunn. "She has no logic in her system. You mean that it was strange for Mrs. Mumsby to get a salmon fly stuck in her hand, when she was fishing for trout?"

"That's it," replied Mr. Winkley. "I'd heard her say often, when I was down here before, that she wasn't interested in salmon-fishing. Mrs. Evans says she never booked a beat on the river, nor even went out with anyone else who was after salmon. There were no salmon flies in the fly-box which lay open beside her, nor did she have a salmon rod out with her today."

"I don't suppose she possessed one," said Gunn. "Everyone knew that she only fished for trout, and not very seriously for them, either."

"I'm sorry to spoil the Old Boys' Reunion, and all that," put in Pussy, "but I really don't see why she shouldn't have been looking at a salmon fly. I can think of half a dozen ways in which she might have taken one into her hand."

"Such as?" asked Mr. Winkley.

"Well, someone might have given it to her, or asked her opinion of it," began Pussy.

"Exactly," replied Mr. Winkley.

"But I don't mean today," persisted Pussy. "I mean, weeks ago. I don't fish at all, but I have a trout fly that I keep because he" – nodding towards Gunn – "once gave it to me. She might have been looking at it for sentimental reasons."

The two men appeared to ignore her.

"What sized fly was it?" asked Gunn. "After all, you can get anything in a salmon fly from the specially small low-water pattern, which isn't any larger than a big trout fly, up to those enormous monstrosities they use in Iceland."

"That's not easy to say offhand," replied Mr. Winkley, "because different makers still make their hooks to different scales. I should say it's made on a two-inch hook similar to those described in Hardy's catalogue as 'taper-shanked, down-turned-eyed'."

"And how far was it embedded in her hand?"

"So deeply that the barb was completely covered, and the body of the fly rested along the palm of her hand."

"And she died from shock." Gunn thought it over for a moment. "Of course, you can get a nasty wound from one of those flies," he reflected, "and if you had a heart as groggy as hers, it might be enough to kill you. It's a nauseating kind of pain, like cutting your finger on the edge of a rusty tin. But I don't see how it could have got so deeply into her hand."

"I can think of several ways in which it might have done so," replied Mr. Winkley, "but they all argue the presence of some other person. The whole thing is right for natural death – atmosphere, details, everything fits into the picture. She was fishing; she landed for lunch; she put her rod down on one side of her and an open fly-box on the other; she handled a salmon fly, stuck it accidentally into the palm of her hand, and died of heart-failure brought on by shock. It's all in order, and yet that fly looks out of focus to me."

"So you really think," said Gunn doubtfully, "that someone else handed her the fly, pulled it into her hand by the attached gut, and beat it?"

"I do and I don't," was the unsatisfactory reply. "You see, there was no gut attached to the fly when I found it, and no sign of any gut lying around. I'm sorry," he added as the look of incredulity deepened on Gunn's face, "but you brought all this on yourselves. If you hadn't been so damned inquisitive, I should have gone over all this by myself, and decided that it was all nonsense. I warned you that it was a hunch, and wouldn't stand the test of logic. Look here, let's forget all about it, and I won't go into it any further. It's probably my brain working overtime, anyway. It hasn't had time to grow accustomed to the holiday atmosphere."

"Oh no, you don't," said Pussy. "If your hunch is enough to drag you out of a warm hotel on a cold evening like this, there must be something in it. You're one of those unemotional individuals like me, and you don't put yourself out for nothing. This is the first bit of excitement I've had in three weeks, and I'm going to enjoy it properly. Of course I'd rather sleuth with you two, but if you don't want to go on with it, I shall ask in the hotel for volunteers. I should think they'd jump at it. But whatever happens, I shall sleuth."

Gunn looked appealingly at Mr. Winkley.

"If you really think there's anything to find out, we might as well go ahead," he said. "She'll do what she says, you know, and it will only make her unpopular with the others. It might be fun, and if there should be something in it –"

"Oh, all right," said Mr. Winkley, "but don't blame me if there isn't."

"You haven't told us yet what you were looking for by the lake," said Pussy.

"The fly, of course, stupid," said Gunn.

"You mean the one that was stuck in Mrs. Mumsby's hand? Did you find it?"

Mr. Winkley nodded.

"But lots of people lose flies by the lake." she objected. "How do you know that you found the right one?"

Mr. Winkley took a folded piece of paper from his pocket, and opened it on the table in front of them. On it lay a salmon fly, its hackles unrecognizably dark and stiff.

Pussy clutched at Gunn's shoulder as she peered forward.

"What's that dark stuff on the hook?" she asked.

Mr. Winkley gave an apologetic little cough.

"I'm afraid it's blood," he said.

"Bleeding hooks!" exclaimed Gunn. "Good Lord! Bleeding Hooks! That's what Major Jeans always says!"

CHAPTER XIII

The following morning, Mr. Winkley and Gunn went fishing, but they did not occupy the same boat. Mr. Winkley took Mrs. Mumsby's boat, apparently because he had lent his own ghillie and boat to Gunn, but really because he wished to see whether the ghillie could give him any further information about the events of the previous day. They had decided that each visitor at the hotel must be unobtrusively interviewed, and as the name of Major Jeans had cropped up among them, it had been decided that Pussy should question him as soon as the opportunity should arise.

When, therefore, Major Jeans walked into the hall the same morning, wearing tweeds which were not sufficiently discoloured and baggy for fishing, she thought that her luck was in. But as she had about as much knowledge of fishing as Miss Haddox, she embarked on the task with some trepidation, and called to her aid all the things she had heard in the hall since her arrival.

"Not going out today, Major?" she asked, looking up at him through her blonde lashes.

The Major cleared his throat, and looked as awkward as a small boy caught bird-nesting in his Sunday suit. He moved towards Mrs. Partridge, who was seated near her daughter, and clutched the back of her chair, as if for support.

"Not today," he said. "Giving the little devils a rest, so that when they see my new fly, they'll wag their little tails for joy, and leap at it!"

"I shouldn't have thought you could buy any new flies in this place," said the girl.

"Buy 'em?" barked the Major. "Who said anything about buying 'em? Never bought a fly in my life. No, I make 'em, my dear young lady. Have done since I was a boy. Don't know what I should do in the winter if I didn't spend my time making flies. No fishing from November to February in these islands. A fellow might as well be dead!"

Mrs. Partridge drew a careful silk thread through the linen she was embroidering, and joined in the conversation.

"Why don't you go abroad in the winter?" she asked. "You'd get fishing all the year round then. There's nothing to stop you. You're a bachelor with no family to consider."

"Can't help that," he returned brusquely, as if he resented the interruption. "I do go sometimes, but when I don't, I make flies. I've got all my paraphernalia with me. I never travel without it, in case of a rainy day. Would you like to look at it?" He addressed Pussy, and ignored her mother.

"I'd love to," she replied, while her thoughts said, *Silly old fool! I do believe he's making up to me. I wonder why, he's never taken any notice of me before – seemed to dislike me, in fact. Perhaps he knows that we're making inquiries about old Mrs. Mumsby's death. So what?*

"I can't bring it down here very well," went on the Major, playing with his fringed moustache. "There's so much of it, and it's all little bits and pieces. Would you mind coming up to my room?" He glanced quickly at Mrs. Partridge and added, "It will be quite –"

"Oh quite," laughed Pussy. "It won't be the first time that I've been in a man's bedroom!"

Major Jeans regarded her with a curious look.

"No," he said slowly, "I don't suppose it will," and led the way upstairs.

The Major's bedroom combined the untidiness which seems characteristic of most bachelor rooms, with the careful neatness of the old campaigner's. Combs, brushes, shaving tackle, and all the paraphernalia of his toilet were packed tidily away in zipped leather cases. Old newspapers and sixpenny detective novels were scattered on the bed. An amazingly long line of boots and shoes were taut on their trees. Empty tobacco tins littered the mantelpiece. A kitbag bulged in one corner and, behind the door, layer after layer of old coats, cardigans, and mackintoshes covered a single hook.

On the table in the window was screwed a small iron vice. Mrs. Evans, luckily, had a good memory for the idiosyncrasies of her regular guests, and always had a table brought up from the scullery for the Major's room.

He made his way across the room to this scrubbed deal table, and unscrewed a fly which was held in the teeth of the vice.

"There! Isn't it a beauty?" he exclaimed. "If that doesn't make their little mouths water and their teeth chatter tomorrow, I'll kill myself with one of my own hooks! Silver body, red hackle, Junglecock wing, you see. That'll fetch them. Isn't it a beauty, eh? Do you know what I call it? 'The Blinkin' Bastard.' Good name, eh?" He rubbed his hands together and chuckled in delight, then suddenly recollected himself. "Oh!"

His face assumed a more serious expression. "Shouldn't have mentioned it. Lady present. Apologize."

Pussy restrained her laughter with difficulty.

She could cap it with a few fancier names than that, she thought, but you had to be so damned careful with the older generation; they were so touchy. And parents were the touchiest of the lot. Queer, really, because by all accounts their morals and language hadn't been by any means blameless during the war, when she'd been born. As for the generation before that, well, she'd heard her grandfather tell tales of Boat Race Night at the Empire which surpassed the escapades of any modern youth. It was curious how people who were really good fun seemed to change completely as soon as they became parents. Perhaps she'd be the same. Still it was stupid of them not to realize that language which had shocked the first audiences of *Pygmalion* was considered quite innocuous by the younger generation today.

"I'm afraid I don't understand in the least what the hackle of a fly is." she said, to assist the Major over his distressed silence. "I always thought that a hackle was the hair on the back of a hound that shows when he's in a bad temper. These artificial flies have no shape, to my eyes."

"It's all a question of getting accustomed to them," said the Major. "I'll tell you what I'll do. I'll make one for you. Live and learn, you know."

He took a clean white linen handkerchief from a drawer, put a selection of fur and dyed feathers on to it, and opened a box containing eyed hooks of assorted sizes.

"I think I'll make a salmon fly," he went on. "It's larger, and you'll see it more clearly."

He poked his forefinger amongst the hooks.

"Aren't you afraid of getting one of those stuck in your finger?" asked Pussy.

"What? Oh no, no," replied the Major. "It wouldn't hurt much if I did, though if the barb gets under your skin it takes a bit of juggling to work it out again. Reminds me of a thing that

occurred on the lake one day. This very lake, too. Some tyro of
a fellow came here one year, all dolled up in the latest outfit,
with every contraption for fishing that you could think of. He
fairly made me sick with all his talk about what a fine
fisherman he was, and how many trout he'd caught on Lady X's
beat on the Test. The Test! Any child could fish on the Test.
Why, the trout queue up to be caught because they enjoy the
exhilarating rush through the air, like the man on the Flying
Trapeze. Well, he didn't know how to cast on this lake, with a
stiff wind blowing in squalls round his head, and he couldn't
get his line out, however he cast. At last he did whip it out, felt
a tug, and struck. D'you know what he'd done?" Major Jeans
let out a hearty bellow of laughter. "He'd hooked his ghillie
through the nostril, and they had to row ashore and find a
doctor to cut the hook out!"

"Oh!" exclaimed Pussy, more interested in this incident
than in the rest of the story.

"Yes. And do you know what that ghillie did? He just turned
to the fellow and said, 'I'm sorry I didn't give you better sport,
sir.' Stout fellow, eh? Quite true. Now look..."

He inserted a salmon hook in the vice, so that its jaws held
the vicious-looking barb from view, and screwed it until it was
rigid. He looped a strand of coloured silk round the body of the
hook behind the eye, and twisted it once or twice, then rubbed
it gently with cobbler's wax. He stripped the fibres from the
extreme end of an orange-dyed feather, and attached it by
means of the silk, then took up a pair of hackle-pliers, and
wound the feather tightly round and round, again securing it
with the same strand of gossamer-like silk. He whipped the silk
evenly along the hook, and secured in it some rabbit's whiskers
for the tail. He added a wisp of the fur to the body, which he
twisted in an open spiral with wide gold wire. Then he added
wings of a freckled snipe's feather, and finished it off with little
dabs of varnish.

Pussy watched, fascinated to see the delicately wound fly
take shape under the Major's service-hardened, spatulate

fingers. At length he took it out of the vice, and handed it to her.

"See!" he said, not a little proud of his achievement. "When this you see, remember me. Wear it in your hat." Pussy held out her hand and the Major dropped it lightly into her palm. She scarcely restrained a shudder as she renumbered that other, blood-stained fly which had so recently lain embedded in Mrs. Mumsby's hand.

"Thank you," she said, "it's very interesting. What do you call this fly? Or is it unprintable?"

"Lord bless you, no!" he replied, gathering together the little pieces of feather from partridge, corncrake, blackbird, tomtit, and jay, and fur from mole, fox cub, hare, and otter, and placing them in the drawer. "I call it 'The Avenging Murderer'. It isn't much like one, perhaps, but by Jove, does it work!"

"Yes," shivered Pussy, "I'm sure it does. I think it's awfully clever of you to make them so neatly."

Major Jeans rubbed his big hands together to express his pleasure at this compliment.

"Oh, good Lord, no," he said. "Any of the ghillies can tie a better fly than that, with far worse materials. Why, that ghillie of mine can make a fly out of a few cuttings from a pullover and a few of his own grey hairs, and he has no vice, either."

"Oh, I'm sure he hasn't," said Pussy. "He looks a very decent, sober sort of man. What's that windmill arrangement for?"

She indicated a wheel with four wooden spokes which stood on the table.

"Oh, that!" replied the Major, in the truculent tones of a man whose enthusiasm has been damped by lack of understanding. "That's a wheel for drying my line after fishing. It rots if it's left wet on the reel, you know."

"It's a very thick line," remarked Pussy.

"Usual salmon size."

"Salmon!" she exclaimed in surprise. "I thought you only fished for trout at this time of the year. Why, I've heard you making dreadful fun of poor General Haddox for fishing for salmon instead of trout."

Major Jeans looked uncomfortable.

"I thought I'd like a change yesterday." he explained. "The General has a pet fish that rises off one of those big rocks in the western bay – I call it Cuthbert. I thought I'd like to wipe his eye by bringing it in, that's all."

Pussy was unconvinced.

Cuthbert indeed! she thought. *I don't believe it!*

"The western bay," she repeated. "Isn't that the place where Mrs. Mumsby – died? Don't you think it was awfully sad for her to die alone like that?"

"Everyone has to face death alone when he or she is old," said the Major sententiously.

Pussy thought him callous.

"Oh, she wasn't old," she protested.

"Awful woman," said the Major. "Mutton dressed as lamb. 'Fat ewes per live hundredweight' –"

"But it is pretty rotten to think that she had no one to help her, when so many people were near at hand," persisted the girl. "I suppose you weren't so far away yourself. You would have heard if she'd called for help, wouldn't you?"

"I might have done," was the reluctant reply. "The Westons were nearest to her, then the Pandas" – his nickname for Mr. and Mrs. Pindar – "doing a little canoodling, and old Fish-eyes and her brother farther over to the left. I was near the road, but I might have heard if the cry was loud enough."

"Did you stay there the whole time?"

"Yes, of course. I don't usually go for a ten-mile walk when I'm out fishing."

"You didn't go away for a teeny weeny minute?"

"No. Yes. Well..." The Major stared at her. "What's the idea of all these questions, young lady?" he asked. "What business is it of yours what I was doing, eh? What are you getting at? The trouble with you is that your mother spoils you. You're nothing but a – a –"

"Blinkin' Bastard," suggested Pussy.

Major Jeans took in a deep breath, looked as if he might suddenly explode, decided that he would not, and screwed up his eyes into a smile.

"It's a good name, isn't it? A good name, eh?" he chortled. "You know, you're a girl after my own heart. No nonsense about you."

He sidled up to her, and before she could move away, he had slipped his arm round her, above her waist, and had brushed her cheek with his moustache.

"Your mother said we ought to get on well together. Do you like me at all? Do you think you could get fond of me, eh?"

He punctuated each question with a squeeze.

A look of the utmost loathing passed over Pussy's face. With a quick twist of her slight figure she freed herself, and landed a stinging slap across his face.

"Sugar-daddy!" she hissed, and ran out of the room.

CHAPTER XIV

Pussy swung down the wide stairs into the hall and found that Miss Haddox and Mrs. Pindar had joined her mother and were engaged in desultory holiday chat. At least, Miss Haddox was.

"...of course I said to him when I saw the laundry, 'My dear *dhobi*, do you really take me for an American tourist?' You should have seen his face, he was dreadfully ashamed, but you have to be very smart out East, or you'd pay through the nose for everything, and what I always say is –"

Mrs. Partridge looked up, and smiled at her daughter.

"Well, dear, did you enjoy your little chat with the Major?" she asked.

"And how!" scowled Pussy. "I think he's a rotten, low hound."

Mrs. Partridge looked surprised.

"Oh dear! I thought you'd get on so well together," she said. "You're both very unconventional, but, of course, if you don't like him –"

"I do not," said Pussy in very decided tones, "and if he's the best you can find for me, I must say that I don't admire your taste."

Mrs. Partridge flushed. She folded her embroidery, and zipped it into her workbag, then, with a glance at her wrist-watch, and a vague smile to the others, she rose from her chair, and walked along the corridor leading to the lounge.

"Oh Lord!" sighed Pussy, sinking into the vacated chair. "Now she's doing her injured cricketer stunt. I can't cope with parents!" She met Mrs. Pindar's inquiring gaze and explained: "Retired hurt, you know. Oh well, I'll give her time to cool off, and then I'll go and smooth her down again. She soon gets over it, that's one blessing."

Miss Haddox regarded her disapprovingly.

"I don't wonder that your mother feels hurt," she said. "You're always so rude to her, but I suppose you modern girls think it sounds clever. I wish my niece, Marigold, were here, then you'd realize that it's possible to be both modern and polite. Marigold's a charming girl, and so pretty. Some people say she's the image of Greta Garbo, but I can't say that I agree with them because I've never met the woman, but you can tell that she must be quite up to date, and her manners, I'm glad to say, are very old-fashioned."

Mrs. Pindar saw the glint in Pussy's eyes, and hastened to change the subject.

"Are you going to take up fishing at last, Miss Partridge?" she asked.

"Me! Rather not! Whatever put that idea into your head? Oh, this." She held up the fly which Major Jeans had given to her. "No, I shall never take up that kind of fishing, thank you! It's too boring by half. This is just an ornament for my beret."

Miss Haddox leaned forward.

"It's just like the fly that killed Mrs. Mumsby," she remarked. "At least," she added hastily, "it's a salmon fly, isn't it? – they all look alike to me because I don't fish, but I'm sure I've seen one like that before, if you see what I mean –"

"I suppose we shall all have to go to the funeral tomorrow," said Mrs. Pindar. "I haven't a thing suitable to wear for it."

"We'll all go in black fisherman's coats and hats, and carry reversed fishing rods," suggested Pussy, glancing slyly at Miss Haddox, who ignored the challenge.

"I shall certainly not attend Mrs. Mumsby's funeral," she said coldly. "I'm no hypocrite, if everyone else in this hotel is. I didn't like the woman, and I never could see the sense in changing your opinion of a person just because she dies. Dying can't reform anyone, and, if I've said it once I've said it a hundred times, she was a bad lot, and I'm not sorry she's dead. If she'd lived, she would have led that stupid Weston boy into trouble, and if it hadn't been him, it would have been someone else, and perhaps someone else in this hotel. She was a dangerous woman."

"Oh, I don't know," said Pussy. "She was a go-getter, of course, and maybe a gold-digger as well, but she was kind-hearted. Perhaps she wasn't a lady –"

"She was definitely not a lady," interjected Miss Haddox.

"– but she was a good sort, and all that. However much you hated her, you couldn't wish her to die all alone in that way. I must say that I can't understand how it was that none of you heard anything at the time. I suppose that you and Sir Courtney were some distance away from her."

"We were nothing of the kind," replied Miss Haddox. "There's only a narrow strip of land round that part of the lake where the boats can be beached, and though it goes right back to the road, you know what these anglers are like – they always sit where they can look at the water. You think they'd get tired of it after sitting for hours on a hard piece of wood, looking at the lake all the time, and would be glad to look at the mountains, or even at a stone wall for a change. But fishing is a disease with all of them. No doubt it's very soothing, if you can stand it, and no one knows better than I what it has done for my brother, but I'm quite a different temperament altogether, as any of you can see, and it would bore me to tears. I suppose it must be because I have a particularly active brain, or at least that's what my doctor thinks. 'Miss Haddox,' he always says, 'you have a particularly active brain.'"

"Well, I haven't." admitted Pussy, "and it bores me, too. I must say that I hand the laurel to Mrs. Mumsby for the way she went out day after day in any weather, fair or foul. I couldn't enjoy that."

Miss Haddox sniffed.

"She didn't enjoy it, either," she said. "She only went fishing so that she could talk about it afterwards with the men. She was really angling for a two-legged fish, and thought that it gave her a pull over all the other women in the hotel. She only stayed here because the majority of the visitors are men. She'd been a widow too long, that's what was wrong with her. She was man-mad."

"Aren't we all?" murmured Pussy, winking at Mrs. Pindar. "So you were within earshot of Mrs. Mumsby," she went on. "Was your brother with you all the time after you'd joined him for lunch?"

"What do you mean?" demanded Miss Haddox. "Of course we were together all the time. Courtney doesn't enjoy eating alone, and his day would be quite spoilt if I didn't see him off in the morning, and join him at lunch-time. He's just a great baby of a man really."

"All the time?" persisted Pussy.

"Certainly," replied Miss Haddox. "What do you mean?"

"He didn't slip away for just five minutes? To reply to the call of Nature, you know."

Miss Haddox got up hurriedly.

"Your remarks are in exceedingly bad taste," she said stiffly. "In my day, young girls did not speak of such things."

"No? But they did them, I hope," returned the irrepressible Pussy.

Mrs. Pindar again tried to make peace.

"Don't you think you take the younger generation a little too seriously, Miss Haddox?" she asked in her soft voice.

But Miss Haddox would not be appeased.

"No, I do not." she replied firmly. "As I have said, my own niece is both young and modern, and yet possesses tact and good manners. As for the modern young man, you have probably had more experience in that direction than I."

Mrs. Pindar flushed – unnecessarily, Pussy thought, but certainly Miss Haddox's tone was offensive.

"I must say that I quite fail to understand the reason for this cross-questioning about my movements yesterday," Miss Haddox continued to Pussy. "But if you really wish to poke your nose into affairs which do not concern you, I should advise you to find out what your mother was doing out there at lunch-time, when she was supposed to be walking on the other side of the lake, and why she did not appear when we all went to look at Mrs. Mumsby!"

CHAPTER XV

"Of all the old cats!" exclaimed Pussy, after Miss Haddox had taken a triumphant departure. "I always think that women associated with titles are the worst when it comes to scandal-mongering."

Mrs. Pindar smiled.

"Haven't you rather underestimated the influence of the Army?" she asked. "The General was once in the Indian Army, you know, and socially that's about the most snobbish organization in the world."

"Do you think so?" asked Pussy. "I think the General's rather a pet, and all the Indian Army officers I've met –"

"Ah yes, the men," interrupted her companion, "but it's the women who make the social life out there. The men are for too busy to bother. I never can understand why the women who go out to the Eastern stations will insist on keeping alive the narrow conventions which lead to such snobbery and cattiness. They're really dreadful, and there seems no reason for it, unless you can assume that every woman who marries into the Indian Army is of a low intelligence type, rather in the same way that the boy who could never get a job used to be sent into the Church, not so long ago. They live in a foreign country, and ought to live in happy little communities, yet they spend their time back-biting, leaving cards, and shaking in their shoes lest the Colonel's lady will refuse to meet the Major's wife."

"I see the point of view, though," said Pussy, who was bored. She always did feel bored when anyone made a long speech, partly because it meant too much sustained mental effort to listen, and partly because she never could understand why anyone should want to talk at such length. Nothing ever touched her so deeply that she wanted to make a speech about it, and even if it had, she would have been at too much of a loss for words to make one. "I expect it's the same in the Navy, isn't it?"

"I really don't know," replied Mrs. Pindar.

"I thought you'd know because Mrs. Mumsby said Mr. Pindar was a sailor, or something."

Mrs. Pindar hesitated, then said quietly:

"You've said that before, you know. Mrs. Mumsby was as big a gossip as Miss Haddox. That's why they hated each other so. It so happens that I am not married to a sailor, and you might remember it."

"Sorry and all that," replied Pussy, quite unabashed. "By the way, talking about Mrs. Mumsby, were you fairly near to her yesterday?"

"Yes. As Miss Haddox said, there's only a certain amount of space for boats to land, and there were six boats altogether. We were all cut off from one another by walls or bushes, but we were all within earshot, I should think. It's strange," she mused, "how everyone tries to get away from his neighbours. We were all fishing, and all keen on the same sport, and you'd think that we should have joined together in one big party for lunch. Instead of that, we all tried to hide from one another. I know we did."

"I don't blame you," said Pussy. "I'd do the same if I were on my honeymoon. Now don't deny that, or it will break Mrs. Evans' heart. She always likes to have one honeymoon couple in the hotel, for luck. Were you..." she broke off abruptly.

Mrs. Pindar laughed.

"I don't mind your questions in the least," she said, "but as a matter of fact that one is superfluous. Given three hours in a boat, followed by a large lunch and liquid refreshment, the time inevitably follows when, as you so poetically put it, the call of Nature must be satisfied. In mixed company, this usually means departures at different times, or '*dames*' to the right and '*messieurs*' to the left. I was alone for two or three periods of a few minutes each after lunch."

Pussy chuckled.

"Of course it's only common sense," she said, "but if people won't answer a simple question, it makes you think they were doing something they don't want you to know, and that always rouses my curiosity. You'll think me an awful nuisance, I know, but somehow, I can't believe that no one heard Mrs. Mumsby cry out. Are you sure you didn't hear any noise?"

Mrs. Pindar smiled at her tolerantly.

"That all depends on what kind of noise you mean. There were dozens of different noises all the time, you see. The lapping of the water on the stones, for instance. I remember Jack quoted Tennyson,

'I heard the water lapping on the crag,
And the long ripples washing in the reeds'"

Pussy suppressed a shudder. She could not bear the sound of poetry, even if it did not rhyme. The only rhythm for which she had any liking was swing. At least, you could dance to that.

"There was the distant sound of a waterfall from the opposite side of the road," went on Mrs. Pindar, "and the rumble of a cart. As for cries, the air was full of them."

Pussy looked incredulous.

"From birds, I mean," explained Mrs. Pindar. "There were a good many gulls flying over the lake. Our ghillie says that they breed on the rocky islands in the lake in summer. Then there were smaller birds among the reeds – dabchicks and waterhens, I think, and the cry of the curlew never ceased. Unless we'd been listening for any special kind of cry, we should never have noticed any strange sound. I suppose you do mean a strange cry?"

"I suppose I do," agreed Pussy, "but I'm hanged if I really know what I do mean."

She sat in unaccustomed thought, rubbing one long-nailed finger up and down the high bridge of her nose with unusual lack of concern for her make-up.

Mrs. Pindar regarded her quizzically.

"It all sounds very mysterious," she said at length. "After all, Mrs. Mumsby is dead now, so it doesn't much matter whether she cried out or not. I wish you'd tell me what you're driving at. Perhaps I could help you."

"I'd rather tell you than anyone," said Pussy earnestly, "but it's not my secret. The only hint I can give you is to say that I have reason to believe that certain people in this hotel are living under false pretences."

To her amazement, Mrs. Pindar leapt up from her seat, and confronted her with the fury of a young goddess.

"Interfering busybodies!" she exclaimed, and her voice trembled. "First Mrs. Mumsby, and now you! You know what happened to her! Why can't you mind your own business?"

CHAPTER XVI

While Pussy was making herself unpopular by her persistent questionings, Mr. Winkley was drifting down The Big Lake in Mrs. Mumsby's boat, while Gunn followed, a few drifts behind, in Mr. Winkley's.

To a non-fishing man or woman, this exchange of boats and ghillies might have appeared strange, but no one at the Fisherman's Rest would have considered it worthy of comment. They knew that whenever Mr. Winkley came down to fish the lakes, David Griffiths was reserved as his ghillie. It was, in fact, Mr. Winkley who had first made David's name among the ghillies and visitors, by bringing in over a hundred sea-trout in a fortnight at a time when David was held to be a mere boat-puller, and thereafter, David's name had gone up in Mrs. Evans' list as one of the best six ghillies in Aberllyn.

On the other hand, Gunn was a beginner, and had no fixed ghillie of his own, merely hiring any ghillie who was free by the day, and not by the week. It was, therefore, quite natural that Mr. Winkley should lend David to him for a day, much as the host of a shooting party might lend one of his best loaders and retrievers to the most likely youngster, so that a future enthusiast might thereby be encouraged. Mr. Winkley could not be expected to share the same boat with a beginner, any more than the host of the shooting party could be expected to share the same butt.

Every sporting man wishes to interest others in his favourite pastime, every ghillie or loader wishes to see his future assured by the advent of potential employers. This arrangement of Mr. Winkley's, therefore, was pleasing to everyone, and most pleasing of all, perhaps, to Mrs. Mumsby's ghillie, John Jones.

John had seen a certain two pounds a week disappear, and doubted whether he would even receive the money already due to him from his late employer. A day's fishing with Mr. Winkley meant an extra ten shillings, and possibly twelve-and-six, for Mr. Winkley was not a mean man. It would be an enjoyable day, too, for Mr. Winkley, with his collection of round, yellow tobacco tins, and square, blue cigarette boxes, was one of the best fishermen who visited the district, and knew as much about The Big Lake as any man alive.

It was all the more surprising, therefore, that Mr. Winkley should express the desire to drift towards the bay at the west end of the lake, when the wind was blowing from the north, and it was obviously a day for the Glasyn River drift on the opposite side.

"The wind's in the north, sir," remarked John.

"I know it is," replied Mr. Winkley, slashing his line into the wind with a two-handed cast.

"A north wind's no good in that bay, sir, no good whatever."

"But it won't stop us drifting, surely?"

The ghillie spat over his left shoulder.

"Oh, we can drift, indeed, but not over the trout. That bay is very deep, sir, and the only place you can get trout there is between the shore and the Black Ledges. And you know yourself, sir, we can't get near the Black Ledges today."

Mr. Winkley looked up at the gathering clouds.

"I've fished it in a north wind before now," he said. "Besides, the wind will change before long. We'll give it till lunch-time, anyway."

And fish it they did, though the set of John's shoulders as he turned the boat a little into the wind with one oar, expressed disapproval.

After an hour, the wind dropped altogether, and the water looked pale-grey and oil-smooth. Mr. Winkley's flies dropped into a slack, depressing heap on the water before he could adapt his casting to the changed conditions. Using his rod as a two-handed salmon rod and sweeping his line in a wide circle over his head for each cast was the tiring order for the next half-hour, at the end of which time an impish puff of wind blew the wet flies into his face. He had barely enough time to struggle into his black oilskin coat and sou'wester hat, before slow, heavy raindrops became the centres of intersecting circles on the smooth surface of the lake. But with the first cast, which cut neatly across the pock-marked water, he hooked and landed a trout, thus confirming his pet theory that fish rise when the pressure is released from the surface of the water.

As long as this heavy shower lasted, he hooked trout, but in less than half an hour's time the rain had ceased, and the wind was back again in the north.

He glanced at the shore, then at his watch, and said:

"We'll land for lunch now. It's early, but it's no use fishing in this wind."

John slipped the other oar into its rowlock, and pulled for the shore without hesitation.

"Best to do that, indeed. We were lucky to get those fish. This bay is no good whatever in a north wind," and Mr. Winkley let him have the last word.

The ghillie made to land at the exact spot where he had beached his boat on the previous day. By suggesting lunch when he did, Mr. Winkley had ensured that the man would do so, for the boat had been in a direct line with that part of the shore. As they approached it, Mr. Winkley saw that another boat was already drawn up just beyond the wall, and as he reeled in his line, and fixed the tail fly to the cork covering of the butt of his rod, he remarked:

"Mr. Gunn is here already."

John Jones rested for a second on his oars, and glanced at the boat.

"That's not Mr. Gunn, sir," he said. "That will be him away over there."

He pointed to the opposite side of the lake, where Mr. Winkley could barely discern the small, humped speck indicated by the ghillie, which to his eyes might equally be an island or a rock.

"Are you sure, John?" he asked. "I said we'd meet Mr. Gunn for lunch, and this looks like David's boat."

To him all grey boats looked alike.

"'Tis not, indeed," returned the ghillic. "I might as well not know my own boat, for the two of them were built by the same man down there on the quay, and my brother it was who bought the timber. Besides, David would never bring the young gentleman to fish this bay in a north wind."

And when they landed, Mr. Winkley saw that this boat was named the *Dobell* whereas David's was called more pretentiously *Queen Mary*, and he marvelled at the keen eye-sight which could so easily distinguish one long, grey boat from another over the whole width of the lake.

While John took the basket out of the boat, he strolled across the wet, crisp grass and looked over the wall to see who had arrived before him, but no one was in sight. He turned, and deliberately seated himself in the same spot which Mrs. Mumsby had occupied on the previous day, and John's nervous start of apprehension when he saw him, did not escape his notice.

He settled himself against the large, grey boulder, and motioned to the ghillie to seat himself within conversational distance. He did not as a rule encourage such an arrangement, although the reason was not snobbish in origin. To chaff a ghillie and share one's cigarettes with him during the long hours in the boat was one thing: to share his off-time duty was quite different. In his experience, even the best of ghillies could not withstand taking advantage of the familiarity implied by the latter procedure. But he had engineered this man here (skilfully he hoped) for a purpose, and he knew that in their present respective places, no man of John's mentality could refrain from introducing the conversation which constituted that very purpose.

"It gave me quite a turn to see you sitting there, sir," he said, as he opened the newspaper containing his meagre lunch.

Mr. Winkley nodded.

"You mean Mrs. Mumsby, poor woman? I suppose it gave you a bit of a shock to see her like that, John."

"Yes, indeed, sir. I can't help thinking that if I'd done what she really wanted me to do, she might have been alive now."

"Oh? How was that?"

Mr. Winkley appeared to be more interested in his food than in Mrs. Mumsby.

"Well, I waited around till she gave me a cup of coffee and some of her food – she was always kind like that." He eyed Mr. Winkley's plate of chicken and ham enviously. "The lunch they give the ghillies is a disgrace to the hotel. Nothing but great hunks of bread and a scraping of butter, and meat so tough that –"

"Yes, yes," was Mr. Winkley's hasty and unsympathetic interruption. He knew the food was poor, but he knew also that it was due to the ghillies' increasing demands for more free drinks from the bar.

"Well, she had often asked me to sit and have my lunch closer to her, as I'm having it now, sir, but I always went as far away as I could, round the rocks and away across the road, so that she wouldn't be calling for me all the time. 'If I don't hear her,' I think, 'I won't be blamed for staying away.'"

"That's rather a high-handed way to treat your customers." remarked Mr. Winkley. "How could you know when she wanted to start fishing again? She might have wanted to go out in a hurry."

John laughed.

"Not she." he said. "She was never what you might call keen on fishing. A waste of time it was to go out with her at all. Besides, on a fine day she always went to sleep for at least half an hour after lunch, so I knew I was safe."

Mr. Winkley balanced a piece of yellow pasteurized cheese on a biscuit, and his voice was as mild as the cheese as he asked:

"Did you like Mrs. Mumsby?"

"Like her?" asked John bitterly. "God! I could have murdered that woman many a time. She was dangerous, I'm telling you. If you had never been in a boat alone with her, you wouldn't know what she was like. She paid me well; she knew that she had to. She liked me, you see. She had to take old Lloyd when the other ghillies were busy, but she. would always rather have a younger man if she could get him. I hated the job, but I'm getting married next year, and I needed the money."

"You didn't come back to speak to her again before she died then?"

"Not I," said John, and Mr. Winkley, catching a glimpse of his oddly assorted eyes, wondered fantastically whether a man could be colour-blind in one eye only, and if so, what the result would be. "I knew her too well. Why, she never stopped talking once she started, and I needed a bit of rest."

"I don't suppose she did much talking yesterday, though," he said. "She must have been feeling rather off colour."

"Yesterday? She was worse yesterday than ever, Mr. Winkley. How I kept my hands from her throat, I don't know. She said she felt better than she had done all her life. Something had pleased her a good deal – perhaps it was the trout she had caught the day before – but she talked more than ever. She was full of pranks, too. She was skittish, and kept asking if I thought she had sex-appeal. She would not fish, but lay in the boat, and dabbled her hands in the water. And on a lake like this which is full of the best sea-trout in Wales!" he finished in disgust.

"I wonder what she was so pleased about. Did she talk of anyone she knew?"

"No, no," replied the ghillie, "unless it was Will. She was often talking lately about him."

"And who is he?" asked Mr. Winkley.

"I don't know, sir. She talked all the time but I never listened. After a time, your ears just hear noise and an odd word or two, if you don't want to listen." He paused for a moment, then said, "You don't suppose that anyone did away with her, sir, do you?"

Mr. Winkley looked startled.

"What makes you say that?" he asked. "Do you know of anyone who had threatened her?"

John laughed.

"Oh no, sir. But I can think of a good many men who wanted her out of the way. She was a menace to the fishing, sir. She made a laughing-stock of all of us, ghillies and visitors alike."

"I suppose you didn't get rid of her yourself, did you?" asked Mr. Winkley.

John shook his head almost regretfully.

"No, sir. She paid me too well."

And Mr. Winkley, not for the first time, thought that the Royal Standard was incomplete without three money bags rampant to represent Wales.

"Well, she won't talk to you any more," he said, as he got up and stretched his long legs. He took a cigarette from his case, offered one to John, and lit them both. "By the way, I lost something out of my pocket yesterday. I might have dropped it somewhere around here. A little bottle, not of any value, but I might as well have a look for it."

John grinned.

"You'll find plenty of bottles here, sir, under those bushes or behind the rocks, but they won't be little ones. Nor milk bottles!"

He gathered the luncheon debris together, packed it in the basket, and carried it down to the boat.

Mr. Winkley walked about in drunken fashion, peering at the ground in places where it was improbable that anyone could have dropped anything by accident. He had not gone many yards before he was aware of a figure who, with head thrust forward, was apparently engaged in a similar search. He hurried forward.

"Hello. Lost something?" he asked.

General Sir Courtney Haddox straightened himself in some embarrassment, and Mr. Winkley saw that his hands trembled.

"It's a bad day for salmon," he said vaguely. "Yes, I was looking for something I dropped here yesterday. It doesn't really matter, but I thought I'd take a look round as I was here. It was a fly, a salmon fly."

"Oh," said Mr. Winkley in an expressionless voice. "What kind was it?"

"A Bloody Butcher," replied the General.

CHAPTER XVII

The three self-appointed investigators met together after dinner to pool their information and discuss what progress they had made.

Gunn was annoyed, and made no secret of it.

"I believe you did it on purpose," he said to Mr. Winkley. "All that talk about meeting for lunch was eyewash. All the time, you were laughing up your sleeve, knowing that you'd given instructions to David to keep me on the other side of the lake so that you could get on with some secret investigation of your own!"

Mr. Winkley laughed.

"I assure you I did nothing of the kind," he said, "but I admit I ought to have foreseen that David would never bring you across the lake in a north wind. I had the devil's own job to persuade John Jones to row me over there, and he never stopped grumbling. You see," he continued, as Gunn remained adamantly unappeased, "when a ghillie is lent to anyone in that way, it puts him on his mettle to show what he can do. He tries to take you over as many fish as possible, and to bring in as many as he can. David knew that he would risk having a blank day if he brought you over to join me on my side of the lake this morning. You would have had a poor opinion of his ghillying in consequence, and would probably have forgotten to tip him, and these Welshmen have money-boxes instead of hearts."

"You brought in as many fish as we did," growled Gunn, still unconvinced, "so the fishing can't be so very different."

"That was just my good luck," returned Mr. Winkley.

Pussy laughed.

"Mr. Winkley really means that it was his good fishing, but he's far too polite to say so. Poor lamb!" she chaffed. "Were you made to fish against your will while Mr. Winkley had all the fun, then? Why didn't you hit the ghillie over the head with an oar, or stick a few fly hooks into him?"

"You really didn't miss much," said Mr. Winkley, and went painstakingly through the events of the morning.

Gunn soon forgot his grievance as he listened.

"But I don't see why you were looking for a bottle," he remarked at length, "unless it was a blind, and you were really expecting to find something else."

"Oh no," replied Mr. Winkley. "I did expect to find a bottle."

"What kind of a bottle?" asked Pussy. "Perfume, beer, sauce, or baby's?"

"A killing bottle," was the reply.

"Come again, I'll buy it," retorted Pussy. "You'll kill *me*, if you don't explain things a bit better."

The two men ignored her, as usual.

"You mean a cyanide bottle for killing butterflies and moths?" asked Gunn.

"Yes," replied Mr. Winkley, leaning forward and stubbing out his cigarette in the ashtray on the table in front of him. "You know how they're made. Lumps of cyanide are placed at the bottom of the bottle and covered with plaster of Paris, so that the gas rises through the porous plaster, and forms a little lethal chamber. A lot of fishermen use them for collecting specimens of flies which they find on the lake or river, so that they can match the ones which the fish eat, with artificial flies."

"But no one would carry a killing bottle about with them so late in the season as this," objected Gunn.

"I think they would," returned Mr. Winkley, "if the specimen they required was a human one."

Pussy threw back her head and yowled at the ceiling. Gunn looked at her, and laughed.

"Do you mind explaining?" he asked. "Pussy can't understand words of more than one syllable, as you know, and I'm not quite sure that I see what you're driving at myself. Are you suggesting that Mrs. Mumsby was poisoned?"

Mr. Winkley nodded.

"But you said that the bleeding hooks killed her," protested Pussy, relishing the adjective.

"So they did, but only because they were poisoned. I've suspected it ever since I saw the body: the way it was twisted, for one thing, and of course, the cyanosis of the face. You're a medical student. You'd have spotted it immediately if you'd seen her."

Gunn accepted the implied compliment without any demur.

"Of course," he said excitedly. "Someone used the word cyanosed to describe the purple flush on her face after she was dead. I remember now, but at the time it conveyed nothing sinister to me."

"That's interesting," remarked Mr. Winkley. "It's not a word that the average person uses much. Do you remember who said it?"

Gunn frowned in his effort at concentration.

"No, I'm afraid I don't," he said. "They were all in the lounge at the time, and it might have been anybody. I've a vague idea that it was your mother," he added, turning to Pussy.

"Don't talk rot," replied Pussy sharply. "She wasn't there when Mrs. Mumsby died."

"No, of course not," agreed Gunn. "Then I'm afraid I don't remember." He paused for a moment, and then said,

"You think then, sir, that someone had previously decided to kill Mrs. Mumsby, and came prepared with the salmon fly, dipped it in cyanide from the killing bottle, and pulled it into her hand, so that the poison was injected into the Wood stream?"

"I always said that the shock of the hook in her hand wouldn't be enough to kill her," triumphed Pussy. "But, of course, if it was poisoned, that's a different story altogether."

"Yes. You see the idea that anyone forced that hook into her hand, knowing that she had a weak heart and might die from the shock of the pain, seemed very far-fetched to me," explained Mr. Winkley. "The method was too unreliable."

"I quite agree," said Pussy. "Anyone who wanted to kill her in that kind of way would think of something much more startling than a fly-hook – something really terrifying, I mean. I've often thought that that horrid old monkey of Claude's might be too much for some people. The way it hurls itself through the air and lands on your neck is enough to –" She stopped speaking, and put a hand up to her mouth as if to hold the words back. A look of apprehension crept into her bold, green eyes. "But I'm sure it was the poison," she concluded lamely.

The others appeared not to have heard her.

"That's all very neatly constructed, Mr. Winkley," said Gunn, "but how much cyanide would it take to kill anyone in that way, and could the small hook hold the fatal dose? I rather doubt that it could. I suppose you've got all that worked out?"

Mr. Winkley lit a cigarette, exhaled the smoke through his nostrils like a benevolent dragon, then offered his case apologetically to the other two. Pussy refused with a shake of her head – she never smoked anything but Russian cigarettes – and wondered whether Mr. Winkley always remembered to use his battered silver case because he bought his cigarettes in fifties or hundreds so that he could use the empty tins for fishing tackle.

"It wasn't cyanide." replied Mr. Winkley. "I've been examining the fly from Mrs. Mumsby's hand, and, as far as I can see, there's no trace of any substance on it except dried blood. Cyanide would have left a little crystallization. No, a liquid poison was used."

"Prussic acid!" exclaimed Pussy. "I once read a book where some old professor-josser killed himself by dipping his cut finger in prussic acid."

"Hark at her!" jeered Gunn. "She once read a book. Ye Gods and little fishes! Who would have thought it possible? Prussic acid, my angel, is a gas, and if you can tell me how to fix some gas on to the end of a salmon hook, you're the world's marvel, and when you peg out, they ought to stuff your body and present it to the British Museum!"

"But it distinctly said that he dipped his finger into a glass of prussic acid," protested Pussy.

Gunn sighed.

"I wish they'd teach elementary chemistry in these exclusive girls' schools," he said. "I remember lending that book to you, and the old josser, as you call him, was a chemist and mixed potassium cyanide with hydrochloric or some strong acid which liberated prussic acid gas in the liquid."

"I've no doubt that you're right," said Mr. Winkley, "but don't you think you're quibbling a bit? After all, although it must have been used in some liquid form, it was the prussic acid which poisoned her. The trouble is that it is so unlikely that anyone has ever been killed before by having a poisoned fish-hook in her hand, and that, short of trying it out on someone, I don't see how we can prove that it did actually happen."

"We could try it on a poor little guinea-pig," suggested Pussy.

"Don't be so 'Citadel'," retorted Gunn. "And anyway it wouldn't help. We couldn't be sure that the same amount which killed the guinea-pig would be fatal to a human being."

"One person knows the amount," put in Mr. Winkley, "and that's the murderer. It's a dangerous piece of knowledge to possess, and it's well known that one murder leads to another."

Gunn nodded his head.

"A nasty thought," he said. "By the way, I take it that the killing bottle you're talking about wouldn't be the usual kind, except perhaps in shape, otherwise the plaster of Paris would absorb the liquid, and leave you with the gas to suspend on the hook."

Mr. Winkley nodded.

"That's so," he said. "I doubt whether you could chip the plaster out of that kind of bottle, either. I just call it a killing bottle because it kills, and I imagine the murderer would have procured a bottle of that shape because it would excite less comment if he kept it, as I imagine he did, among his fishing tackle."

"By Jove!" exclaimed Gunn, clasping his hands behind his head as if to ease his brain from so much concentrated thinking. "The whole thing's damned clever. If you hadn't spotted that salmon fly and thought it queer, no one would have suspected that she died of anything but heart failure. Dr. Rippington Roberts has already signed the death certificate."

"Well, it ought to be easy enough to find the murderer," remarked Pussy. "All you have to do is to find someone who is good at chemistry, like that Professor."

Gunn ran exasperated fingers through his hair.

"Pussy, my pet, as a sleuth you're the eighth wonder of the world."

Pussy took a deep breath.

"The Pyramids of Egypt, the Hanging Gardens of Babylon, the Tomb of Mausoleus, the Temple of Diana at Ephesus, the Statue of Zeus by Phidias, the Palace of Cyprus (the stones of which are cemented with gold), the Colossus of Rhodes," she said without a pause.

The two men gaped at her in silence.

"All right, I'm not crazy," she said, laughing. "I once took a course of shorthand and typing, and if you'd hammered that out as many times as I did, you'd know it off by heart, too."

"Well, as I was saying," continued Gunn, "the murderer doesn't need to be a chemist. Why, any schoolboy knows the preparation of prussic acid: he uses the constituents for... for..." He faltered, and Pussy cocked an eye at him, like a curious bird. "Well, for lots of things," he concluded lamely. "I suppose you suspected poison when you yelled out to me in the dark, not to touch your hand," he said to Mr. Winkley.

"Yes. I didn't know then what poison had been used, and thought that the hook might still have been impregnated with it. And, incidentally, although you're right in saying that the murderer need not be a chemist or a professor, I think that he must be familiar with the use of chemicals and able to obtain them without difficulty, although, in these days of highly skilled amateur photographers, perhaps that isn't worth considering. Anyway, I've scraped the deposit off the hook for analysis, and have given the fly a general clean-up so that you can now see what it looks like. We shall have to find out what kind it is, and where it was made. It's not a familiar pattern to me, but then I don't know much about salmon flies, as I usually fish for trout. It's the only clue we have, and we must make the best of it."

"I don't see how you can possibly find out where it was made," remarked Pussy. "It won't have a label sewn inside it, saying 'Taquin' or 'Norman Hartnell'."

"No, we can't hope for a label." smiled Mr. Winkley. "Do you ever make your own clothes, Miss Partridge?"

"Occasionally," replied Pussy, bridling a little at a question which verged on the personal. She frequently made more personal remarks to other people, but felt doubly embarrassed when the compliment was returned.

"Could you pick out, say, a blouse which you had made, from half a dozen made by other people?"

"Yes, I think so."

"And how would you recognize it?"

"Oh, I don't know. By the general look of it, I suppose. The stitching, and the finish of the seams, and that sort of thing."

"Exactly," replied Mr. Winkley. "And that's how you can recognize the make of a fly. Every tying has a characteristic look about it. Amateurs usually tie the silk or twist the hackle in a different way from professionals. On the other hand, it would be impossible to mistake a 'Dayson' for a 'Hardy' even though both are professionally tied, and it's usually quite easy to spot some difference between the fly-tying of different amateurs, although you may need a magnifying glass to do it. I expect that Major Jeans has one marked characteristic, and General Haddox another."

"I'll go and fetch the fly Major Jeans made for me today," said Pussy.

She swung out of her chair and dropped a kiss lightly on Gunn's hair as she passed.

Mr. Winkley took an envelope out of his pocket and shook the much-discussed salmon fly on to the palm of his hand. Then he placed it on the table with the white envelope as background, and the two men looked at it with careful eyes. Mr. Winkley had cleaned the blood from the feathers, and the fly glinted up at them. It had the thin, threadbare appearance of a favourite fly which has caught many fish, but otherwise it appeared in all its brave colours, and Gunn marvelled again that such an innocent-looking object could have become the implement of a murderer.

Pussy, swinging her slim legs in their black velvet evening trousers, came down the stairs in dance rhythm, and *chasséed* across the intervening parquet blocks of the hall. She put her arm around Gunn's broad shoulder, and gazed down at the white envelope. Then, with a swift movement of her hand, she placed the Major's fly beside the one which had killed Mrs. Mumsby.

"Snap!" she cried.

The two men gasped as they stared downwards.

As far as could be seen with the naked eye, the two flies were identical!

CHAPTER XVIII

"Well," said Mr. Winkley finally, leaning back in his chair and rubbing his eyes, "I can't see any difference between them. They both look the same size, same colour, same tying, same everything. There might be some slight difference in detail, but they're both amateur-tied; neither of them has the slim finish of a professional fly. I'll have them properly examined, of course, but the trouble is that it won't help much. Even if they should both happen to be Major Jeans' flies, it doesn't mean that he is responsible for her murder. He might have given one away, or someone might have taken it from his collection. You were in his room, Miss Partridge; were the flies kept locked up?"

"Oh no," replied Pussy. "Anyone could have walked in and snaffled a few while the Major was out fishing. But all the same, I think he killed her. Miss Haddox said that Mrs. Mumsby turned her attentions away from him as soon as she set eyes on Claude. You see, she was a wealthy widow – the Major knew that – and he was furious at the idea of losing all her money if she didn't marry him. The Major has obviously got to the age when he's attracted by anything in skirts, and when a man gets that way, he's capable of anything."

"Hey, hey," exclaimed Gunn. "What's the old boy been up to now? Play fair, Pussy. You can't condemn a man as a murderer just because he's been gloating over your legs, if that's the trouble."

"Not in these trousers!" retorted Pussy. "I can't think why so many people think trousers are indecent on women. They're really far more respectable than short skirts and silk stockings."

"We won't go into that here." said Gunn. "If you can think of anything likely to be useful in connection with that fly, let's hear it."

Pussy thought seriously for a moment.

"Well," she said at length, "Miss Haddox recognized the fly which Major Jeans made for me as the same kind that was in Mrs. Mumsby's hand. Mrs. Pindar didn't react to it at all, but I'm sure she's hiding something she doesn't want us to find out."

"And your mother?" asked Gunn.

"You can't possibly suspect her!" cried Pussy, as if that settled the matter once and for all, and the others did not pursue the subject.

"General Haddox dropped a salmon fly near Mrs. Mumsby yesterday, and went to look for it today," said Mr. Winkley. "But it wasn't this fly, if we can believe him. It was a Bloody Butcher."

"Well, so is this," said Pussy.

"No," explained Mr. Winkley, secretly thinking that she was quite one of the least intelligent females it had ever been his lot to meet. "That's a different kind of fly altogether. It's –"

"I know," returned Pussy blandly, "but this is a bloody butcher all the same."

"Shut up," ordered Gunn, softening the words by kissing her hand. "It amounts to this, then," he went on, turning to Mr. Winkley, "Mrs. Mumsby was killed by a poisoned salmon fly. The murderer dipped the barbed hook into a bottle containing a solution of prussic acid, and pulled it into her hand by means of a piece of gut threaded through the eye. Then he cut the gut off close to the eye, and went away leaving the fly in her hand."

"Why did he leave the fly?" asked Pussy. "If it hadn't been for that, Mr. Winkley would never have suspected murder."

"Because, numbskull, he knew that someone might come along at any minute, and catch him removing the fly. It would have to be cut out, and he might get blood on his hands, and certainly would get it on the knife. Also, he wanted the fly to stay in her hand as long as possible, so that the poison would do its dirty work properly."

"All right," returned Pussy. "I accept your apology. Go on, Shylock."

Gunn did not bother to correct her.

"We haven't got the bottle. It may either be still in the murderer's possession, or else at the bottom of the lake, but if we did happen to find it, still corked, on dry land, we should know that it was the right one on account of the smell, because Scheele's acid, which I presume was the particular form of prussic acid used, smells stronger than cyanide. Am I right?"

Mr. Winkley smiled.

*"A masterly exposition, Mr. Gunn. Please go on," he said.

"We haven't got the bottle, but we have got the fly. At the moment it seems to throw suspicion upon Major Jeans, but that may be the murderer's intention. So the best thing to do is to keep our eyes open, and go on asking questions until we find something else out. I shall get into the police force yet, at this rate."

"Your feet are too small, and your head's too big," retorted Pussy.

"You've made one mistake," said Mr. Winkley. "The gut was not cut off the fly in the way you have suggested. I ought to have told you about that, but you could have deduced it for yourself if you'd looked carefully enough. You know that gut is attached to an eyed fly by a knot of some kind. It's usually a turle knot or a half-hitch jam which is used, but I have known fishermen who couldn't tie anything better than a granny. Anyway, if you cut the gut off the fly, you always leave the knot behind, and there was no vestige of gut left on the fly in Mrs. Mumsby's hand."

"He might have undone the knot," suggested Pussy.

"That's not as easy as it sounds," smiled Mr. Winkley. "It would probably take several minutes to untie a knot from gut even with the aid of a pin, and the pull on this fly would have made it so tight as to render such a procedure almost impossible. I think that if we are right in saying that the murderer pulled the fly into her hand, then some form of delayed slip-knot must have been used."

"Or else it was spirited away by magic," said Pussy.

"There's too much magic about it altogether for my liking," returned Gunn. "Too much theorizing and guessing, too. The only thing to do is to go on asking questions, and to compare the answers until we find some discrepancy between them. The trouble is that we can't do it openly, and from Pussy's experience so far, it looks as if everyone is ready to resent being questioned."

"Yes," agreed Mr. Winkley; "but it's very natural. Most people in this world have a secret of some kind to hide, however small, and they naturally resent inquisitiveness from casual acquaintances. Besides, everyone poses a bit on holiday; it's part of their enjoyment to pretend to be a little better or worse than they really are. Take the old examples of the shop-assistant who poses as a society lady, or the duke who pretends to be his own valet. Those are big examples, certainly, but we are all guilty of similar pretences in a lesser degree."

"I'm not," returned Pussy. "I'm what I am, and I don't pretend to be anything else, and anyone who doesn't like me can do the other thing."

"That's where you are mistaken," was Mr. Winkley's reply. "You're one of the people who make themselves out to be worse than they are. Or else you really are that *rara avis*, an honest woman."

Ignoring Gunn's murmured, "He's calling you a bird, dearie," Mr. Winkley went on:

"The only thing we can do is to keep our ears open and find out as much as we can without appearing to be over-curious, and we must pool our information."

He picked up the scraggier of the two flies, and dropped it into an envelope, which he sealed and placed carefully in his black morocco pocket-book.

"Do you want to keep Exhibit B as well?" asked Pussy. "You can if you like."

"No," replied Mr. Winkley slowly. "Wear it in your hat as you had intended, but mind you don't lose it. Remember, it's evidence."

"Right," she replied, picking it up. "Come on, Piggy. I'll play you a hundred up before dinner."

"Oh Lord!" groaned Gunn. He was about to run his fingers through his hair when he realized that it was glossily brilliantined for the evening, and smoothed it lightly down instead. "No peace for the wicked," he grinned.

"By the way," remarked Mr. Winkley as they were marching off, arm in arm, "you two haven't answered any questions yet. Do you mind telling me where you were yesterday morning? We shall never make good detectives unless we suspect one another. There must be no exceptions."

The two young people smiled at him as if they had nothing to hide.

"We drove the Iron Lung up to Hafod-y-llyn, and fished," said Gunn. "I thought you knew that."

"Oh yes, I knew that," replied Mr. Winkley, "but I was talking to the ghillie you took with you, and he told me that you only stayed up at the lake for an hour. You were no sooner in the boat than you wanted to get back to the hotel, according to him."

"I suppose it was a bit of a blow to him," said Gunn, "although I paid him for the full day, so he didn't lose by it. But neither of us is terribly keen on fishing, and that mountain lake is so gloomy, and the scenery so bleak, that we got bored and gave it up. That's all."

"What time was it when you got back to the hotel then?"

"About twelve, I think."

"I see. Mrs. Evans says that you were not in to lunch. Do you mind telling me where you were between one o'clock and ten past two, when Mrs. Mumsby was killed?"

Pussy clung tightly to Gunn's arm, and gazed apprehensively at Mr. Winkley.

"Oh no!" she exclaimed in alarm. "We couldn't possibly tell you that!"

CHAPTER XIX

Mrs. Mumsby's funeral had been fixed for the following morning at twelve o'clock, and half an hour before that time, a group of guests, as sombrely attired as their holiday clothes would admit, gathered together in the hall.

Miss Haddox, true to her principle, was not present; she and the General had booked Hafod-y-llyn, the small lake named after the water-lilies which fringed its edge, and had gone up there over an hour before in their car. Mr. and Mrs. Pindar had gone for a day's sea-fishing. ("And you couldn't really expect them to bother about funerals on their honeymoon, the dears!" said Mrs. Evans.)

The rest of them eyed one another with justifiable curiosity.

Gunn's tribute to the occasion was expressed by a black tie, and evening-brushed hair. Mr. Weston was impeccable in a navy-blue pin-stripe suit. Claude wore grey, with a broad-brimmed black felt hat of the kind associated with Spanish grandees and Mr. de Valera. Major Jeans was most strikingly dressed in black morning coat, striped trousers, and top hat.

Mrs. Partridge wore one of her favourite black-and-white ensembles, while Pussy, they all noticed with some relief, had exchanged her pullover and long, flapping trousers, for a neat, short-skirted costume, in which she lost a great deal of personality. On her head she wore a black Basque beret, adorned with the Major's fly.

For some reason the fly seemed to fascinate the other visitors, and from time to time they stole glances at it, until Pussy, always sensitive to personal criticism, exclaimed irritably:

Tm sorry about the family crest, but it happens to be made on a barbed hook, and it won't budge without tearing the material. I really don't see why I should ruin a perfectly good beret for the sake of the late lamented Mrs. Mumsby, and it's the only hat I've brought with me. Of course, if you'd rather see me walk into church without –"

"We were all admiring it," Mr. Weston interrupted, in his pleasant voice. "That colouring looks so pretty against the black background."

"Major Jeans made it for me yesterday," explained Pussy, somewhat mollified.

She noticed that the Major was smiling at her, and frowned in response.

It's a pity I can't be nice to him, she thought, *but he'd only take advantage and try something else on. Really, he's quite distinguished-looking when he's dressed in something smarter than those awful old fishing tweeds, and so few men look well in formal morning or evening clothes. Piggy always looks as if his evening suit will go baggy at any minute when he's at a dance, and his tail-coat never has that stand-by-itself look, although he goes to a good tailor. But I must say that I give the "Galloping Major" – funny how catching this habit of nicknaming people is! – full marks this morning. Mother looks jolly nice, too. I wish she'd let me wear black-and-white outfits; they're so becoming. Come to think of it, they make rather a nice pair standing together. Mother's about the right age for him, too. After all, Father was killed in 1917, a few months before I was born, and Mother must have felt pretty lonely all these years without a man. But what's the use of thinking of things like that with a man like the Major who only makes love to girls young enough to be his daughters? He must be fifty if he's a day – even older than the Merry Widow.*

This thought jerked her back to the present, and she remembered that she definitely suspected Major Jeans of being Mrs. Mumsby's murderer.

It's strange that he's dressed so suitably, she thought. *He looks like the chief mourner. I know that I never go away, even to a fishing hotel, without packing the odd evening dress, but I should think it's unheard-of for a man to take morning coat, striped trousers, and, above all, a top hat with him on a fishing holiday. Unless – well, unless he had reason to believe that he would need to wear them at a funeral like this. They look brand-new, too. But would any man be so callous as to go and order a new suit, so that, after he had murdered someone, he could attend the funeral suitably dressed? It's pretty hard to believe, yet murderers are always vain, they said: that's partly why they're easy to catch.*

This thought encouraged her to speak.

"That's a nice suit you're wearing, Major," she remarked in her most blatant voice. "I don't suppose the natives of Aberllyn have seen anything so beautiful in a hundred years."

Even Gunn was embarrassed by her words, and tried to nudge her into silence, while her mother frowned.

Major Jeans glanced at the girl, ran his finger round the inside of his stiff collar like a boy about to recite, cleared his throat, and tried to make the best of it.

"Not unsuitable, though, I hope," he said rather hurriedly. "I can't leave clothes like this at the Club; the moth gets into them. My last suit was ruined by the little blighters – I had to get measured for a new outfit. I always keep one in case anyone in the family dies, and dying is a little habit that everyone develops sooner or later. But the moths are a nuisance. I've tried everything for them, even cyanide, but that's no good after a day or two, so I decided that the only thing to do is to carry them around with me and give them plenty of fresh air. I suppose you thought I was expecting a funeral, eh?"

He sounded uneasy, and so succeeded in confirming Pussy's suspicions, especially as she had never heard of anyone killing moths with cyanide before.

"Well, I didn't suppose you were expecting a wedding," she retorted.

Major Jeans looked as if he would have enjoyed turning her over on his knee and getting to work with a slipper, but Mrs. Partridge achieved better results with a few well-chosen words.

"Don't you think you've got too much lipstick on, Pansy?" she said. "Remember we're going to church."

"No, I don't," snapped Pussy. "If God can see me in church, He can see me here. You know I never take it off for anyone, except the dentist."

But Mrs. Partridge noted with some satisfaction that her daughter's cheeks showed a natural red beneath their rouge.

At that moment they heard voices coming through the reception office from the adjoining sitting-room, and soon afterwards, Mrs. Evans, in full mourning, joined them in the hall. She was accompanied by a thin, bloodless-looking man with greying hair, wearing horn-rimmed spectacles and morning dress, and carrying a top hat and gloves. As soon as he saw the top hat, Major Jeans stepped forward and shook hands, before he knew who the man was.

"Mr. Proudfoot, Mrs. Mumsby's lawyer," explained Mrs. Evans, as she pulled on a very tight black kid glove.

The lawyer shook hands correctly, and amended this perfunctory introduction by saying to everyone at large.

"Of Proudfoot, Greensleeve and – er – Proudfoot."

"He must be 'and Proudfoot'," Pussy whispered to her mother, but Mrs. Partridge did not smile in reply, for the lawyer's advent had in some manner contrived to make the atmosphere more funereal than before.

I suppose they get used to attending funerals, she thought, *and they put on a suitable manner. I'm sure he says "er" to sound more impressive. It probably goes down well with his clients.*

But in this she wronged him, for his hesitating manner of speaking was quite natural. He always spoke like that at home. With a wife like his, he had to sound apologetic.

"Very sad for Mrs. – er – er – to die so suddenly," he said. "She was a – er – lady who had a great zest for life."

"Aren't any of her relations coming today?" asked Mrs. Partridge.

"No, no. I'm afraid the poor – er – lady" (he was not, thought Mrs. Partridge, the only one who hesitated before using the word in connection with Mrs. Mumsby) "was quite alone in the world. She told me that she had found – er – friends and a – er – haven in this hotel."

"There!" said Mrs. Evans. "She always said she'd be happy to end her days here, and I hope she was. I'm sure Evans and I did everything we could to make her comfortable, and we were so fond of her, poor dear."

She produced a clean handkerchief, but found no tears to wipe away, and Pussy, remembering her quarrel with Mrs. Mumsby in the office the day before she died, did not wonder at this.

"She must have had a pretty penny to leave to someone," remarked Mr. Winkley. "I suppose she made a will."

Pussy and Gunn exchanged glances, while Mr. Proudfoot looked offended at Mr. Winkley's bad taste.

"Oh yes," he said. "She made a will."

Claude, who had been sitting beside his father on a small settee in the corner of the hall, suddenly jumped to his feet.

"Stop it, can't you? Stop it!" he cried. "She's dead, as dead as a – a fish. Can't you leave her in peace even now? You all hated her when she was alive, all of you; now you're pretending that you doted on her, and all because you're hoping to get some of her money. I can't stand it, I tell you, I –"

"Claude!"

His father laid a gentle hand on his son's shoulder, and Claude sat down heavily, and buried his face in his hands.

The noise of crunching tyres came to their ears.

"The hearse!" exclaimed Mrs. Evans.

She moved to the front door and began talking to a man with clammy hands, who had swung down from beside the driver.

The little church was not far from the hotel, and no cars had been ordered. The visitors formed themselves into a procession of self-conscious pairs, and walked slowly behind the four ghillies who, as bearers, followed immediately behind the motor-hearse. All the population of Aberllyn who were not bed-ridden or in their cradles, kept pace with them in jostling groups on either side of the road.

As they moved slowly forward, Mrs. Evans wondered whether Mrs. Mumsby had kept her promise about the thousand pounds, and what she could do about it if she hadn't.

Mr. Proudfoot wondered how the case of Frazer v. Frazer was progressing, and whether he'd be able to catch the three o'clock train back to London.

Mrs. Partridge remembered that Pussy's father had never had a funeral. *"A bomb fell just where he was standing... He was my friend as well as one of my best officers. I can only offer you my sincerest sympathy..."*

Major Jeans was thinking that if he was not very careful, he would end up in as lonely a death as Mrs. Mumsby. He could think of worse ways of dying than when holding a trout rod in his hand, though, and they suddenly seemed near to him.

I wish I hadn't made an exhibition of myself, thought Claude. *I must pull myself together. They're all beginning to notice things and to talk, but they don't understand. I should never be able to make them understand...*

Mr. Weston's thoughts were all of Claude.

Gunn wondered whether there was a Supreme Being, and whether Mrs. Mumsby had met Him yet. It was difficult to know what to believe in these days. One day he'd know...

One day, thought Pussy, *I shall be dead and Piggy will be dead and Mother will be dead and – oh hell! why did I come to this miserable funeral?*

I wonder which of them really murdered her? thought Mr. Winkley.

CHAPTER XX

Pussy Partridge and Gunn edged away from the little group in the churchyard as soon as they decently could. They had sat holding hands in the back pew of the bare, grey church, not unimpressed by the simple burial service, and had followed the heavy coffin, its brass fittings glittering in the sunshine, reverently enough. But the vicar's exhortation to them to move near the grave's edge and gaze for the last time on the coffin, struck that artificial note which so unexpectedly crops up in religious ceremonies, and so readily offends the realism of modern youth.

When they were out of earshot, they both made noises indicative of a desire to be sick, laughed, and immediately felt better.

"It makes you want to be married in a register office," remarked the girl, with an inconsequence which Gunn understood.

"Yes," he agreed. "I quite like going to church, but you have to be such a blooming hypocrite to stomach it sometimes. Of course, this doesn't concern us really because we hardly knew Mrs. Mumsby, but if anyone you loved was being buried, and you believed in God and Heaven, and all that, how could you be expected to sob over the wormy parts in public, so that the local busybodies could go home and say, 'It was a lovely funeral; we all enjoyed it; I wept like anything'? It's all very fine for us to be told that we ought to conform to old customs, but you and I and our children are the people of the future; why don't they conform to our ideas a bit? Yet the Church is all right on a big occasion. They did the Coronation jolly well. I still remember those trumpets."

They walked in unaccustomed silence for a few minutes.

"It makes you want to do something about the murder." said Pussy suddenly. "I mean, she ought to be alive in this sunshine, and not lying dead in the ground. We don't seem to be doing enough, somehow. Do you think Mr. Winkley's all right?"

"What do you mean?"

"Well, he said we'd never make good detectives unless we suspected one another. He's obviously a bit suspicious of us, so perhaps it's time we began to suspect him. After all, he's done some rather queer things – like going out in the dark to look for that fly, for instance. We've only got his word for it that he did find it down by the lake, and for all we know, he might have found some other clue besides. It seems to me that we've really got as much cause to suspect him as the others."

"Oh, nonsense!" laughed Gunn. "He's a decent sort. You can't suspect him."

"Oh, can't I?" retorted Pussy. "They're all decent sorts, and one of them did it. There isn't one of them that I don't like, except Major Jeans, and he's just silly."

"I thought you were convinced that the Major was the murderer," returned Gunn. "You never know where you are with women: they never think the same thing for two days running. And anyway, you dragged Mr. Winkley into this affair. He wasn't sure that she had been murdered, until you started telling him of your suspicions. He might just have gone down to look for that fly because he'd noticed that it was a special kind, and thought he'd like to try it for himself."

"But no self-respecting man would do a thing like that."

"No. But a fisherman might; he'd do anything which would help him to bring in more fish than the next fellow."

"Well, if we're suspecting the others of murdering Mrs. Mumsby, we might as well include him." persisted Pussy. "He had as much opportunity as anyone else, and as much motive, too, because no one seems to have any at all. He did get hold of the fly that killed her, he suggested poison, and did you notice how he walked to the church today right behind everybody else? We do exactly what he tells us to do, and for all we know, it may be part of a deep scheme to put us both off the scent."

Gunn sighed.

"If you've begun to suspect him, I suppose we shall have to do something about it," he said. "You really are the most obstinate creature I've ever come across. If only you'd set your heart on marrying me, there'd be some sense in your pigheadedness: it's wasted on old Winkley. Look here, Pussy, the one person in the hotel who knows more about the visitors than anyone else is Mrs. Evans. If we stroll back towards the churchyard, we shall meet the others coming away, and perhaps we could talk to her."

"Sorry, darling." said Pussy, "but I must get into some comfortable clothes." and they continued on their way to the hotel.

As Gunn held open the door with his lengthy arm, under which Pussy passed without ducking her head, he said, "I must get some cigarettes." and they both turned into the office.

Of all the parts of The Fisherman's Rest, the reception office was the most modern. It had recently been built on the site of a dark cubby-hole which used to house the hotel stationery, spare electric light bulbs, old account books, and all the odd buckets and spades, dried seaweed, cheap novels, knitting, and scarves, left by visitors. Its lath-and-plaster walls were hidden behind imitation oak panelling, on which a series of coloured pictures of salmon and trout literally rubbed shoulders with highly glazed advertisements for fishing tackle and the wares of local tradesmen. Near the single, low window, stood a large, mahogany, glass-fronted show-case, which, in the height of the season, was filled with reels, baits, priests, lines, and the less necessary luxuries of fishing. Now, only a single spinning reel and a few boxed Spoons and Devons could be perceived on its spacious shelves. The lower half of the case was divided into narrow drawers, which held casts and glass-covered divisions for flies of various kinds. A wide oak counter, with a hinged flap, extended across the width of the office, and held the Visitors' Book, and packets of chocolates, cigarettes, and postcards. A glass door at the back of the office led into the Evans' private sitting-room which was a kind of Bluebeard's Chamber to all of the visitors except children, who emerged from it with biscuits or toffee-apples clutched in their hands, and slightly shamefaced looks on their faces.

Gunn pushed Pussy in front of him through the office door, and tapped on the counter.

There was a rustling of paper, a wet, squeaking sound, and then the small, slight figure of Mr. Evans rose from behind the counter. His grey hair was scanty, his eyes small and set too close together, his forehead low, and his face as pale as a white rabbit's. Pussy noticed, with disgust, that he wore no collar, but had only a stained and torn woollen cardigan over his coarse flannel shirt.

As he looked at them, his moist red underlip protruded, and catching the thin, silky edge of his moustache with an experienced flick, sucked at it with every appearance of enjoyment.

"Twenty Churchman? Ta. Everything go off all right?" he said.

"Oh yes, I suppose so," replied Gunn, stripping the cellophane from the green packet, and throwing it on to the floor. "That's if you are referring to the funeral. I should have thought that some of the others might have got back by now, but I didn't see any sign of them."

"Ah, they'll have gone into the vicarage for a glass of wine I dare say," said Mr. Evans, pulling his lips back from his teeth, like a horse, and sucking his discoloured dentures. "The vicar doesn't get much chance of a gossip at this time of the year. We're mostly chapel people in Wales, and chiefly his congregation are summer visitors. He gets lonely, and he'd be glad of company."

"I see," said Gunn. "By the way, I'd better have a few flies while I'm here."

"Trout flies, sir?"

"No, salmon."

He cut short Pussy's exclamation of surprise by treading on her toe, and winked as he apologized for his clumsiness.

"If you know what you want, yourself, Mr. Gunn – Mrs. Evans usually serves the gentlemen with their fishing tackle, and I've heard them say that she knows as much about flies as any of them. Quite an expert at tying them, she is, too, but I don't know much about them myself."

He lifted his coat from a chair, and struggled into it, then lifted the flap of the counter, and came towards them. Pussy saw that the coat did not match his trousers, and felt suitably revolted.

What a man for a hotel proprietor! she thought. *No wonder his wife keeps him in the background as much as possible.*

Mr. Evans opened the miniature drawers in the case, and apologized when he saw that most of the labelled divisions were empty.

"Rather low in flies we are at this time of the year, sir. The season will soon be over, and it's not worth our while to order more."

"I dare say I shall find what I want here." returned Gunn. "You must find things very quiet with so few visitors staying in the hotel."

"Yes, indeed, but we are glad of it. Such a rush that we have in the season, and the hotel full of strange maids and them all quarrelling, and the visitors ringing bells all day, and children being sick! We're always glad when the rush is over, though we like counting the money we make, oh yes!"

Pussy was surprised to find Mr. Evans so eager to talk with them. He was usually a taciturn individual who passed by with no other greeting than a surly nod. Today he was quite garrulous.

"Do the same people come every year?" she asked, for she had by now perceived the trend of Gunn's thoughts, and did not want to be left out of things.

"A lot of them do, miss," replied Evans. "The fishing's good here, the best in Wales, so they say, and Mrs. Evans has a way with her. Major Jeans comes in July and stays till the last day of the season. He always has the same bedroom, number five, the only single one we have with a double bed in it...

Trust him, thought Pussy. *That man lives on hope!*

"Sir Courtney Haddox comes in September. He and the Major are old cronies, always chaffing each other about their fishing. Very jolly indeed. He never brought his sister with him before, but always used to sit at the Bachelors' table in the dining-room with the Major and Mr. Winkley and the other gentlemen."

Pussy stared.

Jolly was not an adjective she would ever have used in connection with the General. Perhaps he was different, though, when old Fish-face wasn't with him. She didn't blame him for that: she found Miss Haddox rather exhausting, herself.

Gunn placed two flies on the palm of his hand, and turned to the corridor in order to see them better.

I wish he wouldn't, thought Pussy, with a shudder. *Flies on the palm of a hand will always remind me of Mrs. Mumsby, just as a hand in a silk stocking always reminds me that I want another pair.*

Apparently they reminded Gunn of her, too, for he remarked:

"Mrs. Mumsby lived here permanently, didn't she? She must have known all these people as well as you did."

Mr. Evans jerked his head in assent.

"Oh, better, sir, better. She was always a great one for the men, and I've thought that some of them came to see her as much as they came for the trout."

"They weren't so keen on catching her, though," laughed Pussy.

"I wouldn't say that, miss. She was a fine-looking woman, and attractive to some. I don't care for these skinny women myself. She was a widow, too, with plenty of money, and she wasn't mean with it. You might call her a very good catch indeed."

"What about the others?" asked Gunn. "Were they regulars too?"

"I never saw Mr. and Mrs. Pindar before," replied Evans, sucking his moustache, "nor Mr. Weston and his son, nor you, sir, for that matter. But I've seen your young lady a good many years ago when she made sand-castles on the beach, and played about the hotel in rompers."

Pussy grimaced.

"And of course your mother has been here for the last three years, miss, in July or August. Mrs. Mumsby used to admire her clothes, and they saw a lot of each other. Your mother will miss her."

"That must have been when I was abroad," said Pussy slowly, "but I didn't know..."

She broke off abruptly, as she felt Gunn's hand on her arm.

"I'll take this one," he said to Mr. Evans. "How much is it?"

"Half a crown, sir."

"Good Lord!" exclaimed Gunn. "What a price! I can get about ten sea-trout flies for that."

"There's a lot more dressing on a salmon fly, sir," returned Mr. Evans. "That's a fairly cheap one. We do have them as expensive as six shillings. They go partly by the size, sir."

"I suppose you haven't got a salmon fly in stock like the one on Miss Partridge's beret?" asked Gunn.

Mr. Evans stared at the fly, licked his lips nervously, and dried them on the back of his hand.

"No," he replied. "No, I never saw one like that before in my life."

Gunn flipped a ten-shilling note on to the counter, and began to turn over the pages of the Visitors' Book as he waited for change.

"I see that Mr. Winkley hasn't registered," he said.

"That's nothing, sir," said Mr. Evans, "though Thomas Lloyd would have us fined for it if he knew. But we shall have his address at the end of the book with all the other regulars. There'll be his telephone number, too, for I well remember writing it down myself. He was expecting a registered letter the last time he stayed here, and I was to telephone him if it came after he had left. Yes, I remember thinking that he must be with some big business firm in the City, but when I mentioned it to Major Jeans, he only laughed at me, and said I ought to get a wireless. But I don't hold with all this wireless, sir; it isn't natural, and it's my belief that it's to blame for all this international trouble in the world today. Excuse me, sir, but I think that's the telephone."

He handed over Gunn's change, and disappeared into the sitting-room, closing the door behind him.

"Well, we've solved one mystery, even if it did cost me half a crown." whispered Gunn. "We-know now why Mrs. Evans always keeps her husband out of sight."

Pussy frowned.

"What d'you mean?" she asked.

Gunn placed his hand to his lips, and lifted his elbow.

"You should have smelt his breath," he said. "I wonder..." He dived under the counter-flap and reappeared on the other side holding up a bottle. "Here's the evidence, Inspector. Lock him up before his wife gets at him!"

But Pussy was not listening. She was gazing in horror at the last page of the Visitors' Book. Gunn leaned across and looked at the words which the polished oval of her nail indicated.

"Telephone. Winkley. Whitehall 1212," he read aloud. "Pussy, you blasted little fool! Now look what you've got us into!"

Pussy relapsed into the vernacular.

"A flat-foot floogie!" she exclaimed. "But he has quite ordinary-sized feet!"

CHAPTER XXI

In the summer, meals at The Fisherman's Rest were served in a large room which had been added so recently to the other part of the building that, in the sunshine, it smelled like a newly cut jigsaw puzzle. When the "get-rich-quick" season was over, the visitors who remained were transferred to the old, fusty, but cosy dining-room at the front of the hotel. At lunch-time, except on the wildest of days when no boat could get out on the lake, this room was either empty or populated entirely by women, but on the day of Mrs. Mumsby's funeral, most of the

tables were filled, since those who had attended the church
ceremony had not thought it worth while to go fishing until the
afternoon. It was obvious, however, that Major Jeans, Mr.
Winkley, and the Westons did intend to go out, because they
had already changed into the shapeless, nondescript tweeds
which the true fisherman wears on his fishing expeditions, and
which bristled with an assortment of flies, indicating to the
initiated as many years' service as the medals on a
Guardsman's dress uniform.

The four men sat at a rectangular table known as the
Bachelors' Table, which was centrally placed near the hearth,
over which hung the stuffed record salmon caught by a famous
statesman on the fly. The carving-chair, which stood with its
back to the fire at the head of the table, was referred to as "the
Chair of Honour", and for the last few weeks, it had been
occupied by Major Jeans. It was assigned to the bachelor who
had been a regular visitor to the hotel for the greatest number
of years, and so it should have been reserved for General
Haddox, but, owing to the presence of his sister, he had been
relegated (for so he regarded it) to a table for two in the
window, from which he cast longing glances at the "bachelors"
whenever they laughed aloud at a joke, which they frequently
did.

On the Major's left sat Mr. Weston and Claude, and on his
right, Mr. Winkley. Beyond Mr. Winkley, today, sat the lawyer,
Mr. Proudfoot. At first sight, it might seem that neither he nor
Mr. Weston qualified for a place at this table, since the former
was a benedict and the latter a widower, but the happy word
"bachelor" in this hotel was applied to any man who was not
accompanied by a female member of his family. Thus a
husband who spent his holiday alone here was a "bachelor",
while an unmarried man accompanied by his mother was not.

In other words The Fisherman's Rest was old enough to
have developed traditions. It was, for instance, an unwritten
law that no one should wear evening dress for dinner, whatever

the reason. If any man did so on the evening of his arrival, he was regarded, tolerantly, as ignorant. If he did the same on the following evening, he was put down as a bounder.

Similarly, it had become a tradition at the Bachelors' Table that after the preliminary politeness of a conventional greeting, a newcomer should be received in silence until he proved his worth by speech, or by the lack of it. If he was by nature a rather diffident fellow, he would make no attempt to draw the others into conversation, so that for the first two courses, they would ignore him, and begin to converse among themselves. If he joined in, the conversation would be stopped immediately, but if he contented himself with an occasional inquiring look, he might be included, and would thereafter be accepted as a true "bachelor" whenever he chose to visit the hotel. If he happened to be one of those less fortunate individuals who are made uncomfortable by communal silence, he would be provoked into starting a discussion himself. Here again, if he were a well-informed man who avoided *clichés*, and could converse modestly with authority on some interesting subject, he would be given a hearing, and probably would be accepted as a good fellow. But woe betide the man who tried to make conversation for the sake of politeness, or who spoke before the third course!

Mr. Proudfoot was such a man.

He had had no necessity to change his clothes, and so was half-way through his meat course before the others could begin on the soup.

He eyed the little tufts of hair, feather, and silk on the lapels of the four tweed jackets, and addressed Major Jeans in tones of respect, befitting his place at the head of the table. It was, perhaps, unfortunate that his opening words should be reminiscent of Miss Haddox.

"Going fishing?"

The Major nodded.

"Er – roach or dace?"

The Major choked in his soup, and dabbed at his lips with his table napkin.

"This, sir," he exclaimed testily, "is a hotel for the accommodation of fly fishermen. We try in our humble way to catch a few trout or salmon, but to fish for coarse fish out of season is not our sport."

A lesser man than Mr. Proudfoot might have been discouraged.

"I've never done any – er – trout-fishing myself," he said. "Is it very good round here?"

"It's damned bad, sir," said the Major.

"Dear, dear!" Mr. Proudfoot shook his head and assumed a sympathy he did not feel. He was so accustomed to doing this with his clients that it had become second nature to him. "But it's the same everywhere nowadays. Trout-fishing isn't what it – er – used to be. I can't think why you stick to it. You ought to try fishing round the Midlands. You get a lot more – er – sport with roach and – er – dace. I think myself that all this talk about salmon and trout is overdone. You hook a great – er – salmon, and it lies down at the bottom of the river until it's tired. Then you – er – pull it up to the surface, and knock it on the – er – head. You call that sporting!"

The others held their breath. It was some days since anyone so foolish as Mr. Proudfoot had tried to bait the Major. They waited hopefully.

Major Jeans did not disappoint them. He leaned across the table and gazed at the lawyer, as if fascinated.

"Do you really mean to tell me that you sit in a flat-bottomed boat all day, and dangle a worm on the end of a bent pin into the water?"

Mr. Proudfoot looked uneasily at the others, but they were busily eating.

"Well – er – not exactly," he replied, "The – er – bait is attached to a float and when the – er – fish bites –"

"– a bell rings," said Claude solemnly.

The lawyer turned startled eyes towards the sound of this new attack, but everyone looked perfectly serious, so he went on:

"Oh no, no. I never heard of that kind of float. You must be thinking of deep-sea fishing. No, the – er – fish drag the float under the – er – water, and you just land them in the ordinary way."

"Do they ever take the bait without hooking themselves?" asked Mr. Winkley.

"Oh yes," replied Mr. Proudfoot eagerly. "They often do that."

"Ah, the little rascals!" cried the Major. "The tricks they do get down to, to be sure!"

"What can you expect from such coarse fish?" asked Claude.

"I suppose they don't run to much of a size," went on Mr. Winkley. "Half-pounders mostly, aren't they?"

Mr. Proudfoot had just realized that the company was not in sympathy with him. He seized upon this innocuous question with fervour.

"Oh, you'd be surprised. We get some very good – er – fish. They run to a very good – er – size, I assure you. I've seen a man playing a roach of several pounds in weight and it took some – er – playing."

"Ah yes, I don't doubt you, sir," said Major Jeans. "But have you ever seen a fish playing a man?"

Mr. Proudfoot laughed miserably.

"Now you're really pulling my – er – leg," he protested. "I can't swallow that – er – bait."

"This fellow did, though," the Major said, quite solemnly. "It was on this lake, curiously enough. It happened to an army friend of mine, so I know it's true. He hooked a fish and felt the very father-and-mother of a tug, and before he realized what had happened, he'd been pulled out of the boat into the lake. A fellow in the next boat heard him shout out, and went for help.

When he came back he thought he could see my friend in the boat playing the fish. Called out to him, and when he turned his head, what was it but a walloping big salmon sitting in the boat playing the Colonel. As true as I'm alive."

"Oh," said Mr. Proudfoot weakly, "and – er – what happened to the – er – fish?"

"They shot it," came the reply. "You can't have that sort of thing happening on a lake. And now everyone has to take a ghillie in the boat with him for safety. Oh, must you go!"

"Train to catch," murmured Mr. Proudfoot. "Forgot the time. Good-bye, ladies. Good-bye – er – er –"

He walked away hurriedly.

"I want a clean cup, let's all move one place up!" said Claude. "Oh my! Don't I wish I'd had my cards in my pocket! Wouldn't he just make the perfect stooge?"

"You must be careful, Claude," remarked his father. "If you say things like that, people will mistake you for a card-sharper."

He smiled in delight at his son's newly-found high spirits.

And indeed Claude's return to the normal was most noticeable. Pussy found herself thinking that it almost looked as if he had only been worried so long as Mrs. Mumsby's body had remained above ground. As if, now, he had nothing to fear.

She thrust the thought away from her mind, but shuddered a little when she noticed Mr. Winkley eying Claude speculatively, as if he, too, were thinking the same thing.

"It makes me sick to hear a fellow talk like that about trout-fishing!" said Major Jeans. "Talking to me about dangling a bait to roach and dace as sport! Cannibalism, that's what it is! Cannibalism!" He got up from his chair with a yawn. "Oo-ah-h! An indoor lunch is the death of a fisherman. I suppose I'd better go and throw a fly at the little – er – rascals, or they won't go to – er – sleep happy."

"Going out?" queried Claude, in a croaking imitation of Miss Haddox's voice. "Well – tight lines!"

"Bleeding hooks!" replied the Major. Then, as if for the first time aware of the implication of the words, he corrected himself. "Er – tight lines!" he said, and stumped out of the room.

CHAPTER XXII

Whether Mrs. Mumsby's funeral had had an upsetting effect on the fishermen, whether it was that they had missed the all-important one o'clock rise, or whether it was just a bad day for fishing, no one knew. But when Gunn and Pussy came back to the hotel from their walk after tea, the floor of the hall was empty, save for Mr. and Mrs. Pindar's bag of sea-fish; two enormous pollack, a few herrings and plaice, a large crab, and two green, glass net floats, which Mr. Pindar insisted on referring to as "ship's eggs".

"Did you enjoy yourself?" Pussy asked Mrs. Pindar, who was looking particularly well in a canary-coloured polo sweater and orange-flecked tweed skirt.

"It was simply marvellous!" she said. "We sailed as far as that rocky island, and saw the puffins and all kinds of queer sea-birds. It was grand, wasn't it, darling?"

She turned to Mr. Pindar, who nodded in agreement.

"Yes," he said. "She," – indicating his wife with the stem of his pipe – "was sick. It was grand!"

Mrs. Pindar laughed.

"It wasn't the sea," she protested. "It was watching the boatman cutting up those horrid pieces of live, raw mackerel for bait, and thinking of other fish eating them. Ugh!"

"And when Owen said, 'Cough it up, mum', you coughed!"

"You look as if it has done you good, anyway," said Pussy. "You look like one of those coloured advertisements for a Keep-Fit Food."

The hall door opened, and Major Jeans' thickset figure strode towards them, his legs in their riding breeches looking slightly bowed.

Hallo, hallo!" he hailed them. "Somebody caught some fish, eh?" He pushed forward through the little square which the four of them made, catching Pussy unnecessarily round the waist and squeezing her. "God bless my buttons! Roach and dace! You'd better clear them away before the cat sees them."

In spite of herself, Pussy could not help laughing, and the Major took advantage of her unwonted good humour towards him to whisk her away from the others, and whisper, "I've got some chocolates for you up in my room."

She-flung herself away from him, and sought the comforting bulk of Gunn, who was talking to Mr. Pindar, and had not noticed this little *contretemps*.

He must be mad, thought Pussy contemptuously. *Half the time he looks at me as if he loathes the sight of me, and the other half, he's making love to me. Why on earth can't he be his age, and behave like the General or Mr. Winkley? Why does he have to pick on me? Does he really expect me to go to his beastly room for a bribe of rotten chocolates? I wish I could tell Piggy about him, but if I did, there'd be another murder in the hotel. Oh, hell!*

"Some girls wear queer things behind their ears," said a voice behind her.

She turned, to find Claude producing a cascade of tiny cards from the back of her head.

"You are an ass, Claude," she exclaimed, laughing. "Don't you ever get tired of doing that stuff?"

"I can't get tired of it," he said, his eyes admiring her slim figure. "My fingers would soon get stiff if I did, and it's my living, you know. I've got to make good at it for the old man's sake." He changed the Lilliputian cards imperceptibly for a pack of standard size, and swung them in a loose concertina from one hand to the other, dropping one. "There," he said, as he stooped to pick it up. "That's fishing for you. Good for the brain, but bad for the fingers. I'm out of practice. I haven't touched them for two days."

"You haven't got that monkey of yours up your sleeve, have you?" asked Pussy rather apprehensively.

"No. I left him upstairs this afternoon. Poor Petkins! He'll feel slighted. If I'd known that we shouldn't get any fish, I'd have taken him with me, but I couldn't stand him patting them again, not – not after..."

He left the sentence unfinished, and Pussy nodded sympathetically. He turned, and ran lightly upstairs, flicking the cards as he went.

Pussy turned, to find Major Jeans greeting General Haddox who had just come in.

"What, no fish?" he cried. "Not even Cuthbert? Lord! What is the Army coming to?"

Mrs. Partridge had just come down the stairs, and was standing close to them, her head on one side like a listening bird. She looked rather like a robin, too, in a brown angora suit which she wore with a vermilion jumper, and the effect was so attractive that her daughter envied her.

"Who's Cuthbert?" she asked.

"Eh? Oh, it's you, my dear," the Major smiled. "It's a joke between the General and me. There's an old salmon that lives just beyond the ledges in the lake – you know, I showed them to you the other day – and whenever it sees Haddox, it jumps out of the lake and puts its tongue out at him. Fact. It makes the General hoppin' mad, and he's sworn to take it, dead or alive. I just call him Cuthbert – the salmon, not the General."

Mrs. Partridge smiled, and turned to Sir Courtney.

"What have you done with Miss Haddox?" she asked. "Hasn't she come in yet? I thought she went up to the small lake with you."

The General looked down at her through his rather prominent blue eyes, which were as expressionless as those of a china doll.

"Yes," he said, loosening the strap of his fishing bag with trembling fingers. "She came in with me, but I think she went straight up to her room. It was cold up in the mountains and she found it tiring. Who's responsible for the fish?"

"The Pandas," replied Major Jeans. He laughed at Mrs. Partridge's puzzled expression. "Good Lord!" he exclaimed. "Haven't you heard me say that before? I should have thought you'd got used to my little habit of nicknaming people. Pindar the Panda, you see."

"Thousands wouldn't," laughed Mrs. Partridge. "I'd like to know what you call me behind my back."

The Major squeezed her shoulder, and Pussy shuddered at his philandering.

"I can't tell you that," he said. "Not in public."

They all turned as the hall door opened again.

"Hallo! Winkley as ever is! Come and redeem the reputation of the bulldog breed in this fishless hall!" was the Major's greeting.

"Have you got any?" asked the General, peering anxiously at the ghillie's net.

"A few," returned Mr. Winkley, stretching his arms above his head, and yawning. "Why is it that it's twice as tiring to go fishing for half a day as it is for a whole day?"

"It sounds like the old problem about a herring and a half costing three-halfpence," said Gunn, but his words were drowned among the exclamations of wonder and congratulation which greeted the line of sea-trout which the ghillie, aware of his own importance on this occasion, was graduating as carefully as if they were a string of priceless pearls.

"Seven, eight, nine!" sang out Major Jeans. "And all out of a few empty cigar-boxes, or whatever he keeps his tackle in. I don't know how you do it, old chap."

"Nice fish," commented Mr. Weston, who had joined them unobtrusively from somewhere or other.

"Not too bad." said Mr. Winkley deprecatingly, although he secretly thought them very nice indeed. "Not very big, you know, but in good condition for this time of the year."

"How about a drink?" asked the Major as he drew him away from the admiring group.

"Dad!" Claude's voice shouted down from the landing before he came into sight. "Have you got Pet?"

Mr. Weston caught his breath in a hard little exclamation, as if he had a premonition of some piece of bad news.

"No, Claude," he shouted back. "Isn't he in your room?"

Claude appeared at the top step of the ten straight stairs which ascended from the hall, and stood motionless for a moment, staring down at them with scared eyes. Then his slim, straight body seemed to bend like a blade of supple steel, and like steel released, he cleared the stairs and dived towards Gunn, tearing at his coat, and peering inside it, like a demented creature.

Gunn thrust out one of his long, bony arms, and clamped it on the boy's shoulder with a force that nearly lifted him off his feet.

"Now then, what's the trouble?" he asked, in the manner of an unperturbed policeman.

Claude looked at him, his eyes blazing with hatred and fear.

"You know what it is. It's my monkey. I left him in my bedroom when I went fishing, and now he's gone, lost! You've been here all afternoon. If anything's happened to him, you've done it! You always hated him. You said you'd drown him! Oh, I knew something dreadful would happen after *she* died!"

CHAPTER XXIII

A careful search outside the hotel revealed no sign of the missing monkey. Pussy and Gunn joined Claude and his father in a search outside, but the night was pitch dark, and this also proved fruitless.

"Perhaps the call of the wild has been too much for it, and it's somewhere up a tree," suggested Pussy, but Claude shook his head.

"No, he'd be more likely to go where it was warm, into a cottage perhaps. He'd be half-dead from cold by now, and he wasn't even wearing Mrs. Mumsby's knitted jacket."

So they began a cottage-to-cottage inquiry, calling at the constable's, the doctor's and the vicar's, without any result. No one had seen the monkey.

The following morning, Mr. Weston, who appeared to be as much upset as Claude about the monkey's disappearance, formed a search-party of some dozen men who worked as ghillies in summer and as beaters in autumn, and systematically combed the village and the country around. The monkey remained hidden and Claude was disconsolate.

"I can't understand what he sees in that verminous little brute," remarked Gunn. "If it weren't that I like old Claude in spite of these queer fits of his, and don't like to see him looking miserable, I should say it's a jolly good job if it is dead. It makes him look effeminate to be always petting a chattering monkey."

"Oh, I don't know," replied Pussy. "It was part of his music-hall act, and he was teaching it some trick. I dare say he's got fond of it in the same way as other people get fond of a cat."

"Well, I'm not going to look for it any more," said Gunn. "Let's go for a walk by the sea. We shall probably find it there anyway. All kinds of things get washed up by the tide, and they call it ozone!"

They set off gaily down the wooded path leading to the sea, until they came to the smooth stretch of sand, where they behaved like any two healthy young people who find each other attractive, and who, for all they know, may be in love with each other.

They played leap-frog, until Gunn neatly sent Pussy sprawling into a patch of wet sand; they played soccer with a pebble, until Pussy resorted to heel-tapping; then they joined hands, and went to peer into the little aquarium pools which the tide had left behind in the grey rocks, and teased the shrimps and tickled the red, jelly-like anemones until they folded up their crinkling, Medusa-tendrilled hair.

"I'll race you to the sandhills," said Gunn, and arrived breathless, an easy winner, with Pussy, laughing, in pursuit.

But as the girl sat on the soft sand to rest, pulling the slack of her brown, bell-bottomed trousers round her ankles to protect them from the piercing spines of the tough dune-grass, her mood changed. She threw off her gaiety as quickly and as unconsciously as she would have thrown off an evening cloak, and sat, morose and silent, with one elbow propped on her knee, and her clear green eyes gazing at the sea.

Gunn, sensitive as always to her moods, sat close beside her, one arm around her shoulders, very still.

The sea stretched out its deep-green depths serenely to meet the hazy blue sky. A white yacht rode gently at anchor, its sails furled. On the horizon appeared the faint blurred shape of a tramp steamer. In the distance the drone of a plane made scarcely more noise than an errant bumble-bee which taxied over their heads.

Gunn rubbed his tousled brown head against her sleek blonde hair.

"What's biting you? Tell uncle," he said.

Pussy continued to stare at the sea.

"Nothing," she said, and her voice was as expressionless as her face.

"Come on, out with it, or I shall recite to you," he replied, and went on, appropriately enough: "'O, woman, in our hour of ease, Uncertain, coy and hard to please –'"

"Oh Lord. Anything but that!" exclaimed the girl.

She put up a hand and began to play with his crisp hair. He waited.

"Oh, well, if you really want to know, it's Mother," she said at length. "I'm worried about her, and I wish to God I'd never started thinking that Mrs. Mumsby didn't die a natural death."

"Clear as mud," said Gunn.

Pussy gave his hair an unexpected tug.

"Bother you!" she exclaimed. "It's clear enough if you use what few brains you were born with. I don't mind the other people in the hotel being suspected of murder, but I don't like to think that Mother can be connected with it. I know she used to come to Aberllyn when I was a child, but she never told me that she'd been here since, and I can't think why she should keep a thing like that to herself unless she has something to hide."

"I don't see why she should tell you all that she does," replied Gunn. "I'm damned sure that you don't tell her one half of the things you do, or the places you go to."

"No," agreed Pussy. "We always have been fairly independent. She gave up the home after my father was killed, so we were often separated, and of course I've been away at school, and abroad. I suppose Miss Haddox's beloved niece wears white lace and pale-blue silk dresses and indulges in heart-to-heart talks with her mother, but we've never been like that. If Mother had had an affair with some man – bachelor flats, and all that, I mean – I shouldn't expect her to tell me about it, but this seems such an unnecessary thing for her to keep quiet about."

"Perhaps she knew someone in the hotel, and didn't want you to know that she'd met them before, or something like that."

Pussy nodded.

"Don't you see, that's just it?" she returned. "Who could it possibly be except Mrs. Mumsby? I didn't tell you before, but Miss Haddox saw Mother near the place where Mrs. Mumsby died that day, but when all the others went to see what had happened, Mother must have slipped back to the hotel, thinking that no one had seen her. You must admit that it looks suspicious, Piggy."

"But, good Lord!" cried Gunn. "You can't suspect your own mother of murder!"

"Why not?" demanded Pussy. "I should think I'm capable of it. I've got an awful temper, and so has she. She's a very deceptive person altogether. She looks as if butter wouldn't melt in her mouth – all petite and feminine. I know. I've seen men go soppy about her. But she's terribly strong-willed really. I simply daren't cross her sometimes."

"Oh, well, we've all got tempers," said Gunn evenly, "but we don't go about murdering people for all that. I dare say I'd go mad and knock a fellow out if he came nosing around you, for instance, but I shouldn't stick poisoned fly-hooks in him."

"That's very noble of you, I'm sure," said Pussy, "but that book makes it even more suspicious. It's the kind of weapon a woman might use. A woman can't go knocking another woman down, and she hasn't much strength in her hands usually, but any woman could use a poisoned hook. I could have murdered Mrs. Mumsby that way myself."

"Not you, my sweet," returned Gunn. "You'd never think of doing such a thing."

"Why? Too kind-hearted?"

"No, darling. Just not clever enough." He jerked his head away from her retaliating hands and imprisoned them in his own. "Now, now, little girls mustn't be rough," he admonished.

The sound of approaching voices stiffened them into silence.

"The Pindars," whispered Gunn. "Keep still till they've gone by."

He drew her head down to his shoulder and held her in his arms.

But the voices did not grow fainter, and they suddenly realized that Mr. and Mrs. Pindar must have chosen an adjoining depression in the sandhills as a resting-place, and were held by a momentary indecision whether to move away, or to reveal their presence.

Mr. Pindar's words held them where they were. He had a peculiarly clear, cultured voice and they heard him distinctly.

"I can't go on any longer like this," he said. "I've been in absolute hell for the past few days. I think I'd better make a run for it and leave you here. It will look better like that. You say that the Partridge girl is definitely suspicious of us. So was Mrs. Mumsby. It will be like that wherever we go, and we can't go round killing everyone who suspects us, can we? I just can't go on with it any longer."

Mrs. Pindar was crying, and her reply was indistinct. The man's voice grew very gentle.

"Oh, I'm sorry, darling. I know you'd stick to me through everything, whatever anyone found out, but men are different. A woman seems able to live an ordinary life, knowing all the time that a bombshell may burst over her head at any minute, but a man can't endure the suspense. We shall have to separate. It will be hell, but at least there's a chance for me that way. They'll never suspect you of anything wrong."

The only word of Mrs. Pindar's reply which was audible to them, was "coward".

"I deserve every rotten name you can think of," said Mr. Pindar. "I'm an utter cad, and a filthy rotter, and – oh, what's the use? I was mad to have done it – mad! We never ought to have come here. I never ought to have been weak enough to let you persuade me into it, but I don't blame you, darling, I ought to have realized what was bound to happen. I ought to be hanged for it. But I'll see that you don't suffer. It's your life that matters, not mine. I'd willingly lay down my life for you, and the least I can do is to go away from you. People are sure to find out: they're getting nearer to the truth than they realize now. We must separate as soon as possible. There's one other way out of it, of course, but you know what that is."

"Yes, I know." Mrs. Pindar's voice was sad, passionate, obstinate. "But I can't do it. I can't."

"Then there's no more to be said. I'll arrange something before the week-end. Don't hold this against me, my dearest. It was a rotten thing to do. But don't hold it against me. Whatever happens you'll know that I shall always love you as long as I live. I love you, adore you, worship you, and I'll never cease to care for you. It's the kind of love I've always derided before, the kiss-the-hem-of-your-skirt kind. You're so lovely..."

The sand deadened the sound of Pussy's and Gunn's footsteps as they crept softly away.

CHAPTER XXIV

"All fry Pass Smoking into Grilled Salmon," said Gunn. "All fry Pass –"

"What on earth are you talking about?" asked Pussy irritably.

"Just repeating a sentence I made up to remind me of the stages in the life of a salmon. Alevin. Parr. Smoult. Grilse. Salmon. Cute, isn't it?"

"Cute, my foot! Why do you want to talk that nonsense now?"

"So that you won't be tempted to make any comment on the Pindars while we're within earshot," was the reply.

"Humph!" said Pussy, and they walked half-way back to the hotel in silence.

"Well, is it better – or worse?" asked Gunn in the inquiring tones of a solicitous eye-specialist.

"Oh, worse," Pussy said, almost in tears. "I like the Pindars. I think they're a sweet pair. Of course she's older than he is, but it doesn't seem to matter. I can't believe that he's a – a – murderer."

"I like him, myself," said Gunn, "but it has to be someone, and we like them all if it comes to that."

"If only it were Evans!" sighed Pussy.

They returned to the hotel by a route which cut across the main road up a rocky hill, and down by a circuitous path bounded by a mossy stone wall, where, in summer, lizards flattened their bulgy sides in the sun. The wall ended abruptly at the boundary of the hotel grounds, and there they saw Claude Weston dangling his legs idly over its mortared end.

He looked up as they approached, and slid to the ground, and, ramming his hands into the pockets of his grey-flannel slacks, stood rather awkwardly awaiting them.

He smiled at Pussy, and addressed himself to Gunn. "Look here, I'm sorry I made such a fool of myself yesterday." he said, flushing to the roots of his copper-coloured hair. "It must have looked funny to you, but I was damned fond of that monkey, and somehow things lately have been too much for me. It made me feel hoodoo, coming right on top of Mrs. Mumsby's death – as if everyone I get really fond of is doomed to die!"

"Forget it," said Gunn shortly.

Claude's little speech embarrassed him.

If you'd read it in a book, he thought, you'd think it a bit overdone. But Claude always was a bit melodramatic in everything he did. You couldn't judge him by ordinary standards, but he was a decent chap.

"Have you found your monkey yet?" asked Pussy.

"No. Dad is still out with the beaters. I never realized how fond he was of Petkins: he always seemed to think him a bit of a nuisance before. But I've given up hope now. If he'd been anywhere in the village, we should have found him by now, especially as Dad has offered a reward. Someone killed him, that's certain."

"It's rotten luck," said Pussy, "but I can't see why you're so sure about its being killed. It may have gone further than you've been able to look. Or it may have died naturally."

"We should have found his body if he'd died from exposure," replied Claude. "Besides, that's the way I feel about it, as I've told you. I suppose there's as much sense in that as in anything else I feel or do."

"It's strange that you should speak of Mrs. Mumsby and the monkey in one breath, so to speak," said Pussy, as if she were not quite sure how to express what she meant. "I mean, I was wondering whether there might be some connection between them." She noticed Gunn's warning look, and floundered still further in the disturbed sea of her thought. "I mean – you often hear of dogs dying after their masters have died, so why not monkeys?"

"Mrs. Mumsby wasn't the monkey's mistress," remarked Gunn.

"I know that," she giggled, "but they were very fond of each other. No other woman in the hotel would have wasted her time in knitting it a jumper. Sorry, and all that, Claude."

"I don't mind," replied Claude. "Monkeys aren't everyone's choice, I know. Most people are a bit scared of them, and think they breed fleas. Women, especially. You nearly always find that a monkey is a man's pet, and it's queer, really, because women are fond of carrying pet dogs, and even tiger cubs, around with them."

"Perhaps they're afraid that a monkey doesn't provide sufficient contrast," put in Gunn, ducking to avoid Pussy's well-aimed fist. "But, seriously, there might be some sense in what Pussy says, for once, though I never knew that the monkey ever took any notice of Mrs. Mumsby."

"Oh yes, it did," said Pussy. "It was there when she died."

Claude gave a gasp and went deathly pale.

Gunn laid a restraining hand on the girl's arm.

"Have a heart, Pussy," he said quietly.

Pussy smiled reassuringly.

"I think Claude would be glad to talk about it," she said. "We might be able to help."

She rested her hands on the grey stones, and vaulted lightly on to the wall. Gunn, still puzzled, followed suit, and they sat there in silence, waiting for Claude to speak. He stood there for a second or two gazing down at the welted toes of his brogues, and streaked his long, nervous fingers through his shining hair. At last he looked up.

"I suppose I might as well," he said eventually. "I can't keep it to myself much longer. Where shall I begin?"

"Well, if we're going to find the connection between your monkey and Mrs. Mumsby, we'd better go back to the day when she – she died," said Pussy.

Claude looked at her with admiring eyes.

"You've more brains than I thought you had," he said. "I suppose you don't want to hear anything that happened before we landed for lunch that day?"

"No," said Pussy, swinging her legs. "That will do nicely."

Claude paced up and down in front of them.

"Well, we landed earlier than usual," he began, "because Dad wasn't looking too well. He's had a bit of trouble with his heart lately, and I suppose he's been overdoing it a bit. Trout-fishing doesn't do him any harm, but he had a week at the salmon when we first came, and that's pretty strenuous. Anyway, we landed for lunch about one o'clock. We saw Mrs. Mumsby at her lunch as we rowed in, and she waved her hand to us, but when the boat was beached, the wall hid us from view. We saw Major Jeans' boat here, but he wasn't in sight, so he must have gone towards the road."

"Were there any other boats there?" asked Gunn.

Claude looked rather surprised at his interruption.

"Not that I could see," he answered, "but of course that part of the bay twists in and out a lot, and there are high rocks in some places near the water's edge, so they might have been hidden from view. Well, we had our lunch, and I dozed off a bit in the heat. I woke with a pain in my tummy and went off to get rid of it, with a piece of sandwich paper tucked in my pocket for emergencies."

Pussy grinned. She understood this language.

"Did you take the monkey with you?" she asked.

"Of course I did. He went with me everywhere. I took my rod with me, too. I thought Dad would be all the better for a rest, and I'd get a bit of sport fishing off the rocks. I didn't expect to catch anything, you know, but it was something to do, and I'd seen a salmon rise in that deep pool just where the big grey rock slants down to the water."

"Cuthbert!" exclaimed Pussy and Gunn together.

"Yes. Oh, I know it sounds absurd when I can hardly catch a trout, but it was just for fun. They say that salmon never feed in fresh water, and no one knows why they ever rise to a fly or bait in the lakes and rivers, so I thought there was a chance that one might do something silly when it saw my fly. I know that Major Jeans and Sir Courtney always joke about Cuthbert, and I thought how marvellous it would be if I could catch it, and bring it in to put down in the hall under their noses."

"What bait did you use?" asked Gunn.

"I used a salmon fly, of course, if you can call that a bait. I took one out of Dad's fly-book."

"What kind was it?"

"Oh, I don't know. I don't know anything about salmon flies. I just tied it on the end of a plain cast, and flicked it off before I'd been fishing for twenty minutes."

"But what about the monkey?" asked Pussy. "You couldn't keep it on your shoulder while you were fishing, surely."

"No," said Claude. "He always had a light chain fastened to his collar when I had him out, and I tied it to a low bush. He was quite happy there, trying to catch spiders and beetles. After I'd lost my fly and reeled in my line, I picked him up again and climbed to the top of a rock. I had a grand view of the lake and the ground all around me. I saw Major Jeans walking along the road, and two people very close together who looked like the Pindars, and Miss Haddox's red sun-shade beyond them. I could see Dad sitting where I'd left him, and our ghillie still in the boat, and I saw another ghillie coming towards the road from the direction of the river. I saw Mother Mumsby asleep near a large grey rock, and I thought it would be fun to go down and wake her. I knew, of course, that she wouldn't want to sleep too long or she would miss the fishing, so I thought she wouldn't mind if I woke her up. I started running down the slope towards her, and I'd just reached the level ground when I caught my foot in a rabbit-hole and sat down with a wallop. Petkins jumped off my shoulder and disappeared out of sight, and when I'd finished rubbing my leg, I went after him. I heard him chattering, and when I found him, he was sitting on her shoulder, patting her face. It was horrible! I could see that she was dead, and it just turned my tummy upside down. I rushed out of sight in a panic, and was horribly sick. When I came back for Pet, I saw the ghillie there. But I never told anyone that I found her first, because I was afraid."

"I don't see why," remarked Gunn. "What was there to be afraid of? Someone had to find her."

"Yes; but Pet had that habit of jumping on to people. You know how you hated it, Pussy. And I never knew she had a weak heart."

"Well? I don't see what that had to do with it," said Pussy. "What on earth were you worrying about?"

Claude gazed at her, and the old look of panic was in his eyes.

"Don't you understand?" he cried. "Can't you see that I killed her?"

CHAPTER XXV

"Piggy, we've got to do something," remarked Pussy Partridge as she sipped her third pink gin.

It was nearly midnight, and the hotel seemed deserted, all the visitors except themselves having apparently gone to bed.

"Oh Lord!" groaned Piggy, levering up his long body from the low, inadequate chair in which he was sprawling, "can't you even keep quiet for an hour? We'd better go and play billiards, then, though I shall see enough balls for Snooker – this is my fifth double whisky since dinner."

"If you drank a few doubles in the morning, you might see a few more fish," retorted Pussy. "I'm not going to play billiards, and that's flat."

"Thank God for that!" murmured Gunn, sinking back into his chair, and smiling beatifically. Then, struck by a sudden thought, he exclaimed, "You don't mean that you want to go out for a drive, do you? For God's sake, Pussy!"

"Take it easy, my lamb," replied Pussy calmly. "I don't want to do anything or go anywhere now. I mean that we've got to do something about Claude."

Gunn gulped down the remainder of his whisky.

"Oh yes, rather!" he agreed enthusiastically. "Of course we must. Old Claude is a jolly good sort. We must do something about him." He sank down still further in the chair. "But the question is – what?"

Pussy wriggled impatiently.

"You're drunk," she said. "But you're not so drunk that you can't do a bit of straight thinking, and your brains aren't so near the floor that they're in danger of crashing if you shake them up a bit."

She got up, and hauled him to a sitting position; she tousled his evening-sleek hair, and smacked each cheek; then she dropped a kiss lightly on the end of his nose, and slipped back again into her chair. Gunn held his long arms out to her, but she shook her head.

"No. No love-making," she said emphatically. "Only thinking."

She poised a long fore-finger against her temple, and wrinkled her forehead.

Gunn smoothed down his hair.

"You're a tantalizing little devil," he remarked dispassionately. "I can't think why I put up with you."

"Sh!" warned Pussy. "Think! If we don't do something about it, they'll have Claude hung for murder."

"Hanged," corrected Gunn.

"I'd rather say hung," returned Pussy as if that settled the matter, which, as far as she was concerned, it certainly did.

Gunn eyed his empty glass, and stretched a languid arm towards the bell.

"Oh no, you don't," said Pussy. "You've had enough to stimulate that thing you call your brain. I'm not going to let you get sozzled."

Gunn pushed his hand into his pocket, and sighed.

"I suppose you want me to play Dr. Watson to your Holmes," he said. "All right, I'll buy it."

Pussy looked perplexed.

"Dr. Watson?" she repeated. "I thought the doctor's name was Something-hyphen-Roberts."

"Skip it," said Gunn. "I might have known you couldn't understand. Your education is practically non-existent."

"I understand everyone as long as they don't spout quotations at me," replied Pussy, "but what with the Major quoting Jorrocks about 'riding over the sticks', and –"

"He said 'rowed over the Styx'," amended Gunn.

"Same thing."

"It may be to you, darling –"

"It is," finished Pussy firmly. "But as I was saying –"

"What you were saying was absolute drivel, as usual," he said, "but what you want to say is this." He leaned his arms on the small, glass-topped table which held their glasses, and gazed at her solemnly. "If Mrs. Mumsby had been murdered – and may God, if there is a God, rest her soul, if she had a soul! – Claude thinks he killed her by letting his monkey jump on to her while she was asleep, giving her a heart attack. If something isn't done about it pretty soon, one of two things will happen. Either he will be found guilty, and hanged" – he paused, but Pussy made no comment – "and hanged," he repeated, "or else he will be driven by this fear to commit suicide. He's that sort, poor devil!"

"And, of course, he's innocent."

"Yes, of course," agreed Gunn. "But how do you know that? That story about the monkey does sound a bit farfetched."

Pussy leaned her arms on the table, and looked hard at Gunn.

"Why, my simple idiot? Because we know him. He's our friend."

"Very commendable of you, Miss Partridge, I'm sure," said Gunn, in what was, he considered, a very fair imitation of a public prosecutor's voice, "but may I ask how long young Mr. Weston has been a friend of yours?"

"About three weeks."

"And did you know anything about him prior to that? Had you ever seen him or heard of him before? Do you know where he lives, or what kind of life he leads, or who his mother was?"

"No, of course I don't."

"Do you know who murdered Mrs. Mumsby?"

"No!"

"Then how can you possibly know that Claude Weston is innocent?"

Pussy banged her hand on the table.

"Of course I know, Piggy. Claude is our sort. We speak the same language; you know we do. He's the sort of fellow we'd take around to dances and parties, and introduce to our friends. He's the sort you'd lend your last quid to – oh, all that sort of thing. Why do you ask such inane questions when you know the answers as well as I do?"

Gunn, now quite clear-headed, nodded.

"I know, and you know," he admitted, "but you won't convince the police – meaning Mr. Whitehall Winkley – so easily. We shall have to do a great deal more than just feeling in our bones that he's innocent, if we're going to help Claude. Once Mr. Winkley tumbles to the fact that Claude found Mrs. Mumsby's body before the ghillie did, he'll get more suspicious than ever. After all, Claude's story is a bit thin, you know. It sounds as if he's invented it to cover up the fact that he knows more about her death than he's admitted before. The monkey was actually found with Mrs. Mumsby, by the ghillie, and it looks as if Claude destroyed the little beast in case it should give us a fresh clue. The whole affair simply stinks of Claude."

"What on earth do you mean?" asked Pussy. "I thought you said he was innocent."

"I did. But if everyone in the hotel knew it was a case of murder and voted for the murderer, I'll bet that they'd all choose Claude. The setting of the murder is like him. The monkey. The fly that must have been slipped from the gut by what I might call the Claudian Knot – I don't suppose that will bring the light of intelligence to your eyes. No? I thought not And you remember when we were talking about the preparation of Scheele's acid, I said that every schoolboy knows the chemicals used in it? Well, so he does. He uses them when he gives conjuring displays: they can be used in the very trick that Claude did when he turned water to milk and wine to ink. Of course it's a bit amateurish, I dare say, but then some of his tricks were, you know, and it does show that he might have been familiar with the stuff. Besides, the whole thing is so slick and clever, just like his performance that evening, and his hysterical tantrums may be invented to take our minds off what really happened, just as his patter takes them off his sleight of hand."

"Well, we know it wasn't Claude," said Pussy, "so why not try to find out who it was, instead of trying to pin it on to him?"

"Okay, let's start at the beginning. Victim, Mrs. Mumsby, a wealthy widow without relatives, living for four years in a fishing hotel for reasons which we all know. As no other attempt was made on her life during the four years, it would appear that the murderer is someone who has never been to the hotel before. Suspects, therefore, are narrowed down to ourselves – if we exclude the time when you wore rompers – the Pandas, the Westons, and old Fish-eyes. It couldn't have been us, so –"

"I don't see that you can cut the others out like that," interrupted Pussy. "It might be someone who had always hated her, and never had the opportunity to murder her before. Or she may only recently have done whatever it was that caused her to be murdered. Or she might have been blackmailing someone – and they'd just got fed up with it."

"Yes, I see your point," said Gunn, stroking a reflective chin which was beginning to get rough in readiness for the morning's shave. "The last straw on the camel's back, or the last twist to the lion's tail. But I'd like to bet that your reason in mentioning all this is that you hate to leave out Major Jeans."

"I only want to be fair. After all, he does fancy himself as a lady-killer, and for all we know, he may be one in all senses of the words. He made an exact copy of the fly that killed her. He admits that he bought cyanide to poison moths. 'Bleeding Hooks' is his pet expression, and it might be his idea of a good joke to kill her like that."

"And you only want to be fair," mocked Gunn. "God help the man you wanted to be unfair to! I think that if Major Jeans had killed her, he wouldn't have called attention to it by making that particular fly for you."

"He might be plumb crazy so that he always gives the same fly to the person he's going to kill – you know, like the man in *Love from a Stranger*, who always gave his victims the same scarf. Perhaps I'm to be his next victim."

But she had to admit that, when expressed in words, the case against Major Jeans seemed less convincing.

"Then there's General Sir Courtney Haddox, to give him his full title. Mr. Winkley met him looking for a fly which he'd lost near Mrs. Mumsby's body, and he's a queer old cuss altogether. But I can't see any motive. He was always very nice to the Merry Widow, and she positively preened herself when he came anywhere near her. She adored his title, and he wasn't above feeling flattered by her admiration."

"That all gives Miss Haddox a motive," said Pussy. "It's pretty obvious that he preferred Mrs. Mumsby's company to hers, and I can't say that I exactly blame him. His sister gets on his nerves; anyone can see that. Every time she says 'Tight Lines!' he gets tight lines round his mouth, and he hates the way she chases after him, and spies on him. Mrs. Mumsby was just the type of hefty, common woman to appeal to him and make him feel no end of a fellow, and his sister hated that, too."

"But it wasn't his sister who was murdered." remarked Gunn, "and although she had a motive, and always went about saying she hated Mrs. Mumsby, I can't see her committing murder somehow. She could never forget she's a lady." He hesitated for a moment, then went on, "We needn't consider your mother any more. We've talked ourselves sick about that."

"I know you think I'm queer to suspect her when I don't suspect Claude," said Pussy, "but if she weren't my mother, she wouldn't be a particular friend of mine. Oh, I suppose that sounds callous, but parents don't try very hard to be friendly to their children. They never tell you about their thoughts, or how they used to feel when they were young, and to hear them talk, you'd think that they'd never done or said a wrong thing ever since they were born. I really know more about Claude after only three weeks than I've learned about mother in twenty years. I asked her what she was doing by the lake when Mrs. Mumsby died, but she flared up at me, and went off in a huff. She didn't deny it, though. Wouldn't it be awful to be the daughter of a murderess?"

"Oh, forget it!" said Gunn sharply. "I just don't believe it."

"Nor do I really," admitted Pussy. "Who's next? The Pandas?"

"They're far more likely. After all, what we heard him say was as good as a confession. If he hasn't murdered Mrs. Mumsby, he's done something nearly as bad, and, what's more, she's in it, too."

"It seems queer to go round murdering anyone on your honeymoon," said Pussy. "What about the ghillie?"

"Wrong kind of crime," returned Gunn, who now sounded quite sure of himself. "He might have hit her over the head in a fit of anger, but this fly-hook business was definitely more cold-blooded than that. It had all been thought out beforehand."

"Mr. and Mrs. Evans, then. She was going to leave them some money, so they had a motive."

Gunn shook his head.

"I don't think so," he said. "She was murdered before she made a will leaving them the money. They would have taken good care that they would benefit by her death before killing her, or it would have been like killing the goose that laid the golden eggs. No hotel-keeper in his senses would murder his best-paying guest."

"No one in his senses would commit murder anyway," retorted Pussy. "What about Jack the Ripper, or whatever the doctor calls himself?"

"That's rather bright of you," admitted Gunn. "I did think it strange that he should have been within hailing distance of the crime when you'd expect him to have been having his after-luncheon nap, or doing his rounds."

"Sounds more like the milkman," replied Pussy. "I'd be inclined to suspect him if he had a motive, and Thomas Lloyd, too. It seems too much of a coincidence that two people who had no business there should have happened to come along at the right moment. We ought to get Mr. Winkley to make a few inquiries in their direction; he'd find out more than we should. Hallo! Who on earth's coming into the hotel at this time of night?"

The hall door opened quietly, and four men tiptoed inside with elaborate carefulness. The leader put his forefinger to his lips, said "Ssh!" loudly to his companions, and, with consummate buffoonery, made elaborate goose-strides into the hall. When he saw Pussy and Gunn, he stopped, and they all broke into roars of laughter.

Their bodies were padded with layer upon layer of woollens and tweeds, topped with leather coats or mackintoshes, and they carried rugs in addition to the full paraphernalia of fishing. Their faces were red, and their eyes bloodshot.

"You don't mean to say that you've been on the lake till this hour?" demanded Gunn, and Pussy realized that these were the four Welshmen who were so rarely seen in the hotel.

"Oh yes," said one of the men. "We came for the fishing, and by God! we mean to get our money's worth."

"You don't know what real fishing is until you're out with the dawn and home with the milk," said another.

"But how can you see your flies in the dark?" protested Gunn.

"Oh, we fish by instinct," was the reply. "The two boats keep together, and we have a bit of a sing-song, and a bit of a drink, you know. It's all the fun in the world, man."

"I should think you're hungry by now," said Pussy.

"So we are, miss, so we are. But the lady of the house doesn't forget us, God bless her. We shall find our supper waiting upstairs for us. I've a bottle up in my room, if you and the lady would care to join me. No? Well, no offence, I hope."

He went up the stairs, and the other three followed him.

"What about them?" whispered Pussy.

Gunn smiled.

"I'm afraid not," he replied. "Much as I should like to think it. They were all on the opposite side of the lake when she was killed, and that's three miles away."

"Then there's only Mr. Weston left."

"He's the least likely one of the lot," said Gunn, "so if this were a thriller, he'd definitely turn out to be the murderer, I suppose. But he was never alone because his ghillie was sitting in the boat within sight nearly all the time, and when he wasn't there, Claude was with his father. Besides, what possible motive could he have had?"

Pussy yawned.

"He didn't like Mrs. Mumsby making all that fuss of Claude," she said. "But that's just silly. Mother doesn't always like Major Jeans making a fuss over me, but she hasn't murdered him so far. So we're back where we started. Come on, I'm tired. Let's go to bed."

"We'd better turn the lights out," said Gunn, getting up and stretching himself.

But when the hall lights were turned out, they saw that the light had been left burning in the lounge, and they sauntered along the darkened corridor towards it. Gunn touched the switch, leaving only the glow of the dying fire to illuminate the room, then drew Pussy, unresisting, to a low settee, where they kissed, and kissed, and kissed again.

Suddenly Gunn held her away from him, and listened.

"Somebody's coming," he whispered, and they waited in silence.

Footsteps, which sounded muffled even on the bare tiles of the long, central corridor of the hotel, moved nearer, and halted outside the door. Then, their eyes now fully accustomed to the darkness, they saw a tall, lean figure move stealthily forward towards the fireplace. A hand was thrust out, and dropped a packet of some substance on to the embers, which coloured them, as if chemically, until they faded into blackness.

They heard a little exclamation of satisfaction, and the figure withdrew silently from the room, and passed as silently along the corridor. They followed as quietly as they could, and were just in time to see a tall figure, attired in Jaeger dressing-gown, and heavy felt slippers, retreating up the lighted stairs.

"My hat!" exclaimed Gunn. "General Haddox!"

CHAPTER XXVI

In spite of their resolution, neither Pussy nor Gunn did anything further towards elucidating the mystery surrounding Mrs. Mumsby's death, on which they had so light-heartedly embarked. The sight of General Haddox creeping round the hotel after dark had made the whole affair too complicated for Pussy, and she tried to put it out of her mind. It seemed that the only way in which they could help Claude was to keep his confided fears from Mr. Winkley, and this was not difficult, as both she and Gunn had avoided him since their discovery of his connection with New Scotland Yard. As Gunn expressed it, "He's a detective, and I'm no Emil."

In this, however, they wronged Mr. Winkley, whose position at the Yard was, in his own words, that of "a hunch expert". The small room in which he sat for the greater part of the day was a kind of dustbin for all the ragtag and bob-tail of information collected at various times by the various departments, and it was his job to sort out and piece together the many half-facts which had no separate significance. As these facts had already been subjected to the scrutiny of all the experts of the detective force before being sent to him, only a brilliant guess could be expected to make sense out of them, and Mr. Winkley was, therefore, the only man in that building with the widely known telephone number who was encouraged to jump at conclusions.

But Pussy and Gunn soon realized that Mr. Winkley was far from feeling aggrieved at their avoidance of him, and had no intention of seeking their company, except when he came to Pussy to borrow the salmon fly which Major Jeans had made. One morning they missed him from the hotel, and were told by Mrs. Evans that he had had an early breakfast, and had gone to London on business. She did not expect him to return until the following evening.

"There!" exclaimed Pussy in dismay. "He did find another clue, and now he's gone to get some information about Claude. That man's not safe. We ought not to have allowed him out of our sight."

At the precise moment that she made this remark, a man in the police laboratory at Hendon was holding a film, still wet from the fixing, up to the light which penetrated through the north window.

A satisfied smile twitched the corner of his thin lips.

Good enough, he thought. *There's enough evidence on that little strip of celluloid to hang a man.*

The fact did not worry him any more than the extracting of a septic tooth worries a dentist. It was part of his job to gather the evidence to convict a man. He never visualized the mind of the criminal, or thought of him as a human being with a home and wife and children. He never considered the effect which the hanging of a criminal would have on the man's family. That was not his affair. He thought of him only as XYZ1234, or whatever designation was affixed to the article sent to the laboratories for investigation, and it meant less to him than if it had been applied to an arterial road.

His work was a constant miracle to him. Science, far from "taking the colour from the rainbow", to his mind imbued those colours with a deeper significance. It was the difference between enjoying *Der Ring des Nibelungen* for its music alone, and enjoying it for the deeper significance of the Wagnerian philosophy which it depicted. He gazed at each microphotograph and each photomicrograph with the unquenchable enthusiasm of an astronomer who searches a familiar telescopic field for a new star.

A noise disturbed him, a sound so familiar that he did not stop scrutinizing the dripping negative. The hinges of the laboratory door had needed oil for months. There were plenty of substances on the shelves which would have effected an immediate cure, but no one ever thought of applying them.

"If you want those prints," he said, without turning his head, "they won't be ready till four o'clock."

"No hurry," replied an unexpected voice, and he swung round, looking – silhouetted against the window – very much like the chemist in a well-known advertisement, except that his white drill coat was certainly not Persil-washed.

"Winkley!" he exclaimed. "What on earth brings you back to town? Had some trouble with a record fish again, and want me to examine the scales under the microscope for you to see whether it's a grilse or a sea-trout? Is that it?"

"Nothing so simple," replied Mr. Winkley, moving forward, and taking the film from his hand. "What is this supposed to be? The canals of Mars?"

"That, my dear Winkley," retorted the other, "is the most perfect ballistics photograph ever taken. See those scratches? Lovely, aren't they? It was a beautiful gun, superbly made inside and out. I can't understand why criminals never tumble to the fact these expensive weapons leave visiting-cards of the clearest engraving."

Mr. Winkley smiled.

"I'm afraid my sympathies are often with the criminal," he said. "Everything is so difficult for him in these scientific days. Wireless that gathers millions of people into a huge search-party, laboratories that analyse everything from his hair to his toe-nails – why, the poor fellow never gets a sporting chance."

"Oh, well, 'Crime isn't sporting', as we all know. And, incidentally, that's the title of a thriller I've just been reading. I don't remember who it's by, but it's a damned good yarn. You'd enjoy it."

Mr. Winkley took a small, leather-covered diary from his pocket, and entered the name at the end.

"I suppose most people would laugh at the idea of anyone from here or from the Yard reading detective fiction in their spare time," the other went on, "but we all do it. They'd probably expect us to read biographies or even Plato."

"So I do, when I want to read," replied Mr. Winkley, replacing his pencil in the diary, "but detective novels are not real reading, they're recreation. The novelist pits his wits against the criminal, and the reader pits his against the novelist. There's a great sense of satisfaction in solving the crime successfully before the last chapter, and an even greater sense of satisfaction in discovering that the writer has tripped up over some detail that you and I know as well as our own names. It will be a great day for all of us when Hercule Poirot makes a mistake. The man's so confoundedly conceited. But, like the Lost Boy, Slightly, I haven't really any hope."

He was interrupted by an apologetic cough.

"Well, what can I do for you?" asked his companion, in the unctuous tones of a salesman suffering from lack of faith in his ability to please. "Sorry, old man, but we're terribly busy at the moment. That" – indicating a bundle of coarse sacking in a corner – "has just come in. If we can extract a millimetre of oil from that lot, we can prove that the big fire at Millchester was an arson case. But it will take time, and a lot of space."

"I should have thought that was a Home Office job," remarked Mr. Winkley.

"They're too busy with these Irish bombing outrages."

"I see. That's pretty dirty work from all accounts." returned Mr. Winkley, "but typically Irish. It's to be hoped that the Government stand firm over it, but I'm afraid they don't realize that you can't make a friend of a Southern Irishman by giving him what he wants. It only makes him feel twice as discontented because he didn't ask for more. Look here," he went on, sensing the other's impatience, "I won't keep you a minute. It's a case of suspected murder, and this is the only clue."

He took an envelope from his wallet, and shook out the salmon fly which had been cut out of Mrs. Mumsby's dead hand.

The white-coated laboratory worker took it up in a pair of forceps, and examined it closely.

"It seems the right kind of clue for a fishing murder," he answered. "Are you sure you're not pulling my leg?"

"It's hardly worth while travelling all the way down from Wales just for that pleasure," said Mr. Winkley, and explained the facts as briefly as he could.

He then took out another envelope, and shook out the fly which he had borrowed from Pussy.

"I hope you don't want me to unwind them and then tie them again. I never can understand how anyone can make a neat job of these things."

"Nothing like that," replied Mr. Winkley. "I just want you to examine each fly as carefully as possible to see whether there is the slightest difference between them in any way, and whether there's any possible clue in the materials used."

"And if they're identical, the owner of the one murdered the person on whose coat the other was found, I suppose."

"I'm afraid it isn't quite as simple as that," said Mr. Winkley. "It's a case of poisoning. I should like you to estimate how much prussic acid it would be necessary to have on that hook to kill anyone, if injected directly into the blood."

The other ran nicotine-stained fingers through his shock of yellow hair.

"You do think out some pretty problems, Winkley, I must say," he remarked. "I'll tell you now that I can't possibly estimate any such amount without first committing a murder myself. There's no precedent for any such thing on our files. Of course I could try it on a guinea-pig, but that will only tell me how much it takes to kill a guinea-pig in that way. I can't see the Commissioner giving me permission to try it on a human being, somehow, and even if he did, I couldn't swear that every man and woman would react in the same way."

"But I thought prussic acid poisoning was instantaneous," protested Mr. Winkley.

"It may be, and then again it may not," came the reply. "I've seen a dog killed instantly by a spot of prussic acid on its tongue. One yelp, and it was dead. I've also seen a cat walk about for half an hour in agony, after taking a dose which was four times what is considered the fatal amount for an animal of its size. You can't tell until you try it out."

"But if it were injected –" persisted Mr. Winkley.

"I should think it would undoubtedly be fatal, but this wasn't injected in the usual way by hypodermic. All kinds of considerations enter into it: the part of the hook on which the poison was most heavily concentrated, the rate at which the hook sank into the flesh, whether it struck a vein, and all that.

The only person who can tell you what amount was used is the murderer. I'll see what I can find out about the flies. Where shall I send the report?"

He took the address which Mr. Winkley wrote down for him, and turned with an air of finality to his bench with its beakers and dishes.

Mr. Winkley took the next tube to town, and managed to catch the Assistant Commissioner for a few minutes. He was considerably taxed to compose a clear precis of his suspicions about Mrs. Mumsby's death for so short a hearing, and his superior was not impressed.

"It sounds to me like one of those yarns you fishing fellows tell," he said, "or else a plot by a lady novelist." He hummed a tune under his breath, "She never will be missed, I've got her on the list."

"If it had been anyone but you, Winkley, "I'd send him out with a flea in his ear, but, after all, we do pay you to get hunches, and we can't grumble if you like to work overtime, I suppose. I'll have those inquiries put through for you, but please remember that you'll get no backing from us if you're wrong. It doesn't look to me as if there's much in it, but I suppose I shall have to humour you. If you'll leave your address, I'll have the report sent to you. Good afternoon."

Mr. Winkley, finding himself dismissed, and somewhat bewildered by the speed of London after the slow quietness of the little Welsh village, sought refuge in his own room. He found the decorators in possession, and its familiar disorder covered with heavy grey painters' sheets. He retreated to the busy streets, and, fretting because there was no train to take him back to the trout before morning, he wandered into a cinema which had seen better days as one of the old felt-and-plush variety halls.

The walls of the foyer were hung with heavy framed photographs of he-men and glamour girls of the films, but the walls above the steps leading to the circle still boasted the no less artificial photographs of the stars of the 'nineties, as if no one had had the energy to remove, or even to dust them.

On his way into the cinema, Mr. Winkley was too much occupied with his thoughts to raise his eyes above the brass handrail which divided the marble steps, but he came out in a more leisurely fashion after he had seen the programme through, and scanned the old photographs with interested eyes. He halted in front of one which purported to represent "The Great Hei-Wei", evidently a Japanese conjuror.

In view of the recent conjuring performance he had seen at The Fisherman's Rest, the photograph held a special interest for him, and he could not help contrasting this kimono-clad figure with the troubadour-slim figure of Claude Weston.

And so his mind travelled back to the mystery of Mrs. Mumsby's death, and he continued to gaze at the photograph long after he saw it. Then he made his way thoughtfully back to his deserted flat.

CHAPTER XXVII

That same night, Pussy Partridge walked into her bedroom, chewing a candy which she had taken absent-mindedly from the open box on her bedside table, which Major Jeans had driven ten miles to fetch for her. She unbuttoned her tinselled evening blouse, which boasted as many colours as Joseph's coat, and put it carefully over a padded hanger, substituting a somewhat disreputable pink cotton kimono. She tied a silk scarf round her head to protect her hair, drew a chair up to the old-fashioned dressing-table of pale Italian walnut, and began to prepare her face for the night.

For a time she was completely absorbed in the task of slapping wet cotton wool, skin tonic, and cleansing cream on to her face, but when she took up her magnifying minor to inspect the lines and crevices of her skin more clearly, her thoughts began to wander.

It was all very difficult, she thought. Whenever circumstances or her mother were not too much against her, she did exactly what she liked. Riding roughshod over people's feelings didn't worry her in the least, for, in what little philosophy she possessed, it was everyone for himself and the devil take the hindmost. But when she did suddenly take it into her head to be tactful and to try and please everyone, things always went wrong.

Take tonight, for instance.

Usually, of course, she and Piggy spent the evening with Mr. Winkley discussing Mrs. Mumsby's death, which she really could not regard any longer as murder. She never had believed it possible to murder anyone with a fly-hook; that had just been make-believe to enliven the holiday in this dead-alive hole. It had been rather fun to pretend, especially as Mr. Winkley had taken it all so seriously, but now she had other things to worry about, and it wasn't fun any longer.

The trouble had all arisen from her kindness of heart, but, of course, no one would believe that.

Major Jeans had suggested a game of bridge, and as her mother had seemed keen as well, she had made Piggy play, much against his will. She played vilely, of course, but in these days it simply wasn't done to say that you couldn't play bridge, and, after all, she had put in a bit of practice at those dull tea-parties of her mother's, where everyone stared at her as though she were a loose woman, and talked down to her as if she were still ten years old.

She and Piggy had cut as partners, so she sat next to Major Jeans. He had ogled her, and made slightly questionable jokes, at which she had laughed too loudly out of sheer politeness, though she had heard them all years ago and they weren't a patch on the ones out of Piggy's extensive repertoire. Then the Major had talked a lot about a B.W.O., which, it appeared, was a fly called a Blue-Winged Olive, and not what your best friends couldn't tell you. And after that, he had mentioned the salmon fly which had been stuck in Mrs. Mumsby's hand.

"If it had been a nymph, now, it would have been more appropriate," he had remarked, and although she understood that implication well enough, she had thought it rather bad taste to say it in front of her mother.

She had grown bored by his long monologue on fly-nymphs so that, when he had turned his twinkling blue eyes on her, and had asked fatuously, "I bet you can't tell me what a nymph's overcoat is called," she had replied, "Aw, shucks!" in the hope of shutting him up.

But that, apparently, had been the right answer. It had really been rather clever of her, and the Major had felt more encouraged than ever. Mother had seemed pleased, too, but Piggy was in a vile humour, and evidently thought that she was playing up to the Major just to make him jealous, instead of its being all through kindness and one pink gin too many. So, of course, she had had to encourage the Major just for spite, and he had ended by rubbing his leg against hers, and purring like an old tom cat. If Piggy hadn't happened to drop a card, and peer under the table for it, she would have explained everything afterwards, but it had been so rotten of him to jump to the worst conclusions, that she had simply had to snub him a bit more. By the end of the last rubber they owed her mother and the Major over ten shillings between them, and after the Major had offered to take his share in kisses, Piggy was in a temper only to be described as flaming, while his face was as white as a sheet.

Piggy had turned on her when the others had gone, and had seized her arms in a grip that had brought tears to her eyes. His brown-flecked eyes shone with a devil she had never seen in them before, and she had felt rather scared.

"You little rotter!" he had said venomously. "I'll teach you that you can't play around with me! You think that you're clever, making up to that old sugar-daddy in front of me, don't you? You think that because I'm crazy about you, I shall crawl on my knees and lick your shoes. Well, you've got me wrong, Baby. Another woman thought the same thing once: she knows better now. You can't play me for a sucker, and get away with it. Anyway, it's about time that we had some understanding. You'll have to decide whether you're going to marry me or not, before the end of this holiday. If the idea doesn't appeal to you, I'll go away, and never see you again. If you play fast and loose with me, I'll strangle you!"

He had turned to the bell and ordered whisky, and somehow all her pride had melted, and she had tilted her sensuous red mouth towards him.

"Aren't you going to kiss Pussy good night?" she had pouted, her eyes seconding the invitation of her lips.

"No, damn you!" he had shouted. "Go and ask the Major!"

Well, of course, she was very fond of Piggy, but she couldn't allow any man to yell at her like that, so she had come upstairs to her bedroom alone, and the tonic she applied to her eyes did not altogether succeed in concealing her tears.

She smeared her face and neck with cream, and patted imaginary lines with her firm, slim fingers. She took the pins out of her hair, and brushed its rather thin, brittle ends, until they stood out in a fuzzy halo round her head, then she plaited it, and tied the ends with washed-out pink ribbons. She rubbed the bruises on her arms, then dabbed at her face and eyes with pink tissues. Her face, without its make-up, looked peaked and sallow, the bones of her cheeks looking too prominent without the pink softness of rouge.

She slid her wide, black trousers into a sleek, satin heap on to the floor, shed her white scanties and shoes, stepped into green silk pyjamas, and went to sleep with her head on a wet pillow, wondering vaguely whether Piggy meant what he had said about strangling her.

A strange, sharp noise awakened her, and she sat upright in bed.

The thought uppermost in her mind was that Piggy had got over his temper, and was trying to attract her attention with the curlew's cry which he had adopted as his theme song. He usually went out and walked off an ill-humour; perhaps he was standing beneath her window, throwing up pebbles. This had no sooner occurred to her than she was out of bed, tearing at the thick curtains, so that the moonlight streamed into the dark room as if glad to be released.

No light came from the lower windows of the hotel. She peered along the street which led to the little graveyard where Mrs. Mumsby lay so silently. There was no sign of Gunn.

Disappointed, she drew back from the window, and as she stood thus silhouetted against the light, she heard a voice say, "Don't move!"

At the sound, her heart beat so suffocatingly against her breast that she could not utter the scream that came to her throat. And so she stood, like a silver statue, till her pride urged her to turn.

Her quick eyes glimpsed a ghostly head with two hollow gaps for eyes, but before she could call out, she heard a swishing sound, and something cold and sinuous whipped like a lash round her neck, and drew tighter and tighter. She struggled against the relentless pressure while the beat of her heart moved up from her breast and drummed in her ears.

As she sank into unconsciousness, she heard Gunn's voice in the distance, saying:

"Forgive me, darling. I didn't mean to..."

CHAPTER XXVIII

The first person Mr. Winkley saw when the local connection from the London train drew up at Aberllyn Halt, was Gunn, striding up and down the wooden platform like a caged lion taking exercise.

"Hallo!" he said. "Where's Game?"

Gunn gazed at him blankly.

"You know that Major Jeans always refers to you and Miss Partridge as 'Game and Gun', don't you?" He smiled, then, seeing that the blank look still remained on Gunn's face, he said sharply, "What's happened? Not another?" His raised eyebrows supplied the missing word.

"No," replied Gunn, "but there's been an attempted one, I think. It's Pussy, this time, and she thinks it's me. I brought the 'Iron Lung' to meet you so that we could go somewhere and talk. Throw your case into the dicky, and hop in."

He started the protesting engine, and drove towards the sandhills at a pace which literally made Mr. Winkley's hair curl. The hood was down, and he had to take off his hat, so that the wind whipped through his long fair hair, and heaped it in a curly mass on top of his head. He rightly guessed, however, that any protest would only cause Gunn to increase the speed, and, knowing that it was barely two miles to the sandhills, he sat in silence.

"Sorry, and all that," said Gunn, looking at Mr. Winkley's hair after he had brought the little two-seater to a squeaking standstill, "but I feel as rattled as this car sounds. It's a bit thick when the Only Girl in the World accuses you of trying to murder her – accuses me, I mean, of course."

"If you could just begin at the beginning," said Mr. Winkley, in the mild tones which suggested the kindly G.P. asking a nervous patient to describe his symptoms.

"Sorry," said Gunn again. "Well, it's like this. Pussy and I had one hell of a row last night. She's been playing me against Major Jeans lately, and I was about sick of it. When it got to leg-play under the bridge table last night, I saw red, and told her where she got off. I know she was only teasing me, but, hang it all, I'm in love with her, and there's a limit. I admit that I said I'd strangle her, and at the time I meant it, but –"

Mr. Winkley sighed.

"If you could put it all a little more clearly," he suggested patiently.

"That's all there is to it," replied Gunn. "I threatened to strangle her, and someone tried to strangle her last night, so she thinks it was me, and she won't have anything more to do with me."

Mr. Winkley at once became alert.

'That's the last thing I expected," he said. "Have you told anyone in the hotel about it?"

"No. We're both too much upset to talk about it. I came straight out after breakfast to meet your train. I've been waiting for over three hours. Pussy had breakfast in her room, but she didn't eat anything. I watched the tray go in, and saw it come out. She was still in her room when I left."

"Is anyone with her?"

"Only her mother."

"We'd better get back at once."

"Yes, but surely –" began Gunn. "Good God, you don't think –"

He took one look at Mr. Winkley's face, pressed the self-starter, and sent the car hurtling towards the hotel at a speed twice that of the previous journey.

Constable Thomas Lloyd was standing on his little mat in the centre of the four cross-roads just outside The Fisherman's Rest. He flung up his hand automatically as the car approached, and all the power of clutch and brake could not check it until it had passed him.

"What the hell did you pull me up for?" demanded Gunn. "You can see there's no other car on the road."

"Dangerous driving," returned Lloyd in his most officious manner. "I've had my eye on you for some time, sir. There's a speed limit through this village, indeed."

"Oh yes, whateffer," mocked Gunn. "There's no sign up, but I suppose you want another conviction to make them up to even numbers."

Lloyd puffed himself out like an old bullfrog.

"Here, here," he said, "there's no need to talk like that now."

Gunn laughed.

"Loud cheers!" he said. "Insulting police on point-duty, I suppose. You know my name and address; you can put it in your notebook if it gives you any pleasure. But if you haul me up in court, I shall start asking awkward questions about what you were doing along the lake road on the day that Mrs. Mumsby died, when you ought to have been on point-duty."

Lloyd deflated himself, and became more conciliatory.

"Now, sir," he began, but Gunn threw in his clutch.

"Oh, go to hell!" he said savagely. "While you keep me here, there may be murder done!"

"Murder?" exclaimed Lloyd, stepping back.

"Murder," reiterated Gunn.

He turned the car quickly round the corner, and drew up at the side entrance of the hotel in a cloud of exhaust smoke.

Lloyd moved slowly back to his mat, and stood there motionless until he was disturbed by the ringing of bicycle bells. Without looking up, he waved his hand, and a crowd of boys from the near-by preparatory school circled round him delightedly three times on their bicycles, before he had noticed what they were doing.

CHAPTER XXIX

Mr. Winkley walked into the bright bedroom overlooking the road, and was greeted by Pussy, wearing a green knitted jumper-suit and a rather subdued air. The only indication of her extreme perturbation was the fact that she had omitted to "do" her face, which, in consequence, looked pale and thin, and exhibited a remarkable number of unhealthy little spots which her usual make-up skilfully concealed. Her lips, too, lacking the exotic lipstick, looked thin, and revealed a more calculating disposition than one might have guessed when seeing her in full war-paint.

All this Mr. Winkley noted as he stood facing her, legs stretched apart, in front of the fire.

Pussy smiled wanly.

"You remind me of the poem that Stanley Holloway recites, about why dogs have cold noses and men have cold behinds and women have cold elbows. Not that women do have cold elbows these days. At least, mine are always warm enough." She sighed and gave up this attempt to be politely conversational. "I feel lousy," she said. "Did Piggy tell you all about it?"

"As much as he knew," replied Mr. Winkley. "How did you know that I'd seen him?"

"I watched him go out, and saw him come back with you, but you're not to tell him that. Did he tell you why he tried to strangle me?"

Mr. Winkley smiled down at her.

There was, he thought, something refreshing about the candour of this war-baby generation. Younger people were growing old-fashioned again, almost Victorian. That was, to his mind, a great pity.

"Suppose you tell me all about it," he suggested, with what Pussy afterwards called "his bedside manner". "I know that Gunn threatened to strangle you. Just go on from there."

Pussy gave him a vivid description of what had happened in the moonlit room.

"...and if it wasn't Piggy..." she said, but Mr. Winkley interrupted her.

"I'd like to ask you a few questions before we jump to conclusions," he remarked. "Did you look round the room before you got out of bed?"

"No. I looked at the window, and jumped out of bed facing that way."

She put her hand up to her throat as if it hurt.

"So we can take it that you were attacked from behind to prevent your turning to see who was in the room. Did you recognize the voice?"

"N... o..." said Pussy. "It was a croaking voice, like Miss Haddox's, or something like my own is now."

"And you didn't turn round before you were attacked?"

"Oh, but I did." Pussy shuddered. "It was ghastly – like looking at a ghost. There wasn't a face – just a kind of blur with great eye-sockets like a skull, only they were white."

"Can't you give me a better description than that?" asked Mr. Winkley, discrediting, still in the medical manner, sixty per cent of what she said.

"Isn't that enough to raise the hair on your scalp?" asked Pussy. "You ought to try looking at something like that in the moonlight when you've only just awakened from your sleep, then perhaps you'd be more sympathetic."

"And you say you heard a swishing sound just before the thing tightened round your neck. It's a good job that monkey's disappeared, or I might think..." He broke off as if a new line of thought had suggested itself to him, then said, "Do you mind if I have a look at the mark?"

Pussy, entirely unembarrassed, pulled down the polo collar of her jumper, and revealed a thin, purplish-red line cutting into her swollen flesh at the angle at which one prunes a rose tree. Mr. Winkley rubbed his forefinger gently along it, then moved away and wiped his finger on his handkerchief.

"H'm," he said. "It looks something like the cut that a fairly heavy trout-line makes when it gets wound round a fish. I suppose you didn't have all that grease on your neck last night."

"Yes, I had," replied Pussy, ignoring his description of her expensive Crème Amourette. "I always cream my neck at night. I usually wipe it off with a tissue before I get into bed, but last night I forgot."

"You were lucky. It made the loop slip. If it had been pulled straight round your neck, you'd have had such a sore throat that you wouldn't have been able to speak today. As it is, you don't sound much worse than Miss Haddox. Have you told your mother anything about last night?"

"No," replied Pussy. "She hasn't seen my neck, either. I just said I had a sore throat, and she took it for granted that I'd been smoking too many cigarettes, but I said I felt rotten, so she told me to stay in my room. I told Piggy, of course, because I thought he'd done it."

"What makes you think it was Gunn?" asked Mr. Winkley. "I know all about what he said last night, but I've heard him say far worse things to you before, and you haven't taken any notice of him. I don't suppose he's the only person you know who has threatened you in that way either."

"I know," agreed Pussy. "Mother often says she'll murder me if I borrow her best silk stockings, and Major Jeans said the same one day over something else. But it was Piggy's eyes. They really did look full of murder."

"I think you'd better have him in here and ask him," replied Mr. Winkley.

He ignored the girl's cry of protest, and opened the door. He did not even look to see whether Gunn was outside in the corridor before he called him into the room.

Gunn sauntered in, hands thrust in the pockets of his grey flannel slacks, and shoulders hunched forward in his sports coat of smooth check tweed.

"Come along." Mr. Winkley's voice sounded overcheerful in contrast with the glum silence of the two young people. "I want to hear your version of what happened last night."

Gunn looked appealingly at Pussy, noted her air of studied aloofness, and set his jaw in obstinate silence.

"For heaven's sake will you stop this nonsense!" exclaimed Mr. Winkley. "I don't care if you never speak to each other again as long as you live, but I do care about solving this mystery. I believe that Mrs. Mumsby's murderer was in this room last night!"

"But –" said Gunn and Pussy together.

Mr. Winkley clapped a hand to his forehead.

"That's right! Both talk at once!" he said.

"But why does the murderer want to kill me?" asked Pussy.

"I don't think that he does," replied Mr. Winkley. "I think he came in here last night because he believed you had a clue to his identity, and he wanted to remove it. By waking when you did, you startled him, and he attacked you, either to prevent your recognizing him, or else to frighten you. Or, if he really did intend to kill you, he must have been disturbed in some way."

"It sounds nonsense to me," said Pussy. "I haven't got any dues. I've nothing belonging to anyone in my room, and as far as I know, I'm not a kleptomaniac. Anyway, there's nothing missing here, because I've looked."

"The salmon fly," returned Mr. Winkley.

"The salmon fly? The one Major Jeans gave me? But I gave that to you before you went to London."

"I know you did," said Mr. Winkley, "but the murderer doesn't know that."

"But it doesn't make sense," persisted Pussy.

"It will do when we know where it fits in," was the reply.

"Then you do think it was Major Jeans," said Gunn, but Mr. Winkley only smiled.

"Suppose you tell us where you fit into all this," he said.

Gunn began by looking daggers at Pussy.

"You ought to know that I wouldn't creep into your room to murder you," he said. "You drive me mad sometimes, God knows, but even if I got to the point of throwing you into the lake, I should have to dive in and drag you out again."

"Well, didn't you do something like that last night!" retorted Pussy.

Gunn would have turned and stamped out of the room at that, if Mr. Winkley had not said, "Go on," in tones which were anything but mild.

"I said I'd strangle her if she played fast and loose with me again," Gunn went on, "and my fingers were itching to do it last night, I can tell you. But I didn't touch her. I had a few whiskies, and then went up to my room. I didn't undress, but walked about the room for ages. Then I drew back the curtains, and saw that it was moonlight, so I went for a walk."

"Leaving the hotel open?"

"I suppose so. Everyone seemed to be in bed, including the Evanses. I unlocked the side door, and locked it again after I came back."

"That was probably when Miss Partridge woke up," remarked Mr. Winkley, and in answer to their surprised looks, he went on: "It's not unusual for telepathic messages to pass between two people who are thinking of each other. You were worrying about her all night, and she had gone to sleep weeping for you."

Pussy stirred uneasily in her chair, and Gunn, seeing her uneasiness, suddenly laughed.

"Well," he continued in lighter tones, "I'd begun to kick myself by that time for behaving like a lout, and knew I'd never sleep till I'd asked Pussy to forgive me, so I went along to her room, and tried the door. It wasn't locked, so –"

Mr. Winkley looked at the girl.

"Did you lock it?" he asked.

"No," she replied. "I left it open in case Piggy wanted to apologize."

"I like that!" exclaimed Gunn. "Why should you always expect me to –"

"Go on," urged Mr. Winkley.

Gunn shrugged his shoulders.

"I slipped into the room and closed the door behind me."

"He's always discreet," remarked Pussy.

"Then I called her very softly and said, 'Please forgive me, I'm awfully sorry', or words to that effect, but she didn't reply, so I thought she must be asleep. I didn't see any sense in waking her, so I just got out gently, and went to bed."

"But, if she heard what you said, as she says she did, she must have been lying on the floor near the window," said Mr. Winkley. "How was it that you didn't see her in the moonlight?"

"The curtains were drawn across the window," replied Gunn. "I couldn't see a thing."

"I see," said Mr. Winkley, as if he didn't see at all.

"By the way," remarked Gunn, "I take it that some lasso technique was in use last night. Where's the instrument of torture?"

"In the same place as the gut off that salmon fly," replied Mr. Winkley. "Miss Partridge says that there was nothing round her neck when she recovered consciousness early this morning, and there was no sign of it in the bedroom. I imagine that the same delayed slip-knot was used again. It would account for the sudden pressure and gradual release. I've an idea that I've seen something of the kind, but at the moment I don't remember where. It's tucked away in a pigeon-hole in my mind, and will pop out one day. I've got that kind of brain."

"This is all very fine," said Pussy suddenly, "but how do you explain the fact that I heard Piggy's voice before I lost consciousness?"

"You didn't," replied Gunn. "You lost consciousness straight away, then you revived a bit when I came into your room, and fainted off again. Isn't that right, Mr. Winkley?"

"I believe it is," he replied. "You see, Miss Partridge, if Mr. Gunn didn't murder Mrs. Mumsby, he wasn't the person who attacked you last night. You can be quite sure of that."

"Is that so?" said Pussy vindictively. "You're quite sure? Then perhaps you'd better ask him, Mr. Winkley, where he was when Mrs. Mumsby died."

Mr. Winkley looked inquiringly at Gunn, and this time he, also, saw murder in his eyes.

"You filthy little rotter!" Gunn exclaimed. "You know that I can't answer that question!"

CHAPTER XXX

Mr. Winkley went away from Pussy's bedroom feeling that he would never elicit the truth about Mrs. Mumsby's murder by indirect questioning. Fitting oddly assorted pieces of facts into one complete whole was his forte; he was unaccustomed to having to find out those facts for himself. And if, he thought, he could not rely on the straightforwardness of the two young people who had agreed to help him, how could he hope to prise the truth from others in the hotel who would almost certainly regard his inquiries with suspicion?

The worst aspect of the affair was that it was having a bad effect on his fishing. From being feted as the most brilliant fisherman in the hotel, who could be relied upon to bring in the best bag whatever the weather, he had become the Jonah of the party. For when his mind should have been devoid of anything but the thought of catching bigger and better fish than anyone else on the lake, it was filled instead with theories about Mrs. Mumsby's murder. When he should have had eyes for nothing except the top-dropper of his cast as he drew it through the water, he saw only the fly which had pierced Mrs. Mumsby's hand. The consequence was that his line never had that taut expectancy which is the essence of successful fishing. He was never quite ready for the first mild swirl of the water which betokens a rising trout, so that he struck too late. Therefore he only hooked and landed the head-and-tail risers which were all too few at this late part of the season, for even fish are human enough to behave in a more sedate fashion when they settle down to rear a family.

He felt his lack of skill all the more since he could offer no excuse to his nightly critics in the hall. He knew only too well that, at this time of the year, a hooked fish should be a dead fish. Only in spring and early summer could you explain that the fish had a soft mouth and "broke away with a toothache – a two-pounder if he was an ounce, my dear fellow". But towards the end of the season, both salmon and trout were tough in more senses than one, and the cock-fish in particular had strong jaws, the lower one developed already into a pronounced hook with which to dig holes in the gravel bed of his favourite spawning ground.

After a few blank days, Mr. Winkley was filled with the kind of exasperation which, before the days of steel shafts, prompted golfers to break their clubs over their knees.

But fishing has truly been named "the gentle art". No fisherman would give way to his temper at the expense of his rod; it is the darling of his heart and he puts its safety ever before his own. Should unhallowed feet walk near the ground where it is resting, he will rush to the spot and hold it upright at attention, until they have passed. Should he have to negotiate a tricky hazard over rock or ditch, he will hand his rod first to the ghillie, and risk a tumble or wetting, alone. When he returns from his day's sport, his rod must be tenderly wiped, unscrewed, and tied away in its divided case. During the winter, he hangs it on a special hook, lest any warp should appear on its svelte surface. And if, on taking it out for the first time at the beginning of a new season, he does not bestow upon it the kiss which the crusader of olden times used to bestow upon his sword, you may be sure that he feels like doing so.

It is easily understandable, therefore, that when an ardent fisherman becomes exasperated with his lack of prowess, there is no course open to him except to admit that he is stale, and to give up fishing for a day or two. This is what Mr. Winkley decided to do.

Dressed in his most reputable tweeds, he sauntered one morning to the door of the hotel to wave off the others with a smile apparently redolent of pity.

But the morning lacked zest.

He had a late breakfast, wrote an unnecessary letter, and set off for a sharp walk along the sea-shore. But after an hour, his resolution weakened, and he found himself retracing his steps towards the hotel. As he drew near, he came upon the bustle of a late departure, and found a little group consisting of Mr. Pindar, Dr. Rippington Roberts, a ghillie who, he was interested to note, was the same John Jones who had been in Mrs. Mumsby's employ, and three dogs, preparing for a day's shooting.

The dogs were by far the most excited members of the expedition. They consisted of a red setter and two liver-and-white spaniels belonging to the doctor, and named respectively, Lock, Stock, and Barrel. The similarity of the first two names did not cause the confusion one might have expected between setting and retrieving, for all three dogs were skilfully controlled by their appropriate whistles.

Mr. Pindar and the doctor were deep in an argument about the merits of different brands of cartridges when Mr. Winkley joined them.

"Hallo!" he greeted them. "Have you gone stale, too?"

Pindar lifted his dark, handsome face and smiled, but to Mr. Winkley's keen eyes, the smile looked forced, and the face worried.

"Not exactly," he replied. "The doctor here had promised me a day's shooting, and as I may have to cut my holiday short, I thought I'd ferret him out today."

The doctor looked up through shaggy grey brows, which stuck out in untidy wisps overhanging his eyes, and gave him the appearance of an old English sheepdog.

"Gone stale, have ye?" he barked, thus completing the illusion. "Well, so've I. Yes. I haven't caught a fish since Mrs. Mumsby died. Seems to have put a curse on the fishing, that woman. I wouldn't mind so much if she'd been anything of a fisherman, but I grudge an actress like her spoiling things."

"It's strange that women have a reputation for being unlucky in connection with water. Lakes, rivers, the sea, there must be dozens of superstitions connected with them." remarked Mr. Pindar.

"If you saw as much of women as I do, you wouldn't think it so strange." growled the doctor. "You'd know they're unlucky."

"Was she an actress?" asked Mr. Winkley suddenly.

"Who? Mrs. Mumsby?" replied the doctor. "I'm sure I don't know. Looked as if she might have been an overgrown lead in a third-rate touring company, or the woman member of one of those old trapeze acts who spends her time wiping her hands and shouting '*Hola!*', while the men do all the work."

Mr. Winkley looked interested.

"What makes you say that?" he asked.

"Their figures run to fat in the same places," was the reply. "As a young man, I used to work in Cardiff, and I saw a good many of 'em."

Mr. Winkley watched their preparations for a few minutes, then said:

"Do you mind if I join you?"

The doctor looked surprised, and the suggestion seemed unwelcome to Mr. Pindar.

"Can't offer you a gun," said the doctor, "but you're welcome to come with us. I suppose you know enough to keep out of the way. I never withhold fire for anyone, and there's no time to yell Tore' with snipe. If you're in doubt, keep close behind the ghillie. And you'll need your fishing boots. We'll be going over boggy ground, and water in Wales has a habit of running uphill. Yes."

Mr. Winkley went into the hotel to order sandwiches and change into more serviceable clothes, and some minutes later, the little party moved up the narrow lane beyond the hotel towards the wilder, open country.

"You'll remember the day Mrs. Mumsby died, by the twins you delivered, I suppose," remarked Mr. Winkley casually. "Do you always go fishing after you've seen twins into the world?"

The doctor plodded steadily on, his gun resting lightly in the crook of his arm, and his right hand fondling the smooth bowl of his pipe which wore a metal protector to keep the sparks from flying about. It seemed at first as if he did not hear the question, but at length he parried it with another. "Why do you come to Aberllyn to fish?"

"For a rest, and because it's lazy and peaceful," replied Mr. Winkley. "London life becomes harassing after a time."

"Not half as harassing as twins," puffed the doctor. "Hey, Lock, come away out of that! They take longer than usual, and if one dies, it's always the one the mother wanted the most, even if they're identical. Funny creatures, women. Yes. You need to go fishing after delivering twins."

"I get you," said Mr. Winkley. "The people who 'never can see what you like about fishing', don't realize how restful it is. By the way, I take it that you didn't mean seriously what you said about Mrs. Mumsby's death putting a curse on things. I mean, you don't really think that there was anything unnatural about it, do you?"

The doctor glared at him.

"Unnatural? In the name of St. David, what are you yapping about, man?" he asked. "How could it be unnatural for a woman suffering from heart disease to die of it, eh? If you've come along to ask silly questions –"

Mr. Winkley murmured a hasty apology, and turned the conversation into less dangerous channels, but Mr. Pindar remained silent, as if the questions had embarrassed him.

It was one of those blameless October days when the sky is of summer clearness, and the air touched with the crispness of winter; a perfect day for seeing the birds, and an impossible day for fishing. Mr. Winkley was soon congratulating himself on the sudden impulse which had brought him to the open river country with the guns, but for which he might have been tempted to flog the lake without result, and have been reduced to trolling a minnow, a method of baiting fish which the enthusiastic fly fisherman despises.

Dr. Rippington Roberts brought down the first bird which Lock had set, and Barrel, only to be distinguished from his half-brother by an appropriately greater girth, retrieved it with satisfied wags of his stumpy fringed tail.

Mr. Pindar missed his first snipe, and maimed the next, and they all searched for fifteen minutes without finding it.

This seemed to upset John Jones, the ghillie, and he cast the dogs, time and time again, through the clumps of wet, reedy grass, until the doctor gave the signal for them to move on.

By lunch-time, four brace of the long-necked, long-legged, speckled birds had fallen to the doctor's gun, and he was particularly pleased because two of the smaller Jack-snipe were included in his bag – a sure indication of his accurate shooting. Mr. Pindar, on the other hand, was having an off-day, if indeed he was any shot at all, which the doctor began to doubt.

The ghillie, again at the doctor's signal, found a comfortable spot for lunch, pulled the neat packets of sandwiches from his bag, and stood hesitantly in front of the three men as they unwrapped the grease-proof papers.

The doctor looked at him with a knowing eye.

"What's wrong with you, man?" he asked.

"It's that bird, Doctor," was the reply. "I think I'll take the dogs along to see if we can find it. It might not die till the morning."

"Don't be a fool," snapped the doctor. "Sit down and get some food into you. We shall be moving off again soon. It isn't often that I see the birds as clearly as I do today, and I'm not wasting any time."

"I think I'll go all the same," replied John, "if you have all you want."

"I've the whisky-flask in my pocket and that's all that I need at the moment," returned the doctor. "You always were a soft-hearted fool." He watched him out of earshot. "Nice fellow, that," he remarked to the others. "He knows the name and nest of every kind of bird in these parts. He won't rest until he finds that snipe. He'll break their necks quite happily when the dogs bring them to hand, but he won't let one die in agony if he can help it."

"Decent of him," said Mr. Pindar. "A clean, quick death isn't a bad way out for any of us. It's the slow, lingering kind that destroys your courage."

The doctor regarded him curiously.

"Oh, he's decent all right," he said, "but it takes up too much time."

"I suppose you engaged him so that he wouldn't feel the loss of Mrs. Mumsby's money so badly," put in Mr. Winkley.

"H'm," said the doctor. "So you think I'm a philanthropist, do you? Most of my patients think the same, but I'm not. I've had John as my ghillie for years, and I never go out with another man if I can help it. I used to have his father, till the old fellow went blind."

"You had a different man the day Mrs. Mumsby died," remarked Mr. Winkley.

"Never have anyone but John," retorted the doctor.

"But," protested Mr. Winkley, "He was with Mrs. Mumsby; we all know that."

The doctor took a drink from his flask.

"Well, there's no harm in telling you now," he said, wiping his mouth with the back of his hand, "though I can't see why it interests you. John was up with the dawn that morning. He knew where I was – the whole village knew, of course – and he was ready to go out with me. We had two clear hours before he had to go to Mrs. Mumsby –"

"But you never said anything about it at the time."

"Why should I? John was doing no harm. He came over to help me at lunch-time, too, while she was asleep, but why should I tell anyone? If Mrs. Mumsby had known that he was ghillying for me, she'd have been peeved. She paid well for his services, and expected full value for her money. But John never would take a penny from me since I pulled him round from a dose of diphtheria, years ago. Well, he's hoping to marry young Pegi Griffiths in a year or two, and no doubt we can get even again a few months after that. Maybe it'll be twins – the air of Aberllyn seems to produce them in pairs."

"So he had an alibi," murmured Mr. Winkley.

"Who? What? Good God, man! Anyone would think the old girl had been murdered!" He peered at Mr. Winkley through the shaggy curtain of his brows, gurgled a drop of the neat whisky down his throat from the silver-topped flask, coughed, and exclaimed, "Huh! So that's it, eh? Well, Mr. Winkley, I don't know what your job is, and whether you have any right to poke your nose into other people's business or not, but I do know that if ever a woman died from natural causes, that woman was my patient, Mrs. Mumsby, and I warn you that the less you say about your suspicions, the better it will be for you."

He menaced his flask in the air, and Mr. Winkley, stammering earnest apologies, rose hurriedly to his feet and said: "Mr. Pindar – he must have gone off somewhere – I didn't see him go. I think I'll have a look for him. He didn't look well – might be feeling sick – or something."

"Huh!" was the doctor's only reply. Nevertheless he seemed to be disturbed by Mr. Winkley's recent words, and, as he was gathering together the few remains of the sandwiches, he stopped several times as if to consider some irritating thought. "Huh!" he exclaimed again. "The meddling fool!"

He got up and rubbed a rheumatic knee.

Huh! Getting old, he thought. *Ought to know better than to go fishing and shooting in all weathers at my time of life. Always makes me stiff and bad-tempered. Been telling myself that for a good fifteen years, but it has no effect. Well, a doctor can't die peacefully in his bed. No. He must die in harness like a good horse. People expect it. Still, I can't expect my patients to obey my orders when I neglect them myself, can I? No. Take Mrs. Mumsby, now. She knew well enough that she'd been playing a dangerous game these last few years. I warned her often enough, but she was a damned obstinate woman. She would have things her own way, and look what it led her to!... I don't like all this talk about unnatural death. Never expected anyone to start thinking in that way. Damned, impertinent fellow, this Winkley! The best thing is to keep him at arm's length. Tell him nothing, that's the way. Let him guess –*

John Jones strode up to him, dangling a dead snipe by its beak, while the dogs panted along behind him less friskily than they had departed.

"Lock found it, sir," he cried, a smile lighting up his dark face and oddly assorted eyes. "He set it like a new bird, and had Barrel deceived, too. But Stock knew it for a wounded bird, and brought it to hand in a flash. It would hardly have lived till the morning."

The doctor fondled the wet silkiness of Lock's chestnut-coloured ears. He was too stiff to stoop and stroke the spaniel, but praised him with words.

"You're a fool," said the doctor again. "You always were, ever since the day I delivered you into this poor old world, head first."

The ghillie grinned.

"You're shooting well today, Doctor," he said. "You'd have bagged twice as many birds if you'd been alone, instead of giving the honour to Mr. Pindar all the morning."

The doctor fingered over the brown-specked bodies of the birds, which would no more drum their wings in acrobatics for the enticement of their mates.

"Maybe we're both fools," he replied. "I should ask a man if he'll pot a few gulls with me, before inviting him to a decent day's shooting."

"You wouldn't be mistaken in Mr. Pindar, though," said John. "He'd be handy with a gun, by the look of him, but this morning he was worried. I thought it was Mr. Winkley, perhaps, for he seemed to move away from him as if he disliked him. I –"

He was interrupted by a shout which seemed to come from the next field, beyond the hedge which had sheltered them. They heard Mr. Winkley's voice raised in anger, and Mr. Pindar's pitched in a fearful key.

"Don't, Winkley! Leave me alone!"

John glanced apprehensively at the doctor, and they both ran towards the hedge. When they had negotiated the low wall into the next field, they saw the two men struggling together at the far end. Before they had moved forward again, the familiar report of a gun echoed in the clear air, followed by a long cry, and when they reached the end of the field, they saw Mr. Pindar lying on the ground, with Mr. Winkley, gun in hand, standing over him.

The doctor groaned as he forced himself to his stiff knees beside the fallen man.

"I congratulate you, Mr. Winkley." he remarked grimly. "It's a good plan to take a doctor with you when you intend to commit a murder!"

CHAPTER XXXI

When Mr. Winkley next saw Mr. Pindar, the latter was lying in bed propped up by a snowy mountain of pillows. A maroon silk dressing-gown, adorned with golden horseshoes, was draped round him, practically hiding the voluminous bandages which covered his shoulders. He smiled a welcome at Mr. Winkley, and was as suddenly serious.

"I don't know what to say," he began. "Of course you realize that you saved my life."

"So I wasn't wrong." Mr. Winkley sounded pleased with himself. "You really did intend to..." He broke off quickly, and glanced at Mrs. Pindar.

She interpreted the glance correctly.

"It's quite all right. I know all about it," she said. "How he could ever have done such a thing... If he had died, I..." Her lower lip trembled, and slow tears gathered in her eyes. "I shall never forget what you've done for us."

Mr. Pindar made a movement forward, winced with pain, and lay back again on the pillows.

"Oh, I say!" exclaimed Mr. Winkley, feeling considerably embarrassed. "I'm sure you ought not to let him talk, Mrs. Pindar. He's got quite an ordeal in front of him when he gets to the hospital for that X-ray. Wouldn't it be better if he rested now?"

"No, that's okay, Winkley," said Mr. Pindar. "The doctor filled me up with brandy, and the pain isn't too bad if I remember not to move about. We both feel that we owe it to you to explain things a bit. We know that you won't mention it outside this room. Isn't that right, darling?"

Mrs. Pindar nodded, seated herself gently on the side of the bed, and took his hand in hers.

There was a pause, then Mr. Pindar said:

"What would you say if I told you that we were not married?"

Mr. Winkley smiled as if the statement afforded him no surprise.

"I'd say it was just about time that you were," he replied.

"I knew you'd take it like that," went on Mr. Pindar. "You'll probably think me the world's worst cad, but –"

"But it's all my fault," put in Mrs. Pindar. "We've been crazy about each other for two years, and he's asked me to marry him in every letter, and whenever he was on leave, but I always refused."

She paused for a moment.

Mr. Winkley, who saw a great deal more below the surface of things than most people imagined, did not ask the obvious question. He looked instead at the golden sheen which the sunlight from the window reflected in the natural waves of her hair, and at her lovely skin and features, and thought that, in all probability, he would never see a more beautiful woman.

"I refused," she repeated, "because I am ten years older than Jack, and I knew it would never do. You don't notice the difference in our ages now, and of course that scar of his makes him look older, but a woman who marries a man younger than herself loses her peace of mind. She is bound to envy younger women as the years go by, and will try to look younger than she really is. I could foresee a hectic round of beauty parlours in another ten years' time, and myself running like a lost soul in search of my youth while I destroyed his. When he is forty, I shall be fifty. When he is fifty, I shall be –"

"– still the most beautiful woman in the world," finished Mr. Pindar.

"Idiot! Mr. Winkley, I was sure that I was right to refuse to marry him, but because we love each other we came away together. I persuaded him that we had the right to do so, and I still feel that there is nothing wrong in it. For a week or two, it was heavenly, but lately, people have grown suspicious of us. I've been asked all kinds of intimate questions, and the deceit of it all has spoiled everything. Jack still wanted to marry me, but I refused again, and we decided to part. You know the rest. As soon as I heard that he'd gone out shooting, instead of fishing, as he'd said, I knew what he meant to do."

"So you're going to marry him after all," said Mr. Winkley benevolently.

She raised her troubled eyes to his.

"What else can I do?" she said. "I should never forgive myself if anything happened to him."

"It won't be so bad, darling," said Mr. Pindar, adoring her with his eyes. "I can always pretend that you're my mother when I meet my school pals!" He drew her hand to his lips and kissed each separate finger. "Shameless hussy!" he teased.

Mrs. Pindar bent over and kissed the puckered scar which ran from his temple to the corner of his mouth, then got up from the bed.

"I must go and see what arrangements Dr. Roberts has made about getting you to the hospital," she said. "You can have a heart-to-heart talk with Mr. Winkley," and she moved, graceful and straight, towards the door, and closed it softly behind her.

Mr. Winkley was not aware of his thoughts until Mr. Pindar put them into words.

"It's like the sunshine going out of the room, isn't it?" he said. "Do you wonder that life doesn't seem worth living for me without her? Look here, I'm terribly sorry to have dragged you into this, but if it hadn't been for you –" He broke off in sudden embarrassment.

"Never mind that," replied Mr. Winkley. "But as I am in, I wonder if you'd mind clearing up one or two points for me. Not if it's too painful to talk about, of course," he went on in his most diffident manner. "You see, I so nearly didn't save you from killing yourself. You left the gun in my hands, and yet you were still able to pull the trigger. I hadn't time to point the muzzle right away from you, and that's how you got shot in the shoulder. I shall worry about it for weeks if you don't explain. I've got that kind of mind, you see."

Mr. Pindar drew his lower lip hard between his white, young teeth. The interview was already beginning to tire him, and his shoulder was throbbing steadily and painfully.

"I was a damned fool!" he exclaimed savagely. "Of course I'll tell you. I owe you that at least. It was an arrangement with a piece of string, and it seemed foolproof to me when I thought of it. You see, I thought it would make the whole affair look more accidental if I didn't touch the trigger with my finger. My finger might have tightened on it when I – when I was dead, and it would have been bad for her." He bit his lip again, and spoke with an effort. "I threaded the string through the trigger with a special slipknot that gives a double action. It pulls suddenly tight, and then springs apart. The idea being that when I pulled it, the string would tighten on the trigger, discharge the gun, and drop off on to the ground. No one would see the string, the gun would fall down with me on top of it, and everyone would think I'd tripped over it, and had forgotten to put the safety catch down."

"A piece of string," said Winkley thoughtfully.

"Well, it was really a piece I cut off my fishing line," explained Mr. Pindar. "It's green, and I thought it wouldn't show up on the grass. I don't know where it is now."

"In my pocket," explained Mr. Winkley, pulling it out. "It's strange that I've been looking for a piece like this. Number two Kingfisher, isn't it? That your rod?"

He indicated a two-piece greenheart rod standing, ready for use, in a corner of the room. He walked towards it, and Mr. Pindar watched with interest as he compared the cut ends of the line.

"Rather a heavy line to use with a light rod like this," he remarked. "What kind of knot is it that you used?"

"I don't know what it's called," replied Mr. Pindar. "I picked it up from young Claude Weston when he did that sleight-of-hand show. You remember the trick with cords that you and I helped him with?"

"I remember the trick," said Mr. Winkley, "but I'm damned if I know how it was done."

Mr. Pindar puckered his brows in pain.

"It isn't easy," he admitted, "but, you see, I'm used to tying all kinds of knots. They're part of my job."

"R.N.?" queried Mr. Winkley.

"Yes. Mrs. Mumsby guessed right, and it was damned queer because I'd never set eyes on her until we came to this hotel. That's why we had to be so careful, and why the idea that anyone might guess we weren't married scared us. Mavis has visions of a long and honoured career for me, and any suspicion of an affair like this would soon put an end to that. The Royal Navy doesn't object to its officers making use of prostitutes, but to take a woman of your own class and not marry her – well, you know the old code. 'The Navy whereon, under the good Providence of God, the wealth, safety and strength of the kingdom chiefly depend' – that kind of thing, you know. They seem to think that the state of matrimony was instituted especially for the benefit of the Senior Service. All we use our swords for, nowadays, is for making archways at weddings –"

"Do you think you could teach me how to tie that knot?" asked Mr. Winkley, who had been too busy with his own thoughts to pay much attention to what Mr. Pindar had been saying.

"I'll try, but it's rather difficult to get it right. It's like the evening ties with a tapered end; if you turn the end up at one particular point, instead of down, you get the whole thing wrong, and have to start again. With this confounded shoulder, I can't do it for you."

Mr. Winkley seated himself in a low chair beside the bed, and took the length of fishing-line in his hand.

"Left under right," gasped the wounded man, now seriously much distressed. "Bring the two ends down. No, I'm sorry, up. Now take the left one over. No, that's not it. I'm frightfully sorry. I'm afraid I can't –"

A light tap sounded on the panel of the door, and Mrs. Pindar walked into the room. She looked straight across at Mr. Pindar, sweating and gasping against the pillows, and held open the door.

Mr. Winkley, perceiving in her eyes a look similar to that which he had seen in the eyes of a sheep collie bitch which resented the attention being paid to her puppy, rose hastily, murmuring apologies, and walked out into the corridor.

CHAPTER XXXII

"Now what have you been up to?"

Pussy Partridge addressed Mr. Winkley in the tone of voice in which, at home, she was wont to reproach her two cats, Djinn and Ginger.

She and Gunn had evidently made up their quarrel in a way known only to themselves, and were waiting, Mr. Winkley noted with some dismay, to waylay him in the hall as he descended from the Pindars' bedroom.

And just when I'm getting along so much better by myself, he reflected.

"Well," continued Pussy, "what's all this we hear about you trying to murder Mr. Pindar?"

"Oh no," said Mr. Winkley, "that was all a mistake, I assure you. There was nothing like that at all. I only –"

"You needn't try that old-fashioned stuff on me, because it won't work," interrupted Pussy. "A bargain's a bargain, and you promised to let us in on all your discoveries, or else! So cough it up, as the ghillie said to Mrs. Pindar when she felt seasick."

Mr. Winkley sighed, and wondered why he had ever considered Pussy's blatant outspokenness an asset. However, he realized that he would have to give some explanation of the shooting sooner or later, and, hoping to point a moral to the two young people, he said, not quite truthfully, that the Pindars had quarrelled rather violently, and that Mr. Pindar, in his distress, had tried to commit suicide.

But the reception accorded to this piece of information was disappointing.

"The silly so-and-so!" exclaimed Pussy. "If you ever did a thing like that, Piggy –"

"Who? Me?" asked Gunn. "Not bloody likely! Quotation. George Bernard Shaw, so it counts as literature. No woman's worth killing one's self for, in my opinion."

"Quite right," agreed Pussy, "and no man either."

Mr. Winkley sighed again.

He quite despaired of understanding these two. When they were on good terms, they agreed with each other about everything; when they quarrelled, they disagreed about the same things. He realized that he took them too seriously, but it was difficult for a bachelor, almost old enough to be their father, to do anything else. He wondered what kind of men and women they would become, and tried, ineffectually, to remember whether he had been quite so gauche, and yet so sophisticated, in his twenties. He decided that one good point in their favour was that they had so far treated his confidence with respect, and he wondered, for the hundredth time, whether they were quite as foolish as they appeared to be. He could not see that there was anything to be gained by making a mystery about the Pindars' affair, so he proceeded to fill in the details, withholding only the fact that they were not married.

"I'm not sure that you're telling the whole truth and nothing but, s'welp-me-bob," remarked Pussy, regarding him with quizzical eyes, "but it seems to clear them of Mrs. Mumsby's murder."

"I don't know so much about that," replied Gunn. "They might have murdered her, realized that we were suspicious, and planned today's performance to put us off the scent. That piece he cut off his fishing-line may have been the very piece he used to try and strangle you. He thought we had tumbled to that knot, and hoped to lull out suspicions by coining dean. He may even have pointed that gun at his shoulder to ensure Mr. Winkley hitting him, just to make it more realistic."

"Rather far-fetched," replied Mr. Winkley. "Besides, why did he kill the monkey?"

"He didn't. Or, if he did, it was a red herring," replied Pussy with her usual high disregard for metaphor.

Mr. Winkley shook his head.

"I don't agree," he said. "There must be some connection between all these events involving Mrs. Mumsby, the salmon fly, the monkey, and your midnight visitor. There were other incidental coincidences as well, but those four things are in the main line of deduction."

"Says which?" gasped Pussy.

Gunn explained patiently.

"He means that we've collected a lot of facts together and that some of them don't mean a thing, but that some of them are connected with the murder, and these are the salmon fly, the monkey, and you."

"Cheribi for da organ, da monkey, an' me," sang Pussy in a highly unmusical voice. "But if he knows that, my darling Pig, he must know who done it."

"I've a pretty good idea," said Mr. Winkley. "When I get some information from the Yard, I shall be sure."

"You think it's Claude, I know you do!" cried Pussy. "Oh, why did he lose a fly, or have a monkey, or tie that knot!"

"Shut up, Pussy," said Gunn. "You know, Mr Winkley," he went on, "I can't help thinking that we've been taking this murder from the wrong end. You know that American criminal lawyer, Perry Mason...?"

"That gas-bag!" exclaimed Mr. Winkley.

"Maybe he is, but he's clever all the same. He says – I wrote it down in my pocket-book – yes, here it is – 'In the long run, the essence of all successful detective work lies in reconstructing the life of the victim. That gives motivation and motivation makes murder.' Has it occurred to you how little we really know about Mrs. Mumsby? No one here ever met her husband when he was alive, and she seems to have no friends or relations."

"It was partly because it had occurred to me that I went up to London." replied Mr. Winkley. "But while I'm waiting for results, it might be a good plan to clear up some of these conflicting side-lines which you both seem to have collected so easily. We've cleared the Pindars, or we may assume that we have for the moment. What about yourselves?"

Pussy and Gunn grinned at each other, but neither of them spoke.

"Perhaps it may simplify things if I tell you what I've found out about you for myself," went on Mr. Winkley. "You have no alibi for the time of the murder. You went up to the small lake with no intention of staying there, and Mr. Gunn caught a decent-sized trout within the first twenty minutes, so your reason could not have been that the fishing was bad, and you felt bored. You came into the hotel before luncheon, but you didn't have a meal in the dining-room, yet no one noticed you going out again. You may be interested to know, Miss Partridge, that your chambermaid went to take your laundry into your bedroom at about one-thirty but found the door locked. Of course, if you could prove that you were inside between then and two o'clock, that would clear you of suspicion, but I'm afraid you can't."

"Did you try the door for yourself?" asked Pussy. "There's a little piece of linoleum which sticks up inside, and you have to force the door to open it."

"I did try the door," agreed Mr. Winkley, "and I found that a piece of linoleum had recently been cut to look as if it jammed the door, in case anyone started to ask awkward questions. But it only acts as a wedge if someone is inside the bedroom to arrange it."

"We give you full marks," said Gunn. "You really deserve to be told all about it, though, as it happens, Pussy and I had already decided that you ought to know. You see –"

"Let me tell him," said Pussy. "It will sound better. He might have old-fashioned ideas about these things. In fact, I'm sure he has."

Mr. Winkley glanced questioningly at her, and waited.

"Have you ever tried to make love in a hotel?" she went on. "No, on looking at you, I'm pretty sure you haven't. Well, it isn't exactly easy – even the Major could tell you that – and when you have a doting parent hanging around you, it's practically impossible. Oh, I know that Piggy and I kiss each other in dark corners, or on the sand-dunes, but all the time, we keep looking over our shoulders in case someone may be looking. We've got the 'Iron Lung', of course, but it's a two-seater, and the clutch gets in the way, and whenever it's drawn up in a lane anywhere around here, that long-nosed policeman always seems to smell it out. Besides, it's too cold to sit out in it in this weather. So we just got desperate and decided that we must do something about it. After all, how am I ever to decide whether to marry Piggy or not if he never makes love to me? Well, we booked the small lake on the day that the Merry Widow passed out, just to encourage Mother to go out herself, and stay out. She goes out walking, with a packet of sandwiches, if she has neither of us to lunch with. We stayed up there just long enough to give her time to get well away from the hotel, then we packed up, paid the ghillie, dropped him at his cottage, and came back here."

"And then?" asked Mr. Winkley.

"Then we went to my room. That's why the maid couldn't get in."

This was one of the few things that Mr. Winkley had not guessed, and he looked suitably shocked.

"Now you can see," Pussy finished blandly, "why Piggy couldn't tell you where he was at that time. He was afraid of giving me a bad reputation if it leaked out. Even he is old-fashioned enough to worry about that."

"Yes, oh yes," jerked out Mr. Winkley. "But of course I wouldn't dream of telling anyone that anything like that occurred."

"Anything like what?" demanded Gunn.

"Like – well, like that," was Mr. Winkley's inadequate reply.

But his face was expressive, and Gunn read it correctly.

"Look here!" He grew belligerent, while Pussy's green eyes mocked at the two of them. "We told you because we thought you were a sensible sort of chap who wouldn't misunderstand us as most of the others would. We thought you knew us better, but I suppose all people of your generation are too full of prejudices to see the truth in certain things. We locked the door, and we made love to each other, but nothing happened for you or anyone else to get het-up about. I can see now that the worst possible thing we could have done was to refuse to tell you about it when you asked. You were bound to think that we had more to hide than we really had. I'd have told you that day, after she'd been attacked, but I couldn't tell you without her consent, and – well, you know what she was like then. She tried to make you suspicious because she was mad with me, but she didn't mean it really. You see, she's such an awful tease."

Mr. Winkley nodded wisely.

"Strip-tease," he amended.

CHAPTER XXXIII

On the following morning, Mr. Winkley received a letter from London. He read it carefully, and looked thoughtful when he set out as usual for The Big Lake.

It was a wild day, and the wind whipped the surface of the lake into white-tipped waves, so that the boat had to crawl crabwise under the lee of the shore to reach the head of a drift, and then was blown down it in less time than it takes to land a well-hooked trout. Had any ghillie been foolhardy enough to venture to row out into the open water in the middle of the lake, his boat might have capsized.

Mr. Winkley shouted a remark to his ghillie, but the wind blew the words around his head and away to the seething water as soon as he had uttered them. It was bitterly cold, and he drew his knitted fishing mittens, which covered the backs of his hands, leaving the palms free for handling the rod, over his cramped, purpling fingers.

Before lunch-time, it began to hail, and the regular swishing sound of the hailstones echoed across the water with the precision of belted machinery. Luncheon itself was a miserable affair, consisting of wet lobster and sodden sandwiches snatched in the boat under the meagre shelter of an over-hanging bush. To catch fish under such conditions as these, held no charm for even such a keen fisherman as Mr. Winkley, and at three o'clock he signalled to the ghillie to return to the head of the lake. Leaving the man to tie the boat securely, and wedge her sides with slats of wood and rocks, he walked sharply towards the hotel, chin tucked inside the turned-up collar of his black waterproof coat, and water dripping on to the end of his nose and chin. The dull thud of his heavy rubber waders mingled at every step with the cheerful rattle of tins in his pockets.

The wind blew directly in his face as he turned the corner of the lake road, and he wondered whether he dared risk appearing at dinner in the presence of ladies, without shaving.

He had a delicate skin, and the very thought of running his safety razor over the tingling surface of his chin and lip made him shudder.

No fisherman, he thought, was likely to see anything poetic in the epithet "wind-kissed" – nor in "sun-kissed", for the matter of that. Unless you indulged in lake-fishing it was impossible to estimate the strength of the sun's rays in the British Isles. In the bad summer a few years ago, he had returned to work after a holiday in Wales, looking as healthily tanned as any cowboy, and to this day his colleagues at the Yard believed that he had been involved in some romantic escapade abroad.

It was all a matter of reflected light from the water. You got the same kind of thing in Switzerland, where the dazzling light from sunlit snow was strong enough to cause snow-blindness. Hats could protect you from the direct rays of the sun, but were useless to shade you from the glittering reflection from the water. Men suffered more than women. Contrary to popular opinion, their skins, being unprotected by expensive foundation creams, were more sensitive than those of the sex, which nowadays likes to be called fairer, but not weaker.

In October last year, alternating days of sunshine and wind had wrought such havoc with their faces, that he and the others had been forced to improvise face-masks with linen handkerchiefs or scarves. Major Jeans, he remembered, had made himself even more impregnable by wearing, under a hat of plaited rushes, a long piece of black material which hung down to his shoulders like the protective veil of a beekeeper. He had two slits for his eyes, and it gave him the appearance of a negro minstrel. Black, with two slits to see through, like the eye-sockets of a skull only they were white...

The thought vibrated a chord in his memory. That was it, of course. Why hadn't he thought of it before?

The wind slung a snatch of conversation to his ears, and looking up he saw Mrs. Partridge and Major Jeans, bending towards each other, and talking earnestly. They were a few yards away, and he quickened his steps, having by this time no qualms about eavesdropping, and caring not at all if he heard no good of himself.

"...But I tell you I am doing the best I can to make her fond of me," Major Jeans was shouting. "She only looks at me as if I were a salmon suffering from furunculosis. It can't be because of my age. Look at the way she encourages that fellow Winkley, inviting him into her bedroom when she had that sore throat, and all that sort of thing. If I walked into her bedroom, she'd probably scream and go all Victorian. No, she just hates the sight of me, and I'm terribly cut up about it. My fault? How can it be? I've been as nice as pie to her, given her chocolates, made flies for her. I tell you it's no good. Why, she even slapped my face when I tried to kiss her! You can laugh if you like, but it was all your idea. I told you it would be best to pop the question right away! She'd have got used to the idea by now, and we should have had no more trouble from her. As it is, people are beginning to talk, damn their eyes, and I'm working against time! If I don't get her on my side within the next few days..."

They turned into the hotel drive, and Mr. Winkley heard no more. He waited for some minutes before following them into the hotel, and when he at last entered the hall, he found it deserted. He divested himself of his wet clothes and gave them to Taffy, the porter, to hang in the furnace-room. Then he ordered tea, and went upstairs to get his red leather bedroom slippers.

When he entered the smoking-room, which, like the bachelors' table, was reserved for men only, he was somewhat surprised to see that another tea-tray had been placed beside his own on the red plush cloth which covered the large centre table. He decided that Sir Courtney Haddox had at last succeeded in evading his sister's close vigilance, and intended to go to ground for a brief respite. He was unprepared for the appearance of Major Jeans.

"Well, well," exclaimed that gentleman, rubbing his hands together as he made his way across the room to the fireplace, "if it isn't the all-conquering Winkley himself! Do any good?"

"Not a bite," Mr. Winkley replied. "It was too rough. I had a few rises, but the wind blew the flies out of their mouths. Did you have any luck?"

The Major shook his head.

"I cracked off half a dozen new flies, and lost a brand- new cast round the gunwale of the boat. What a day!"

He sat down in a large leather arm-chair, and, with a concentrated air, dropped five lumps of sugar into his cup.

"What are you doing in here?" asked Mr. Winkley. "Have you grown tired of the ladies?"

The Major finished pouring out his tea before replying.

"No. They're tired of me," he said. "I'm beginning to think that I've lost my touch. Used to be considered a regular ladies' man at one time, but women want too much these days. I don't wonder they wear trousers."

He began to eat his tea in gloomy silence, but Mr. Winkley reflected that he did not appear unduly upset, as he watched him finish hot scones, sandwiches, bread and butter, jam, biscuits, and half a large currant cake. At length he gave a replete sigh, and accepted one of Mr. Winkley's cigarettes.

A year ago, thought Mr. Winkley, *I should have said that this man was to be trusted. We've met in this same hotel year after year, and I could have sworn that he was a decent, honest fellow. But what do I know about him really? Very little. I don't know for a fact that he's entitled to be called "Major", though I imagine that General Haddox would have found him out by this time if he were masquerading under a false title. There's no doubt about the General, that's certain; he's well-known all over the country. But the Major is up to some little game, innocent or not.*

He took from his pocket the letter which he had received in the morning. From it he abstracted the two flies which he had left at the Police Laboratory a day or two earlier. "Can you tell me anything about these?" he asked, casually. Major Jeans placed the two flies on the padded leather arm of his chair, and fumbled in the pocket of his Donegal tweed jacket for the combined compass and magnifying-glass which he habitually carried with him. He examined each one with the careful intentness of a watch-maker. Then he looked up.

"Thought you'd catch me, eh?" he chuckled. "D'you think I don't know my own tying?"

"You're sure that they're your own flies?"

The Major grunted.

"Huh! I ought to be sure. I've been tying flies since I was a boy, and that's more than forty years ago. Why, what's wrong with 'em? Clues for murder or something, eh?"

"Not exactly," replied Mr. Winkley, thinking hard. "The one with the new hook is the one you made for Miss Partridge; the other one killed Mrs. Mumsby."

Major Jeans jumped as if he had been shot, and banged the open palm of his hand on the arm of the chair. When he lifted it again, one of the flies was sticking up from the flesh of his hand.

"Now look what you've done!" he exclaimed. "Do you mind getting it out for me? These barbs are the very devil when they get under the skin."

Mr. Winkley manoeuvred the hook out with experienced ease, and dabbed the wound with the iodine pencil which most fishermen find it necessary to carry in their pockets for this purpose.

If Major Jeans had wanted to prove his innocence of Mrs. Mumsby's death, he could not have devised a more effective method. Mr. Winkley had been watching his face closely, and could have sworn that no flicker of fear had shown in his eyes when the barbed hook struck his flesh.

"I believe that you've some idea that she didn't die naturally," said the Major. "The doctor won't be too pleased with that, I fancy, and, mind you, he's by no means the frowsty old fogey that he pretends to be. In my opinion, he's good enough for Harley Street, only he's too fond of fishing and shooting to settle in a town." He stared at Mr. Winkley for a few seconds, and then began to laugh until he shook in the chair. "Ho-ho-ho!" he roared. "You don't think that I bumped the old sheep off with a fly-hook, and then left it in her hand so that you could identify me, do you? Upon my soul, that's rich! It's such a lady-like way of murdering her that I shouldn't wonder if you'd expected me to wear white kid gloves while I was doing it, like old Dicky Wagner used to do when he conducted Mendelssohn. I admit that I hated the sight of the woman. She made my life in the hotel a positive misery with her ogling, and her 'dear Major' this, and 'dear Major' that. I might have hit her a conk on the head with a priest, but a fish-hook...! Good God, Winkley! What will you think of next? That's the worst of being at Scotland Yard; you're always looking for a mystery, like an eel looking for a salmon pea." He suddenly held out his arms, hands clenched. "Well, here I am. Where are the handcuffs?"

"There's no need to take it like that," began Mr. Winkley.

"I think I'm taking it damned well," returned the Major. "It isn't every man who gets accused of –"

It was now Mr. Winkley's turn to interrupt.

"No one's accusing you of anything, Major," he said. "I just want to ask you a few questions to help me to clear up this matter, and I want you to promise not to let this go any further."

Major Jeans grinned.

"All right. Carry on, Sergeant."

"Let's go back to the day of Mrs. Mumsby's death. Did you notice anyone behaving strangely during the time when we were all supposed to be having lunch?"

"I didn't see anyone at all until her ghillie came running along to say she was dead."

"Not even Mrs. Partridge?"

The Major glared at him.

"So you know that, do you?" he snapped. "Well, what of it? Why shouldn't I invite her to meet me for lunch? I had something private to discuss with her. There's nothing wrong in that, I suppose?"

"No," replied Mr. Winkley. "But why did she run away when the others went to look at Mrs. Mumsby?"

"Run away? Good God! What nonsense! She walked away. As a matter of fact, I walked a short distance down the road with her, and it was when I returned that I heard all the commotion about the Merry Widow. We didn't want the whole hotel to gossip about us. We were discussing a – business matter, and wanted to keep it to ourselves. How the hell did you come to hear of it?"

Mr. Winkley smiled.

"You've forgotten that Miss Haddox was also lunching there."

"She would see her," exclaimed the Major in disgust. "She's well-named Fish-eyes; she can see all round her like the trout. Now, I warn you, Winkley, don't let any breath of suspicion fall on Mrs. Partridge, or I shall certainly become a murderer. She's one of those dainty, frail little women who have to be protected from such things." He paused for a moment. "At least, I used to think she was," he added rather ruefully.

"There can't be any suspicion attached to either of you, if you were together as you say," Mr. Winkley pointed out. "You give each other an alibi, of course."

"Calloo, callay," chortled the Major with a sudden return of his normal manner. "Oh, call me early, mother dear, for I'm to be Queen of the Mayfly!" He got up from his chair, and pirouetted round the room, holding out the sides of his loose jacket in an imaginary ballet skirt. "And on every box, the picture of a dancing lady!" he sang out in the showman's stentorian voice.

Mr. Winkley looked annoyed.

"Look here, Jeans," he said stiffly, "this is a serious matter, and I want your help. Did Mrs. Mumsby ever fish for salmon?"

The Major became more serious, and strolled back towards the fireplace.

"Never. She hadn't either the skill or the patience. It requires a different technique altogether. Any fool can catch an occasional sea-trout, and there are brownies which hook themselves, and are highly prized by the novice. But catching salmon is a different kettle of fish altogether. Mrs. Mumsby would never have had the patience to cast for hours with a two-handed rod, and she would not have held on to a twelve-pound salmon. She'd have cut the line, and gone home after ten minutes of it. Why, she had little enough patience for trout. Most of the time, she lay in the bottom of the boat, while the ghillie fished. The night you arrived, she'd caught more trout to her own rod than she'd ever caught in her life."

"And yet on that night of all others, she went straight upstairs without looking at the fish in the hall. Queer. But you see, Major, it was strange that she should be found with a salmon fly sticking in her hand, if she never fished for salmon. Did you ever give away any flies like that?"

"Lord bless you, yes!" replied the Major. "It was a good killer, and I suppose I gave one to anyone in the hotel who ever fished for salmon. Big-hearted What's-his-name, that's me!"

"I suppose you can recognize that both of those are your own flies by some peculiarity in the tying – the winding of the hackle, or the waxing of the thread," went on Mr. Winkley.

A knowing look spread gleefully over the Major's sunburnt face.

"It's easier than that," he said. "I can tell you a bit more about it, too. Both those flies were made within the last three weeks. You see, when I first invented that pattern – I called it the 'Avenging Murderer', by the way – I used fur off a rabbit's face for the body. But, as it happens, I didn't bring any of that particular fur with me, so I had to find a substitute." He began to chuckle. "Well, I just grabbed a handful off the face of that monkey of young Weston's. You should have heard the little devil swear!"

CHAPTER XXXIV

The wind blew in a steady gale all through the night, and had not abated by the following morning. The ghillies could not attempt to take their boats out, and gathered in disconsolate groups in the yard of The Fisherman's Rest, hating the prospect of an idle day.

Because there seemed so little hope of going out on the lake, Mr. Winkley found that this day, above all others, was the one on which he most desired to kill a fish. At quarter- hour intervals, he shared with the other fishing enthusiasts the task of going outside the hotel to gaze at the scudding sky, as if to give the lie to the gilded weather-vane, shaped like a salmon, which swung in gusty circles above the coruscated cockscomb of the roof.

Whenever the hall door was opened, the wind swirled round the hall, to the great discomfort of the visitors seated there, and caused Miss Haddox to cling to her elaborate coiffure as if she had reason to suppose that it might be swept off. Nevertheless she remained in the hall long after the others had sought less draughty quarters. Her brother was safely ensconced in the smoking-room, and from where she was sitting she could watch the door, and waylay him when he came out.

Her concentration so impressed itself upon Mr. Winkley that he forgot to watch the weather, and wandered into the smoking-room himself. Here he found Sir Courtney Haddox sitting alone, and nodding a drooping head over a day-old copy of *The Times*. He did not waken as the door opened, and Mr. Winkley thought that he had never seen a man more restless in his sleep.

He tiptoed softly across the thick Turkey carpet towards the window which looked out on to the main road. He could see the cross-roads to the right, and Thomas Lloyd standing on his little mat, with the self-conscious pomposity of a Noah's Ark figure. He heard, rather than saw, the approach of a powerful sports car humming along the main road, and at the same time caught sight of an open two-seater, which might well have been an entrant for the Old Crocks' Race, approaching more diffidently along the side road. He recognized the driver as Dr. Rippington Roberts, and wondered why old family practitioners should remain so conservative in their choice of cars, as if to register a permanent protest against the passing of the old horse-and-gig days.

It was evident that the sports car had both the right of way and the necessary speed to pass the corner before the doctor was ready to cross. Lloyd looked up, but did not make any signal, and the driver took this as an indication of a clear road, and stamped on the accelerator. Neither he nor Mr. Winkley was prepared for the constable's outflung hand when the car's front wheels were over the crossing. The driver braked suddenly. There was a squealing of tyres as the big car skidded, missed Lloyd by inches, made a lurching turn, and crashed across the side road into the doctor's car. With a sudden roar, a sheet of flame shot upwards.

"Good God!" shouted Winkley. "They'll be burned to death! That policeman's a bloody butcher!"

There came a queer, half-strangled noise from the room behind him, and a thin, high-pitched, unearthly scream that turned his flesh cold. He swung round and saw the General tottering on his feet, with eyes dilated, and trembling hands clutching at his throat. Before Mr. Winkley could move forward, he had fallen in a convulsed heap on to the floor.

The door burst open, and Miss Haddox rushed in. She shot one glance full of hatred at Mr. Winkley, then ran to her brother. She squatted beside him, lifted his head on to her lap, took a thin wedge of ivory from his waistcoat pocket, and, with the swiftness of long practice, slipped it between his teeth. She chafed his head and hands until the twitchings of his body ceased, then looked up.

"Brandy," she said, "and keep everyone out."

Mr. Winkley, reflecting that she looked more competent than he had ever seen her before, obeyed the command in her voice, and ran outside. The hall was empty, and he guessed that the accident had drawn everyone out of the hotel, a surmise he confirmed when he found the bar also deserted, and had to help himself to a bottle of brandy. He returned to the smoking-room, poured some of the spirit into a glass, and handed it to Miss Haddox. She took it without a word, and, from time to time, poured little drops down her brother's throat, until his breathing grew calmer. At last she seemed satisfied, and signed to Mr. Winkley to help her to lift the General into a chair, placing a smaller chair for his feet.

"He'll sleep now," she said.

"Won't you take a little brandy?" suggested Mr. Winkley. "It must have upset you, seeing him like that."

"No, thank you, Mr. Winkley," she replied. "I'm not in the least upset. I'm far too much accustomed to these turns, unfortunately. But what happened? It's usually some shock."

Mr. Winkley explained.

"Yes, I see. It would be the fire, of course, and you shouting about someone being burned. It's just a relic of the last War To End War," she said bitterly, and her voice sounded even harsher than usual. "Even Regular Army men didn't become generals for nothing, you know. I've been expecting this for some days."

"Ever since Mrs. Mumsby died, in fact," remarked Mr. Winkley.

Miss Haddox looked startled.

"Yes. How did you know?" she asked. "She never was much to look at – of course she was no lady – but she looked particularly revolting when she was dead. I thought that

Courtney might have one of these attacks if he saw her looking like that."

"So that's why you pretended to have hysterics, and why you stopped as soon as the doctor arrived," remarked Mr. Winkley.

She nodded.

"It was the only thing I could think of to take his attention off her," she said. "I know I did them badly, because I'm not by nature a very hysterical woman, as you may have noticed, and it's a good thing that I'm not, or I don't know what would have happened to Courtney by now. I know you all think me a fool, and despise me for running after him all day long, but I hardly dare let him out of my sight. At any time of day he's likely to have a sudden shock like this, and he expects me to be with him when he comes round from one of his attacks. The doctor said it might be dangerous if he found himself among strangers, and he's been so much worse lately that I didn't like to let him come away without me. You don't suppose I enjoy giving up my own holiday to stay in this bleak hotel, do you? The only time I get to myself is when he's out fishing. It soothes him, and he doesn't seem to mind killing the fish, although I'm sure I don't understand how anyone can touch the horrid slimy creatures."

"I thought that perhaps you'd come here this year on account of Mrs. Mumsby," said Mr. Winkley.

"What do you mean?" she asked sharply.

"I mean that you may have heard that she was setting her cap at him," he replied calmly. "You wouldn't have liked him to marry her, I suppose."

"Marry her!" She glared at him vindictively. "How could he be allowed to marry anyone? What woman would ever have the patience to look after him as I have done? Marry her! What nonsense!"

"Exactly," replied Mr. Winkley. "But what could you do to prevent it?"

Her eyes blazed at him.

"Do? I should have killed her!" she cried, and Mr. Winkley believed her.

CHAPTER XXXV

Mr. Winkley went in search of Mrs. Evans.

The office was locked, but he found her, as he had expected, outside the hotel looking at the damaged cars. The flames had been extinguished, and Thomas Lloyd was making futile measurements with a foot rule, and entering them into his notebook. Dr. Rippington Roberts was talking to the driver of the sports car, who had not yet recovered from his pale fury, and Mr. Winkley walked over to them.

"Well, Winkley, you're not the only murderer in the village," was the doctor's greeting. "I'm trying to explain to this gentleman that his only excuse is to plead guilty, and hope to get off with a fine. Lloyd will explain to the Court that he was holding him up because he knew that I was trying to get to an urgent case. He will swear that the man was driving to the danger of the public, and that although he saw the signal, he was unable to stop, and nearly killed the poor doctor. What's more, he'll have plenty of witnesses to prove it."

"But it isn't true," protested Winkley. "You know that it was Thomas Lloyd who caused the accident. You'll have to tell the truth."

"I shall," laughed the doctor, "but no one will believe me. They will say that I'm too kind-hearted to get the man into trouble. There'll be a headline in the local paper, 'Doctor pleads for his attacker'. Lloyd has the gift of the gab; besides, he'll give his evidence in Welsh, and it doesn't translate well. This gentleman is one of the hated Sassenachs, and therefore a rich goose to be plucked. He doesn't stand an earthly chance of winning his case. It will be a heavy fine, man, and I shouldn't be surprised if they promote Lloyd."

Mr. Winkley did not attempt to follow these curious workings of the Welsh mind.

"I hope you're not hurt," he said. "You had a narrow escape."

"Oh no. I slipped out of the car before it was hit. I've seen death too often to want to experience it before my time."

"I must say you sound cheerful enough," remarked Mr. Winkley.

"Cheerful? Of course I'm cheerful, man," replied the doctor, slapping him on the back. "I shall get a new car out of the insurance company at last. I've been hoping to get into an accident for years."

He went off, swinging his worn, leather bag, and chuckling to himself.

Mr. Winkley stared after him.

It was very odd, he thought. If ever an accident had been deliberately arranged, surely this one had. It was difficult to believe that any sane man would do anything so criminally careless merely to hasten his promotion in the force. And surely it was strange that two people who had been so conspicuously close at hand when Mrs. Mumsby had met with her death, should now be involved in an accident, which, but for extraordinarily good luck, must have resulted in another death. Yes, certainly he had been lax in overlooking these two as potential murderers...

He made his way to the office, where Mrs. Evans was making arrangements for the unfortunate driver to continue his journey in the hotel car. He waited until the man had gone out and then told her what had occurred in her absence.

"Why, thank you, Mr. Winkley," she said. "The girl had no business to leave the bar, but you know what it is in a small village like this – they all feel that they must join in any bit of excitement that crops up. I'm as bad myself, indeed. So the General had one of his turns, did he, the poor man? I can't say that I'm surprised. I've been expecting something of the kind ever since poor Mrs. Mumsby died."

Mr. Winkley stared at her in surprise.

"You don't mean to suggest that he had anything to do with her death?" he asked.

Mrs. Evans looked mildly shocked.

"Oh dear me, no!" she said. "And if you're thinking of that old piece of scandal about them, I'm sure there was nothing in it. I don't deny that he was seen coming out of her bedroom that night, but that was only because he knew there was a fire there. Of course, we all knew what she was like, poor thing, and the idea of having a man in her bed-room tickled her to death, though Major Jeans always said she'd die of shock if any man made love to her. But that was just his idea of a joke, and I'm sure that the General is too much of a gentleman to behave like that to any woman."

Mr. Winkley looked puzzled.

"Do you mean to say that General Haddox used to go into Mrs. Mumsby's bedroom at night to warm himself in front of the fire? I'm not much of a scandalmonger, but that sounds fishy even to me."

Mrs. Evans bit her lip.

"Oh dear!" she exclaimed. "Didn't you know? I never ought to have mentioned it, but I thought that you knew all about the General and his little ways as you'd been helping Miss Haddox today."

"It will seem much worse if you don't explain now," Mr. Winkley pointed out.

"I'm afraid it will. Well, I can't see that there's much harm in explaining. After all, a good many visitors know about it already, and you're one of our regulars. It was the war, you know. He was nearly burned to death in a dugout, but his batman managed to drag him clear before the whole thing went up in flames. Three other officers were killed, and he can't forget it. They talk about shell-shock lasting a lifetime, so I suppose you could call this fire-shock. When anything upsets him, he gets this fear that he will be burned alive. He can't sleep at night until he knows that all the fires in the place have been let out. He waits till everyone is in bed, and then goes round the hotel, looking at all the grates. He carries some chemical stuff with him that's supposed to douse the flames. Then he goes to bed, and sleeps quite soundly."

"Has he always been like that?"

"Ever since I've known him, and he's been coming here every year since the Armistice. He caught a chill once when he was out fishing, and the doctor ordered him to stay in bed, and told me to put a fire in his room. You never saw anything like the job we had to keep him in bed. He kept getting up to see whether the fire was all right, and in the end we had to let it out."

"I must say I can't see why he should be so much upset by Mrs. Mumsby's death," said Mr. Winkley.

Mrs. Evans studied him through serious, light-blue eyes.

"Why, Mr. Winkley! To hear you talk, anyone would think you had no feelings," she said. "The General has met Mrs. Mumsby every year for the last five years. They were great friends, and it's only natural that he should feel upset. You must miss her yourself. Now, own up."

"I'd certainly prefer her to be alive," replied Mr. Winkley, somewhat untruthfully, for any regret he may have felt originally was by now entirely submerged in the excitement of his self-imposed chase after her murderer. "You make us feel so much at home here that when one of the family goes, we feel a personal kind of loss. Look how badly young Mr. Weston took her death."

"That seems to me much stranger than the General's way of taking it," said Mrs. Evans. "You see, Mr. Claude had never set eyes on her before."

"Are you sure of that?" asked Mr. Winkley. "I had an idea that they knew each other well."

"No, they didn't, though I'm sure I don't wonder at you thinking that, for she fairly doted on that boy, and all within a few weeks. I used to tell her that she couldn't have made more fuss of him if he'd been her own son, but she only laughed at me, poor dear. You know that hearty way she had of laughing."

Mr. Winkley had thought it more of a bellow than a laugh, and shuddered even now when he caught an imagined echo of it.

"Weren't you annoyed to find that she hadn't kept her promise to remember you in her will?" he asked. "You know, I suppose, that she left her money to charity, and it was a considerable amount."

Mrs. Evans, luckily, did not ask whence he had obtained his information.

"I never knew what she was worth," she replied, "but I know that Mr. Mumsby was a very rich man. She used to tell me about her house. Twelve servants she kept, and she had satin bedspreads and a different coloured telephone in every bedroom. It must have been a big change to come to live here so quietly, but she liked it. No, I never thought any the worse of her for forgetting me. She left it too late, but she always meant to leave me some money. She had a kind heart."

There was a pause.

"I forgot to give you the brandy," remarked Mr. Winkley, lifting the bottle on to the counter. "By the way," he added inconsequently, "what was Mr. Evans doing on the morning that Mrs. Mumsby died?"

Mrs. Evans flushed crimson, and a sudden fierce light blazed in her eyes.

"That's no business of yours, Mr. Winkley," she said, and, swinging the bottle off the counter, she turned and went into her sitting-room, banging the door behind her.

But Mr. Winkley smiled. He knew very well what Mr. Evans had been doing.

He sauntered out of the office just as the front door opened. The wind catapulted into the hall a short stocky figure, barely recognizable in black fishing hat, waterproof, and boots.

"Good lord, man!" exclaimed Mr. Winkley. "Do you mean to say that you've been out fishing again in this gale? You must be mad."

The figure, holding one hand beneath the bulky folds of his coat, strode mysteriously into the centre of the hall. Then, with much rolling of the eyes, and twisting of the mouth, he suddenly produced from under the coat, the long, emaciated body of an old bull-headed, black-scaled salmon.

"Meet Cuthbert!" said the Major.

CHAPTER XXXVI

Just before luncheon that day, Mr. Winkley received a second letter from London. It did not bring to his face any visible signs of the thoughts which it induced in him. The smile of understanding which the information might have brought to the thin lips of Sherlock Holmes, or the gleam which it might have induced in the eyes of Sexton Blake, were not apparent. Mr. Winkley merely shuffled his feet in his old slippers, and felt uncomfortable. He pondered upon it with an air of indecision, untouched by that aura of satisfied alertness which should surround the detective at the successful solution of his case. He pondered upon it as he walked slowly to the dining-room for lunch. He pondered upon it during the meal, so that all Major Jeans' wit evoked no response from him, and he was voted a dull dog by the bachelors' table. He pondered upon it in the hall after the meal, and scarcely noticed the presence of Gunn, who sat with his long legs stretched out towards the fire, with Pussy balanced on his knees.

"Hullo! What's biting you?" asked Pussy.

Mr. Winkley hesitated for a moment, then said slowly:

"I've been following up the life of Mrs. Mumsby, as you suggested, and I don't quite know how best to deal with the results. You see, I still have to guess at the motive."

"Well," replied Gunn, "three heads might be better than one, even if one of them is Pussy's poor substitute. Perhaps we can help."

"I'm afraid you wouldn't want to, if you knew as much about it as I do."

"Oh, rot!" exclaimed Pussy. "We've helped with all the dirty work. I want to be in at the death."

"Very well," was the reply. "Let's see what you make of this." He spread the letter and began to read:

"George Mumsby, theatrical promoter. Owned a chain of provincial variety theatres which he sold to Oleander Cinema Syndicate for a fabulous sum, and retired on proceeds. Died of diabetes in 1933. All money and property left to the dead woman known as Ruby Mumsby. Baptismal name, Gladys May, daughter of a coster named Charles Clew –"

He paused, and looked up.

"It's spelt C-l-e-w," he remarked.

"Gladys Clew," murmured Gunn. "Perhaps there's a clue in the name."

"There is," returned Mr. Winkley, "if you can find it. It's quite simple."

"Clew," repeated Pussy. "I can't see –"

She stopped abruptly, as Claude made one of his lightning descents of the stairs, and almost landed on top of them.

"I'm in awful trouble," he said, and his eyes were moist. "You must tell me what to do. It's Dad. I always knew he had a weak heart. He had to give up salmon fishing because it was too strenuous, but I never knew it had got to this stage. Look!"

He thrust a folded piece of parchment towards them and Mr. Winkley caught sight of the familiar words "Last Will and Testament", before Claude snatched it away.

"It's his will," he explained. "It says, 'To my only son, Claude Lionel Everard...' He must just have made it; it isn't signed yet. He's left me everything. He's always done everything for me all my life, and now he's going to die. I can't bear it, I tell you. It isn't fair!"

"What isn't fair, Claude?" asked Mr. Weston's quiet voice from behind them.

Claude swung round on his heel and reddened to the roots of his faun-like hair.

"It's – I found this," he said, holding out the will. "You didn't tell me anything about it. You left it for me to find out. It isn't fair. It's cruel."

Mr. Weston could not control his cold fury. All that was warm and kind in him seemed to freeze in front of their eyes.

"Do you usually entertain your friends with your father's private affairs?" he asked bitingly. "That is my property. You took it from my room."

Tears trembled on Claude's red-gold lashes.

"I'm sorry, Dad. I ought not to have touched it, but I didn't know at first that it was yours. I kicked up the corner of the carpet in your room and found it underneath, and I was going to give it to Mrs. Evans. It wasn't till I was coming downstairs that I opened it, and saw my name inside. Then I had to say something at once – it was the shock of it, Dad! People only make their wills when they know they're going to die. It can't be true. I've no one but you in all the world. We'll do everything. We'll go to doctors, specialists, abroad. I'll earn the money for you. I know I can. I –"

"Control yourself, Claude," said Mr. Weston sharply. "You're as bad as a man who thinks it's a sign of death to consult a specialist. Anyone who waits until he is at the point of death before he makes his will is a fool and a coward. Fortunes have been lost before now, because people left it too late before making a will. This is merely a wise precaution. You're so impulsive." He stroked the boy's head caressingly. "Well, now you've found it, it might as well be finished. We've plenty of witnesses here," he continued in his normal tone of voice. He took out his fountain-pen and unscrewed the cap. Using his left hand rather awkwardly, he wrote in his name, "William Weston" and signed it at the end. Then he handed the pen to

Mr. Winkley. "Mr. Winkley? Thank you. And you, Mr. Gunn? There, that's done, and don't let me hear any more nonsense about this from you, Claude. Doctors, indeed! What do I want with doctors?"

Mr. Winkley looked up at him.

"By the way, talking about wills," he said. "Did you hear that Mrs. Mumsby left all her money to the Actors' Benevolent Fund?"

Mr. Weston looked politely interested.

"Really?" he said. "A very worthy institution."

CHAPTER XXXVII

Claude thrust his hands deep into the pockets of his navy blue corduroy trousers, and kicked at the tiled kerb surrounding the hearth. Pussy and Gunn had gone to play billiards, and his father had gone upstairs, so that he and Mr. Winkley were alone in the hall.

"I wish I wasn't so hasty," he said, frowning. "I'm always making myself look a fool in front of people because I can't control my feelings. One of these days, I shall fly at someone, and kill them, and then wish I hadn't when it's too late. Just look at the times I've made an exhibition of myself in this very hall! Over Mother Mumsby, and the monkey, and this will. It's absurd, but I can't help it. It's the way I'm made, I suppose."

"You didn't lose your temper with the monkey, and kill it, I suppose," remarked Mr. Winkley.

"What an idea! Of course not!" exclaimed the boy indignantly.

"Somebody did," was the reply. "You said so yourself. You know I can't help thinking that there's some connection between the monkey's death and Mrs. Mumsby's."

Claude clenched his fists.

"You – you mean that my m–monkey killed her?" he stammered. "That's haunted me for days. It would mean that I was guilty of m–murder."

"It wouldn't mean anything of the kind," resumed Mr. Winkley; "and the monkey certainly didn't kill her. No, I mean that the monkey was killed because it had some connection with Mrs. Mumsby."

"But I don't understand." Claude looked completely bewildered. "How could –"

"Let's try and work it out," said Mr. Winkley. "You'd like to know who killed your pet, wouldn't you? Well then, let's go back to the last time you saw Mrs. Mumsby alive, and see if you can tell me anything about her m– er death."

Claude's eyes dilated with fear.

"Murder!" he whispered. "That's what you were going to say, isn't it? You think she was murdered. Oh, my God! Mother Mumsby!"

He passed one slender hand over his forehead, and pressed it against his eyes. Then he looked up tragically at Mr. Winkley.

"That's what you mean, isn't it?" he repeated in a voice which would have done credit to Henry Irving's Hamlet.

Mr. Winkley nodded.

"But how? When? And who would wish to kill her? She was good, kind-hearted, generous. She didn't deserve to die."

"You'd met her before?" asked Mr. Winkley.

"No. No, I hadn't, but I always felt that I'd known her all my life, or in a previous existence, perhaps. You may laugh at that, but all the time something pulled me towards her. Perhaps you didn't think she was attractive, but I never saw her as she was; I saw her as she used to be years ago – slim, fair and vivacious. I never asked if she did look like that. I never even saw a photograph of her. I just knew – like that! We never spoke of it, but she knew how I felt. It was like seeing someone for the first time in a dream, and then meeting them." He broke off and looked confused. "Oh, you wouldn't understand," he concluded.

"I probably understand a great deal better than you do," replied Mr. Winkley. "I suppose you'd like to have her murderer punished?"

"I'd give anything in the world to help." the boy said passionately.

Mr. Winkley crossed one baggy knee of his plus fours over the other.

"If you'd answer a few questions, it might help," he said. "I understand that you landed at the beach that day, after Major Jeans. When you drifted past Mrs. Mumsby, she was alive?"

"Oh yes," replied Claude. "She waved to us."

"That was somewhere about one o'clock, I take it. Then you had lunch. How long did that take?"

"We were slow about it, I remember. It might have taken half an hour. I couldn't be sure."

"Say one-thirty, then. You had a nap then, you said. How long were you asleep?"

Claude puckered his forehead in an effort to concentrate.

"I don't believe I did go to sleep," he said at length.

"But Mr. Gunn distinctly said –"

"I know," replied Claude quickly, "but you know how it is. You can nod off for a minute, and kid yourself that you've slept for an hour. It can't be important, anyway."

"It might be very important," said Mr. Winkley. "Perhaps you'll let me be the judge of that. You were very near to Mrs. Mumsby when she died, and she may have cried out. It may have been that cry which awakened you. Did you look at your watch when you woke up?"

"No," said Claude. "I went by the length of time that anyone can practise casting on land. What would you say was the limit, Mr. Winkley?"

"On dry land?" Mr. Winkley smiled. "Not long, I'll admit. I used to practise on the lawn when I was a boy, but ten minutes was my limit, until I had the idea of using a bucket of water to make it more realistic. You hear a lot about expert fishermen being able to cast a fly on to a threepenny bit, and so they can. But I bet they don't practise with one unless it's under water somewhere. If you knew there were no fish in a lake, you wouldn't enjoy fishing there. But if there were still no fish and you didn't know it, you could get your day's sport just the same."

"You'll admit, then, that I was only asleep for ten minutes," said Claude. "I dropped off with the combined effect of the sun and the lobster. Dad was practising his casting, with no cast on his line, of course. When I woke up, he was still doing it."

"And you didn't look at your watch?"

"No, I didn't." Claude sounded like a rude child.

"And you suddenly decided to go off for a walk?"

"Yes."

"But until that time you were with your father?"

"Yes." Claude was still sulky.

"You weren't away from his observation for even a few minutes? Not long enough, shall we say, to slip over the wall into the next field and back?"

"No, I was not," retorted Claude. "Look here, what are you getting at?"

"I'll tell you," replied Mr. Winkley, placing his forefingers together and waggling them. "If Mrs. Mumsby did not die a natural death, there's a bigger case against you than against anyone else. Those flies didn't get into her hand accidentally; someone pulled them in. They used a knot which you demonstrated in front of all the visitors in this hotel. The same knot was used in an attempt to strangle Miss Partridge, because she was getting near the truth, and a little knowledge, as we all know, is a dangerous thing. The monkey was killed because it carried a clue to the murderer on its body. The fact that it was near Mrs. Mumsby when she died, shows, too, that someone connected with it had been there just before. Now, you admit that you had the monkey with you all the time. Can you deny that it was you who had just left Mrs. Mumsby's body? You've admitted that one day you'd fly at someone and

206 | BLEEDING HOOKS

murder them, and then feel sorry for it. Isn't that just what happened? You've been very clever with all your exhibitions of grief, but you haven't been quite clever enough. I suggest that you slipped away from your father while his attention was fixed on his casting, killed Mrs. Mumsby, and walked on to the rocks where you say you were fishing."

"No, no," cried the boy. "I'll admit that I told Pussy and Gunn that I killed her, but I really meant that the monkey might have killed her by jumping on to her neck, and waking her with the shock. And, as he belonged to me, I felt that I was responsible. But if what you say is true, it couldn't have been that at all. I never meant that I – murdered her."

"Oh?"

Mr. Winkley's smile was full of disbelief.

"I'll admit, too," went on Claude, "that I found her before the ghillie did. I went away to be sick because it upset me so – I'd been eating lobster, and it had made me squeamish. I didn't say that I'd found her, at the time, because I was a bit scared. But she was dead when I found her. I told Pussy all about this ages ago."

"Oh?" said Mr. Winkley again. "It's the first I've heard of it. I suggest that you did kill her. In your agitation, you forgot all about the monkey, and left it behind. When you realized that, you went back and found that the ghillie had arrived a few seconds before. I suggest that lobster for lunch had nothing to do with your being sick. It was the sight of your victim in her death agony. You didn't intend to kill her, I believe that. You did it on one of your devilish impulses, and by the time that you saw her again, you were sorry for what you'd done."

"Anything else?" sneered Claude.

"The fly was one which you knew could be traced back to Major Jeans," continued Mr. Winkley, remorselessly. "It was easy enough for you to get hold of the poison. You almost boasted of the fact when you used the ingredients under our very noses in one of your conjuring tricks, the night before you killed her. All murderers are exhibitionists."

Claude, trembling with frightened anger, stood for a moment, glaring at Mr. Winkley with a look of mingled hatred and horror in his eyes. Then he turned abruptly, and half-ran, half-stumbled, up the stairs.

CHAPTER XXXVIII

After Claude's sudden indignant departure, Mr. Winkley strolled to the front door to take yet another look at the weather. The wind had not abated; it bent the stripped fuchsia hedges down until they kissed the grey wall behind which they were planted, and whipped the sharp rain in a slanting curtain against the windows. Fishing was obviously out of the question for that day, and, shrugging his shoulders fatalistically, he wandered into the billiard room. He was hailed hilariously by Pussy and Gunn, and sat for a time on the slippery, rounded, leather-covered seat which ran round two sides of the room. But he was restless, and soon drifted out across the hall into the smoking-room.

He had only just poked the fire, and lit a cigarette, when the door opened, and Mr. Weston walked in.

"What's all this that Claude tells me about Mrs. Mumsby being murdered, and you accusing him?" he demanded. "I suppose it's a joke, but you've frightened the life out of him."

"It doesn't take a great deal to frighten him, does it?" replied Mr. Winkley. "But this time, he had plenty of reason to be scared."

Mr. Weston moved deliberately over to the fireplace and, clasping his hands behind his back, stood immobile, gazing at Mr. Winkley. The light from the electric bowl, fixed high in the ceiling of the room, cast a light yellow glow over his face, and emphasized the oriental cast of his features.

At last he spoke again.

"My son wasn't very coherent," he said, "but as I understand it, you really believe that Mrs. Mumsby was murdered. I don't see how you make that out. The doctor signed the certificate, and everyone was satisfied."

"I wasn't satisfied," replied Mr. Winkley. "I knew something was wrong, when I saw that salmon fly in her hand. No one could have got a fly stuck in their hand in that position, unless it had been deliberately pulled in. I have every reason to believe that she was killed by means of poison injected into her hand by the hook. Her whole appearance was consistent with prussic acid poisoning."

"Ingenious," remarked Mr. Weston. "And the case against my son?"

"Is a very strong one," said Mr. Winkley, crossing one leg over the other in his favourite attitude. "The only means by which that fly could have been pulled into Mrs. Mumsby's hand was by a delayed slip-knot, such as Claude used in the trick in which I took part. He used a fly made by Major Jeans, hoping to cast suspicion away from himself. But he did not realize at the time that the Major had used some fur off his monkey for the fly's body, thus casting suspicion back to him. When he discovered this, by seeing a similar fly at close quarters in a bright light on a dark background – in fact on Miss Partridge's black beret – he killed the monkey, so that no one else would trace the fur. Rather a foolish thing to do, for of course anyone could still find plenty of hairs off the monkey scattered over Claude's clothes, or, for that matter, on yours. He also decided to get hold of all flies of that pattern in the hotel, which again wasn't clever, but by this time he was in a panic and didn't stop to think it out logically. It's the common psychology of a man unused to murder. Nearly all criminals convict themselves sooner or later."

"And then?" asked Mr. Weston.

"He went to Miss Partridge's room to get the fly, not knowing that I had taken it to London with me to have it scientifically compared with the one which killed Mrs. Mumsby. But he disturbed her before he could finish his search. He was not afraid of being recognized because he was wearing a piece of black material over his head, with slits for his eyes, such as fishermen sometimes use to protect them from the sun. He was not displeased at the opportunity for frightening Miss Partridge, who had been too much interested in his movements, and he had come prepared for such an emergency. He carried a short rod with a piece of trout line already formed into a lasso by means of his slip-knot. The room was high and wide, and Miss Partridge was silhouetted against the window in the moonlight, and he was an expert caster. He succeeded in scaring Miss Partridge, and then, very wisely, let well alone, and made no further attempt to obtain possession of the flies."

"Very interesting," remarked Mr. Weston. "But why pick Claude as the murderer? There must be a motive for murder, and he'd never met her before he came here. Besides, if you've ever seen him fish, you'd know that he's far from being an expert. He could never cast a lasso like that, however good a target Miss Partridge made."

"No? Well, he can explain all that to the jury when he's on trial. If he's innocent, he'll have nothing to fear, of course. But he'll find it difficult to make any jury believe that he's not guilty. You see he's the only one who has no alibi for the time of Mrs. Mumsby's death."

Mr. Weston stood in posed immobility, thinking deeply. Then, as if he had suddenly made up his mind on a matter of vital importance, he felt in his pocket and brought out a cigarette-case of a type much in favour amongst fishermen, in which the cigarettes are bounced upwards, singly, by small springs. He slid back the top, took the exposed cigarette between his lips, replaced the case in his pocket, and took out a nickel-plated lighter. During the whole process, his right hand remained by his side, and Mr. Winkley marvelled at the amazing dexterity of the other.

Mr. Weston inhaled slowly, then turned a grave face to Mr. Winkley.

"Claude is my only son," he said, "the only thing in life I live for. I've brought him up since he was a baby, and shielded him from anything sordid or unhappy. I very much doubt whether you can have any proof for your suspicions, but I can't risk having him dragged into this."

"I thought you'd probably feel like that," said Mr. Winkley, nodding a wise head.

Mr. Weston flung his cigarette into the fire with an air of decision.

"I suppose you know that I killed her," he said in a casual voice.

"Yes," said Mr. Winkley.

Mr. Weston shrugged his shoulders.

"There's nothing for me to say, then. You're a damned good fisherman, Winkley. You know to a second when to tighten on a fish and land him, and you used the only bait I was likely to take."

Mr. Winkley stretched his legs, and got up, standing a good head and shoulders above his victim.

"On the contrary," he said, "there's a great deal for you to say. If you want to prevent proceedings being taken against Claude, you'll have to give me a signed confession."

"Oh, I'll do that," replied the other, "but" – holding up his crippled hand – "I'm not so handy at writing with my left hand as I am at casting."

"In that case –" began Mr. Winkley.

He broke off as he heard the sound of squeals outside, and opened the door in time to see Pussy skidding to a standstill in the hall, while Gunn menaced her from the door of the billiard room. He caught her by the arm.

"You said you'd taken a course in shorthand and typing," he said urgently. "Can you make use of yourself for once in a while?"

Pussy looked completely taken aback.

"Yes, but –" she began.

Mr. Winkley did not wait for her to finish, but propelled her forward into the smoking-room, and locked the door. He waved her to a chair which was drawn up at an oak writing-table, and placed paper and a fountain-pen in front of her.

"You don't mind?" he asked Mr. Weston, who shook his head in reply.

"Mind? It's I who mind!" exclaimed Pussy as soon as she had recovered her wits. "Sitting behind locked doors with two men, treated like a blooming secretary... what's the little game?"

"You said you'd like to be in at the death," said Mr. Winkley. "It was Mr. Weston who killed Mrs. Mumsby. I want you to take down his confession."

Pussy's eyes nearly dropped out of her head.

"Claude's father!" she cried. "Oh no! It can't be true!"

Mr. Weston walked across to the little table, and smiled down at her.

"Yes, Claude's father," he said. "You're Claude's friend, aren't you? I'm sorry I frightened you that night, but I never meant to hurt you. I hope your throat wasn't too sore."

"Then it's – it's really true?" murmured Pussy. "You really did – murder her?"

"I'm afraid so," was the reply. "I'm not sorry, but I wish I could keep the truth from Claude."

He sighed, moved over to the large, centre table, and perched himself on the corner, arms folded.

"Take this down, Miss Partridge," ordered Mr. Winkley, as if she were indeed his secretary.

"But I –" objected Pussy.

"Don't worry. He'll speak slowly, won't you, Weston?" said Mr. Winkley, anticipating the question. "Ready?"

Pussy shrugged her shoulders, French-wise, and took up the pen.

CHAPTER XXXIX

"Mrs. Mumsby was no more entitled to be called Mrs. Mumsby than you or I," began Mr. Weston, with no more emotion than if he were describing a new fly. "If she married Mumsby, she was a bigamist. Her legal name was Weston. She was my wife, and Claude's mother."

Pussy could not hold back the little squeal of astonishment which came to her lips, but neither of the men took any notice of her, and she bent her blonde head again over the table.

"When I first met her, she was parading, under the name of Ruby Lavalle, in the back row of the chorus in a third-rate music-hall show. Her real name was Gladys Clew. She was very slim and pretty, and in those days she had auburn hair."

"She didn't look very pretty on the day she died," remarked Mr. Winkley.

"She didn't deserve to," replied Mr. Weston. "By that time, she had destroyed one man's soul, and was getting ready to sharpen her talons on another's... I was doing a Chinese illusionist's turn at the time, and was just beginning to make a success of it. It was my last engagement in that class of hall, for I had been booked for a turn of the best halls in the larger provincial towns. I had ideas for improving my act, and thought it would go down well with a lady assistant. I offered the job to Gladys, and she jumped at it. Everything went well, and I began to receive offers from managers of London halls." He paused, as if some dim echo of the applause he had earned had come to his ears. Then he shook his head ruefully. "For a time I was a rage, my name was on everyone's lips, but fame on the boards is proverbially fickle. I don't imagine that you would find a single person nowadays who remembers me."

Mr. Winkley looked up.

"The Great Hei-Wei!" he cried.

Mr. Weston jumped to his feet, and acknowledged the tribute by placing his finger-tips, first on his forehead, and then on his breast, in a gesture which was more bastard-Arab than Chinese.

"Even so," he said. He pressed his left forefinger against the outer corner of his eye and pushed the skin upwards. "You can see that it didn't need much make-up to turn me into a celestial. A little sticking-plaster hidden beneath a Chinaman's wig, and a few strokes with a grease stick, gave me what I suppose this young friend" – he emphasized the word – "of Claude's would call 'glamour'. In those days, China was a glamorous country to all who didn't live there. You remember *Chu Chin Chow*, of course, Winkley, which looked as if it would beat Johnny Walker's record. Well, well, all I need say is that my act was a great success, and after I had made a bit of money, I married Gladys. I was madly in love with her, and thought she loved me. It wasn't until afterwards that I found out that she really loved my success. I suppose you couldn't blame her. She'd been dragged up with ten brothers and sisters in a London slum. She was –"

"A gold-digger," suggested Pussy.

"Yes. And the tragedy was that I loved her. Early in 1921, she found that she was going to have a baby, and then I saw her worst side for the first time. Before telling me, she went to every quack doctor she could hear of, and nearly killed herself with the stuff she took to prevent it. Then she cursed me for ruining her figure, and said I was envious of her success in the act. I put it down to her condition, and somehow managed to appease her. Luckily, I had money to buy her presents, and after a time, she rather enjoyed playing the part of an interesting invalid, reclining on a divan in satin negligees all day, eating chocolates. After Claude was born, she started nagging me again. She never got back her slim figure, and never forgave me for it. Of course, it was her own fault, but you couldn't make her see that. You'd have thought that it was really her act, from the way she went on, but all she had to do was to look pretty and bring on the apparatus, and take away the things I produced by my sleight-of-hand. Mine was really a one-man-show, like Claude's."

"When I first saw her," remarked Pussy quietly, "I imagined her dressed in pink tights and a sequined tunic, rather bulgy."

Mr. Weston smiled.

"That was the idea," he said, "but it was a red velvet tunic, trimmed with gold braid. Am I saying too much?" he added, turning to Mr. Winkley.

"No," he replied. "Just keep on as you're going."

"I wish I could have done," sighed Mr. Weston. "The stage is a grand life, and as long as I had money, Gladys would have stayed with us. But when Claude was two months old, my right hand began to get stiff after my performance. I tried massage and exercises, but it got steadily worse, until one night, I failed in my best trick. I managed to cover it up, but both the manager and Gladys noticed it, of course. She accused me of being drunk, but I knew it wasn't that. A conjuror can't afford to get drunk; his living depends on steady hands. I was seriously alarmed. I went to the best specialist in London, and he found some atrophy of the muscles, which he said was incurable. I tried every possible kind of treatment, but all to no purpose. By the time that Claude was six months old, my name had been erased from every playbill in the country. It was then that Gladys left me."

He paused, as if savouring again the bitterness of that moment, then continued.

"According to her, I had ruined her life. I, who had taken her from a career which would almost certainly have ended on the streets for her; who had kept her in luxury, given her a good home, and a son! She ran away with the manager of a touring revue company, named Robins. I don't know where she picked up Mumsby, nor how many men's lives she has ruined in the last seventeen years. But I do know that she won't ruin Claude's."

"I used to think that Claude wasn't really your son," remarked Pussy. "You see, you're always emphasizing the fact that he is, and when people do that, it's usually to hide the truth."

Mr. Weston smiled. His smile was so genuine and friendly, that it suddenly seemed preposterous to Pussy to think that he was a self-confessed murderer.

In a moment, she thought, *I shall wake up and find it has all been a dream. Things like this can't possibly happen in real life.*

"He is my son, that I do know," said Mr. Weston. "I suppose the reason why I'm always talking about it is that he means so much to me. He's the rock I rebuilt my faith on, the only thing that kept me sane during those awful, lonely weeks. He was so small and helpless, and he depended on me so much. I vowed then that he should always have me at hand to help him as long as he needed me. I swore that I would never fail him as she had failed me. Everyone I knew tried to persuade me to send him to an orphanage, but he was all I had left in the world, and I clung to him. How I managed to make enough for us to live on, I don't know, but somehow I got through the nightmare of those early months. All that I knew was connected with the stage, and I naturally tried to pick up a living there. I got a job as a scene-shifter while there was still enough use in my hand, and it was then that I strained my heart. Then I became a stage-doorkeeper, and, after that, I even hired myself out to parade outside a cinema in fancy dress to advertise a film. There were times when Claude and I nearly starved. You see, I'd had no chance to save any money; I'd spent it all on Gladys. When things were at their worst, some friend got the Actors' Benevolent Society interested in me. They found a good job for me with plenty of opportunity, and now, thanks to them, I'm the manager of the Oleander Cinema in one of the provincial towns, and Claude and I can afford to take a fishing holiday."

"It seems poetic justice that her money should go to that Society," said Mr. Winkley. "But why did you kill her?"

Mr. Weston began to pace up and down the carpeted room.

"Can't you see why? I must have explained it all very badly then. From the day that she left me until the day that Claude and I walked into this hotel, I had had no word from her, nor set eyes on her. She had inherited all that money from Mumsby, and had grown into a rich, lonely, discontented woman. As soon as she saw Claude, and realized that the baby she had deserted had grown into a good-looking, talented boy, she determined to get him away from me, and take him for her own constant companion."

"Didn't Claude guess that she was his mother?" asked Pussy. "It was queer that he should call her Mother Mumsby."

Mr. Weston shook his head emphatically.

"I'm quite sure that he didn't know," he said. "He isn't very good at keeping things to himself, as you know, and he would have said something about it if he had guessed. He just called her that because she mothered him and that monkey of his. She wasn't a bad actress when she liked, and she made a dead set at him. They say that blood's thicker than water, but I never believed it until I saw the attraction between those two."

"It was certainly rather uncanny," remarked Mr. Winkley.

"Uncanny?" repeated Mr. Weston. "It was horrible to me. It was almost obscene to see her putting a caressing hand on his arm and smiling at him, when I knew how callously she had deserted him when he was a helpless baby."

"Why didn't you tell Claude all about it?" asked Pussy. "Surely he would never have left you if he had known how badly she had treated you."

"I daren't risk it," replied Mr. Weston, still pacing up and down the room. "There was that great sympathy between them, and it would have been only my word against hers. She would have stopped at nothing to get her own way. Oh, I knew her so well! My only hope was to stave her off until I could work out some plan for getting rid of her. That suited her well enough because it gave her time to worm her way further into his affection. Things came to a head one evening when we walked back from the lake together and she told me that she was making a new will, leaving all her money to Claude, and mentioning him as her son. She dangled the will in front of my eyes, and I snatched it from her. She had filled in Claude's name but not her own."

"That was the will that Claude found today, then," remarked Mr. Winkley.

"Yes. You are a witness to the fact that I filled it up in my own name instead. She only laughed at me when I told her to leave her money elsewhere, and we had a violent quarrel."

"That was the evening when she caught more fish than usual, and never came to see them put down in the hall." said Mr. Winkley.

Mr. Weston nodded.

"I knew then that I must kill her." he said.

CHAPTER LX

"But why?" Pussy sounded bewildered. "Why should you deprive Claude of all that money? He would have been rich. He need never have done any more work. He –"

"Why?" Mr. Weston swung round, and glared at her. "Why? Because there are other things in this world of greater value than money. Character, goodness, a man's soul. Can't you see what kind of a man Claude would have become if he had become dependent on that woman, who would have treated him like a new toy to be taken about and exhibited everywhere? A boudoir lizard! A human lapdog! I heard Major Jeans call him a gigolo once when they were together. Can't you see how much like her he could have become, and how easily she could have ruined my long years of careful rearing? Can't you see what a wonderful future he has in front of him, with those clever young hands of his, and all the tricks of prestidigitation I have taught him? Already he is nearly as good as I was at the height of my career. And surely he owes me something. We Westons have been conjurors of one kind or another for generations. My grandfather took lessons from

Trewey, and specialized in shadow pictures. Besides, Claude has no idea of the value of money. When that fortune came to him, he would have run through it at Monte Carlo or somewhere, and supple fingers can be a temptation when things go badly. Can't you see how he might have ended? As a light-fingered thief. No! She destroyed my soul and my faith in human goodness; I daren't risk her destroying his. She deserved to die, and may her soul rot in hell!"

There was silence in the room after he had finished speaking, although Pussy, emulating all the ranks of Tuscany, barely restrained a cheer.

Then Mr. Winkley spoke.

"I'm sorry, Weston, but however much sympathy one may have with the 'eye for an eye and a tooth for a tooth' philosophy, it doesn't give one the right to take the law into one's own hands. I shall have to pass this information on to the police, and there's only one thing they can do."

"Hang me, I suppose," replied Mr. Weston cheerfully. "Well, let's get the preliminaries over."

"It's all most irregular," frowned Mr. Winkley. "I didn't caution you, for one thing, although you certainly knew that all this was being taken down in evidence."

"Don't worry about that," was the reply. "I'm not going to question the truth of my own words."

"Well," said Mr. Winkley, still looking worried, "in that case, Miss Partridge had better read what she has written, and then it can be written out and you can sign it."

Pussy looked confused.

"You mean – read it aloud?" she asked incredulously.

"Yes, yes. I can't let him sign it without hearing if you've put it down correctly, and I don't suppose he can read your shorthand."

"I'm damned sure he can't," returned Pussy. "I can't even read it myself!"

"This is no time for joking," said Mr. Winkley sternly. "Please do as I say."

"But I – I can't..." stammered Pussy.

"Miss Partridge," said Mr. Winkley, "this man is a murderer. He deliberately took the life of Mrs. – er – his wife. Even if you think that she deserved it, you can do nothing to save him from the consequences of that act. Even if you threw that confession into the fire, I should only get someone else to take down another copy. Please be sensible about it."

"Oh, it isn't that at all," explained Pussy. "I just can't read it because I haven't put anything down."

"You – what?" shouted Mr. Winkley.

"Well, it was your own fault," retorted the girl, reacting at once to his tone. "I tried to tell you that I couldn't do it, but you wouldn't listen. You just stuck me in this chair, and gave me a pen, and ordered me to do as I was told."

"But you said you knew shorthand."

"That's where you're wrong," said Pussy. "I told you that I once learned shorthand, which is quite a different thing. I did begin a course in it, but I never did any good. My spelling is too bad, for one thing, and I can't concentrate, for another. I've no brains."

"You certainly haven't," said Mr. Winkley bitterly. "I shall have to find someone else, and start all over again. I suppose that was the idea. You've done nothing but hinder me ever since the beginning of this case."

"If you'd asked Piggy instead of me..." began Pussy, but Mr. Winkley was already unlocking the door.

"Have I your word that you will stay here till I come back?" he asked Mr. Weston.

"You have," was the reply. "I won't move from this room, I promise you."

He waited until the door had slammed behind Mr. Winkley, then moved towards Pussy.

"Thank you," he said. "I knew I could rely on a friend of Claude's."

Pussy's eyes filled with tears. He seemed such a tragic little man, and she still found it impossible to think of him as a murderer. Such emotions as had been revealed during his confession were beyond her comprehension, and yet she felt indescribably sorry for him.

"I'm glad I could help," she said simply. "You can escape now, can't you?"

He nodded.

"Yes," he agreed solemnly. "I can escape now."

CHAPTER LXI

The hall was empty when Pussy left the smoking-room and closed the door softly behind her. She wandered along the corridor into the lounge, where she found her mother talking to Major Jeans.

As soon as he saw her, the Major jumped up, and pushed his chair forward, but she ignored him rudely, and seated herself instead on the arm of her mother's chair, swinging her shapely legs.

"Ha-ha, the little salmon fry!" said the Major in his hearty voice. "We were just talking about you, my dear. Were your little gills burning?"

"No," said Pussy shortly, without troubling to look at him.

Major Jeans glanced across at Mrs. Partridge inquiringly. She nodded her head.

"Listen to me, Pussy." The Major lowered his voice with difficulty. "Your mother and I have been talking about you. It's rather an important matter, and she has given me permission to speak to you about it." He leaned across, and took her hand in his. "You don't hate me, my dear, do you?"

Pussy snatched her hand away as if his touch had scorched her, and jumped to her feet.

She had just been in contact with stark tragedy, and this old fool must choose this moment to make love to her, she thought. With her mother's permission, too! Well, she'd soon put a stop to it. Her patience had been tried long enough!

"All right," she said, raising her voice. "You've asked for it, and now you'll get it! Yes, I do hate you. How could I help it? Ever since we came to this hotel, you've done nothing but pester me. You can't come near me without putting your arm around me, or trying to kiss me. I can't bear to be mauled, especially by an old sugar-daddy like you!"

'Tansy, be quiet!" ordered Mrs. Partridge.

"I won't be quiet. It isn't my fault. He's an old satyr, I tell you. He can't leave any woman alone. I've watched him stroking your arm, and making goo-goo eyes at you, when he didn't think I was looking. But you didn't know that he was making love to me at the same time, did you? I've put up with it for your sake, because I knew you'd hate to have a scene in the hotel. But when it comes to the two of you dis-cussing me behind my back, and arranging my future for me, I think it's just about time I told you where you both get off." She turned to Major Jeans, and put her hands on her hips. "Now listen to me, old lobster-face," she said. "I don't want to marry you, I never have wanted to marry you, and I wouldn't marry you if you were the last man on earth. And you can tell my mother if you like!"

Major Jeans got up, and sent his chair crashing backwards with a well-directed kick.

"Good God!" he roared. "Marry you? Do you think I'm mad, wench? Don't you know that it's as much as I can do to be civil to you? I don't like your clothes, I don't like your manners, I don't like your painted nails, or your painted face. The trouble with you young fry is that you imagine every man you meet is in love with you. Upon my soul, you're as bad as Mrs. Mumsby! Marry you? I'd sooner marry a fish! You're just about as cold-blooded. Haven't you any eyes in your head, girl? Can't you see that it's your mother I want to marry? Been in love with her for years, but she wouldn't hear of it, until I made you like me as a father. Marry you? God bless all little loaves and fishes!"

He turned on his heels and strode out of the room. They could hear his bellows of laughter echoing all the way along the corridor.

Mrs. Partridge rose to her feet, and perked her small body up and down like a belligerent robin. She spoke very softly.

"I hope you're satisfied, Pansy," she said. "I never believed that a child of mine could be so gauche or so rude. This is all the thanks I get for giving up my life to you. I've stinted myself for years of clothes, and sometimes of food, so that you could go to good schools, and be finished abroad, and have everything you wanted. All I've succeeded in doing, is to make you selfish and self-centred. Nothing is sacred to you. You only laugh at people's feelings. I've been told enough times that I've spoiled you. So I have. But I shall do it no longer. You're so sure of yourself, that you can go your own way in future, and do what you like. You'll have no further consideration from me. I'm going to marry Major Jeans, whether you like it or not. You won't fool me any more."

She turned and walked out of the room.

In the corridor outside, she bumped into the Major.

"Winkley," he said. "Have you seen Winkley? I want Winkley."

He scarcely waited for her to shake her head, but brushed impatiently past her, and a few seconds later she saw him running into the smoking-room, followed closely by Mr. Winkley and Gunn.

She shrugged her shoulders and went upstairs to her room.

Inside the smoking-room, the three men stood looking down at the lifeless body of Mr. Weston.

"He kept his promise," said Mr. Winkley. "I ought to have had enough sense to realize that this was bound to happen, but he seemed so resigned to things that it never occurred to me that he might kill himself. Besides, I left Miss Partridge here with him..."

"You – what?" exclaimed Gunn. "Do you mean to tell me that you left her alone with him, knowing that he had killed one woman already? God help you, if any harm had come to her!"

Mr. Winkley surveyed him through mild blue eyes.

"You don't understand," he said. "He wasn't a violent man. Mrs. Mumsby's murder was purely psychological. He saw it as the only means of freeing his son from her. Otherwise he was a very kind man. He wouldn't dream of attacking Miss Partridge."

"Sez you!" retorted Gunn. "He'd already half-strangled her."

"There's no revolver," remarked Major Jeans, who could only think of one way of committing suicide. "How did he die?"

Mr. Winkley knelt down beside the body, took a small, wide-necked bottle from the floor, and placed it carefully on the table. Then he turned each of Mr. Weston's hands palm upwards. In the right hand, so drawn and twisted, was the upstanding hackle of a salmon fly, its furred body stained with the blood which oozed around it. The forefinger and thumb of the left hand still gripped a length of gut.

"Poetic justice again," remarked Mr. Winkley. "This was the way he murdered Mrs. Mumsby. He thought he'd elude me without a confession, but the *P.M.* will prove it for me this time. The inquest will reveal a verdict of 'Death by prussic acid poisoning', and then we shall be able to exhume Mrs. Mumsby's body, and prove that she was killed in the same way."

"If you do," said Gunn, "there'll be another death on your hands for certain. Thomas Lloyd will expire for joy!"

Major Jeans looked down on the face of the man with whom he had exchanged favourite flies and fishing stories. With some difficulty, he recaptured his habitual flippancy of speech.

"That's the second biggest fish I've seen killed on a fly in these parts," he said.

CHAPTER LXII

A week later, Mr. Winkley, with the tang of the crisp Welsh air still in his nostrils, and the sound of his screaming reel still in his ears, was back again in the little room at Scotland Yard, which was known to his colleagues as " Winkley's Hatchery".

He was talking to Paget, a sparse-fleshed, sandy-haired man, with alert eyes and a confident manner, who was the Yard's recognized expert on toxicology.

"So although they brought in a verdict of 'Death from natural causes' at the inquest," Mr. Winkley was saying, "Weston really committed suicide. Of course you couldn't expect a Welsh country doctor, whose chief job in life is to deliver twins, to spot prussic acid poisoning when he did the *P.M.*, but as Weston was a self-confessed murderer, the whole case will have to be reopened. If that stupid girl had only had the brains of a louse, I should have had his signed confession to put in as evidence, but as it is, the Commissioner will probably take a bit more convincing. I've asked you about it, because I want to be sure that I've got the technical details about the poison correct, before I send in my report."

Paget thrust his hands into his pockets, and perched himself on the edge of Winkley's desk.

"In other words, Winkley," he said with a grin, "you want me to lend my authority to an otherwise bald and unconvincing narrative."

"Well – yes," agreed Mr. Winkley, squirming slightly in his chair (Paget often affected people in that way), "but you needn't put it quite so offensively."

"Very well, then," returned the other, with an even broader grin, "this bloke committed suicide by dipping a salmon fly into something, which you optimistically call prussic acid, and after sticking it into the palm of his hand, expired forthwith."

"Why optimistically?" asked Mr. Winkley.

"Because I've yet to be convinced," returned Paget, "that any prussic acid found its way into his hand at all."

"But surely –" expostulated Mr. Winkley. "There was the bottle with the stopper out, the hook stuck in the man's palm. He obviously died from prussic acid poisoning."

"Oh yeah?" drawled Paget offensively. "Look here," he went on, "what do you really know about prussic acid?"

Mr. Winkley looked uneasy.

"I know that it's the most powerful poison known," he said. "I know that if you take even small quantities of it by the mouth, it is almost instantaneously fatal, and that if it is injected into the blood stream by means of a hypodermic needle, its action is even more speedy."

"And," interrupted Paget rudely, "every criminal carries a small capsule of it in his pocket, which he swallows on the threshold of Scotland Yard, thus relieving Inspector Horn-rims of the necessity of explaining a lot of difficult technical details in the course of the book. And, of course," he added, "the whole of Scotland Yard stinks of bitter almonds for weeks afterwards. Am I right?"

Mr. Winkley opened his mouth to protest, but Paget, who, like most experts, liked to hear the sound of his own voice, continued before he could speak.

"Just let me tell you what the facts are," he said in his best professional manner, taking out a slim gold pencil, and waggling it in Mr. Winkley's face. "Prussic acid, or more accurately hydrocyanic acid, is a gas. Or rather," he corrected himself, "it is an extremely volatile liquid, which boils at the temperature of an ordinary warm room. If you dipped a fishhook, or any other hook, into it, the liquid would evaporate almost before you could withdraw it from the bottle. So that, really, pure liquid prussic acid is nothing more than a laboratory curiosity. What is usually known to the public as 'prussic acid', is a dilute solution of the gas in water, and is known to us as 'Scheele's Acid'."

"Yes, I know that," interrupted Mr. Winkley. "I've realized all along that that was what was used in this particular instance."

Paget changed his rising exasperation into an exaggerated air of patient resignation.

"I believe you said that the room he died in was hot," he said.

"Yes," agreed Mr. Winkley. "I should say it was well over seventy."

"Well then, if you dipped a pin in water..."

"Salmon hook," amended Mr. Winkley.

"Same thing," retorted Paget, with the expert's lofty disregard of the unimportant details. "And if you held it in the air of a warm room for a minute or two, how much water do you suppose would be left on it by the end of that time?"

"Not much," admitted Mr. Winkley.

"Not any," returned Paget decisively. "In fact, I should say that a fish-hook dipped in 'prussic acid' would be a damned sight safer than one out of your fly-box, Winkley, because it would probably be sterilized, and the fellow wouldn't even have been able to give himself a septic hand with it."

"But all this is absurd," protested Mr. Winkley. "Everybody knows that people commit suicide with prussic acid..."

"In books," put in Paget. "The lay public knows so little about it, that it's a positive godsend to the writer of detective fiction. The very name has come to be synonymous with 'sudden death', whatever the circumstances. But consider the facts for a minute, Winkley. You're suggesting that this fellow Weston was in such a hurry to kill himself (before you could get at him again), that he dipped the hook into the acid, stuck it into his hand, and died, all within the space of ten seconds; whereas you and I know perfectly well that in real life, suicides like to do things in style. They rarely stick their heads into gas-ovens, for instance, without first providing a soft cushion to lie on. Now this fellow probably seated himself in a comfortable chair near the fire, dipped the hook into the acid, and then meditated cosily on his past life, and consoled himself with the suicide's usual flood of self-pity. He would have decided several times, probably, to stick the hook into his hand, and each time, he would funk it, and give himself a few more moments to live. By which time, the hook would have been quite harmless, since prussic acid, being a gas," he grinned, "does not leave a deposit similar to that employed by the Jujube Indians on their arrowheads."

He got up, and turned towards the door. Mr. Winkley followed him.

"You think, then...?" he began.

"I'm afraid I think," said Paget, "the fellow probably died of shock. And don't forget that definition that you threw at my head when I once ventured to remind you that I was supposed to be an expert."

"What was that?" asked Mr. Winkley to Paget's receding back.

Paget poked his head back through the door.

"'An expert always knows what can't be done'," he said, with a wide grin.

"But what about Mrs. Mumsby, then?" shouted Mr. Winkley.

But Paget had already disappeared, leaving behind him, like the Cheshire Cat, nothing but his grin, and, to Mr. Winkley's imagination, the faint odour of bitter almonds.

THE END

Lightning Source UK Ltd.
Milton Keynes UK
UKOW06f1705170316

270402UK00005B/216/P